THE SCANDAL OF MERCY

A JOE BOYD SUSPENSE NOVEL - BOOK 3

DAN WALSH

BAINBRIDGE PRESS

COPYRIGHT INFO

The Scandal of Mercy
Joe Boyd Suspense Series – Book 3
Bainbridge Press
Editor - Cindi Walsh
ISBN: 978-1-7341417-6-4
Copyright © 2021 Dan Walsh

PROLOGUE (SCENE 1)

April 26, 1945
Kaufering IV Concentration Camp
A Sub-Camp of the Dachau Complex

SS OFFICER OBERSTURMBANNFÜHRER HANS ZANDER WATCHED in horror as a massive crowd of Jews—essentially, those still able to walk—were being marched away from the main entrance of the camp, heading south on a road toward Dachau. Along with and walking beside the Jews—beating and prodding them at regular intervals—were most of the other SS officers and guards Zander had served with at Kaufering for the past two years. Leading this procession in his staff car was their camp commandant, SS-Standartenführer Franz Heydrich, along with the rest of his key staff members.

Zander's sense of horror stemmed from the realization he was being left behind. Heydrich, and everyone else

Zander was now observing from the front gate, would not be coming back.

Ever.

Recent reports had confirmed the Allies 12th Armored Division, along with units of the 101st Airborne, were less than two days north of the camp. Hence, Heydrich's rapid departure to the *south*.

By rights, as second-in-command, Zander should be sitting in that staff car beside the commandant. This *significant assignment* Heydrich had given him could easily have gone to any junior officer in camp. When Zander had respectfully appealed, Heydrich dismissed him, emphasizing—in front of the entire staff—the *critical nature of the tasks*, saying they could only be handled by someone who still enjoyed Heydrich's total and complete trust.

Zander knew, this was utter nonsense.

The simple truth was…Zander knew too much. He had personally seen enough atrocities carried out directly by Heydrich—or under his direct orders—to ensure the man would hang for war crimes once the war ended. Which everyone knew—but dare not say aloud—would happen within a matter of weeks, if not days.

Of course, Zander had committed his own fair share of atrocities since coming to the camp two years ago, but they were a fraction compared to those done by Heydrich.

This was the real reason Heydrich was fleeing south now.

He was the camp commander. They had heard reports that commanders and leading officers of similar concentration camps were being summarily executed without a trial when the camps had been overrun by Russians in the East.

Heydrich had told Zander since their camp would likely

be captured by the Americans, he needn't worry if they arrived before Zander and the guards helping him could escape. *"The Americans are not animals like the Russians,"* he'd said. *"They believe in the Geneva Convention."*

That may be true, but Zander knew...if he carried out Heydrich's last assignment, the rage generated from seeing hundreds of weak and sick Jewish prisoners freshly massacred could easily make them forget the Geneva Convention.

He turned and surveyed the condition of things in the camp now, tried to imagine how they'd appear to Allied troops who just arrived.

He sighed.

Even to him, it was utterly revolting.

Stacks of dead bodies lay about here and there in plain view, piled high like cordwood. Dozens of confused, emaciated Jewish men in filthy striped garb, meandered about in the dirt, like living corpses. The soldiers would quickly find within the rotting walls of the wooden barracks, hundreds more prisoners too ill to even get up, packed in like sardines, lying on wooden slats. Row after row of them.

All these pathetic souls were Zander's final assignment. He and the guards were to kill them all, so there'd be no one left to testify about what had happened here.

Then he was to burn down the camp headquarter buildings to the ground. He must stay long enough to ensure that all camp records and files were completely incinerated. Once these two things were accomplished, he and the remaining guards could use the Kubelwagen and truck Heydrich had left behind, and join them in Dachau.

"Obersturmbannführer Zander," a deep voice yelled out. "What are your orders, sir?"

Zander turned to see the familiar face of Sergeant Schmidt, the squad leader of the remaining SS guards.

"Commandant Heydrich, he seemed to be...to want us to carry out his orders most urgently. Shouldn't we begin? We need to know how you want us to proceed. Do you have any directions, sir?"

Zander sighed again, looked back down the main road. Only a handful of the multitude marching to Dachau could still be seen. He turned to face Schmidt and the others. "You men gather around. I have something important to say. Something that will be...*difficult* for you to hear. But you need to hear it."

The men looked confused but, of course, they obeyed and came close.

"For the sake of the watching prisoners," Zander said, "stand at attention while I speak. But if they weren't here, I'd invite you to sit around in a circle and we'd speak as friends." That only furthered their confusion but Zander wanted it said.

"I am going to speak to you as men, not as children who must do as they are told, who speak only when spoken to. I am going to tell you things as they are, not as we wish them to be. Everything I'm about to say is from confirmed reports, mind you. But things we have kept from you all until now."

He looked at them, straight into their eyes. They seemed slightly less alarmed. "You men must know by now, the war is lost." *See? No one reacted to this. They really did know.* "It breaks my heart to say this, as I'm sure it does yours. We have not officially surrendered. But the Allied troops are less than two days from here. Even that could be wrong. They could be here tomorrow." Their eyes widened at these words.

"Sir," Schmidt asked. "If I may, if the war is truly lost, why did the Commandant take all the healthy prisoners south to Dachau? It would seem—if they are not to be used to help us defend the Fatherland—why not leave them here with the sick ones, and kill them all along with the rest? Instead of guarding thousands of Jews, we could all be sent to the front lines to fight."

"Not a bad question, Schmidt," Zander said. "The reason this march was undertaken today...it's...well, complicated. The simple answer is, it's a measure to buy some time. That's all. A week, maybe two at the most. The Führer and those leading us at the very top, do not want to face the reality of how the war is going. They refuse to admit what all the Wehrmacht generals know to be true. You can see it for yourselves. Almost every night, hundreds of Allied bombers fly overhead. Do you ever see any Luftwaffe fighters rise up to meet them? No, not for weeks now. The Luftwaffe is kaput. Hundreds of our planes have been shot down or destroyed on the ground. We have no fuel left for those that remain."

Now their faces registered the truth. "In the Ruhr pocket," Zander said, "over 300,000 Wehrmacht troops have surrendered to the Allies in recent days. Why do you think camps like ours in the west are all closing up and fleeing to the interior? In the east with the Russians, things are far worse. We've heard they are near the outskirts of Berlin." He looked right at Schmidt. "There are no front lines anymore, Sergeant. Not on our side. Only the Allies have forces still in the fight. And they are headed here. Right here to this camp."

"Then what are we to do?" one of the others said.

"Well, I'll tell you what we are *not* going to do?" Zander said. "We are *not* going to carry out the Commandant's last order. We're not going to kill the prisoners. It will be bad enough for the Americans to come and see things as they are. Far worse for us if they see hundreds of recently-slaughtered prisoners throughout the camp. I'm sure you realize, the Allies do not hold to our...*views* regarding the superiority of the master race, nor the inferiority of the Jews. They will see everything we have done here as..."

"War crimes?" Schmidt said.

"Yes. War crimes. Crimes that are, to them, worthy of execution."

"Then are we to just stay here till the Allies come, guarding the prisoners? Won't that mean they will—"

"No," Zander said. "When I am done speaking, it will be as if I'm a captain of a ship. A ship that is about to sink. And I'm giving the order to abandon that ship. And then it will be...every man for himself. You are free to leave, to go home or anywhere else you please. But understand, if you are caught by those still loyal to Hitler, you will likely be shot or hanged as a deserter."

He paused, everyone looked at each other, faces full of sadness. But they were nodding and agreeing.

"What about the prisoners?" Schmidt said. "What will happen to them if we just leave?"

"That is not your concern any longer," Zander said. "The Allies will be here soon. Let them decide their fate." He was just about to dismiss them when he remembered something.

"One more thing, men." He pointed to the SS badge on his collar. "You should be aware, if you decide to surrender to the Allies, you may want to consider getting rid of any visible connection to the SS. The reports are, they are treating SS with special harshness compared to regular Wehrmacht troops."

That was it then.

He looked at everyone, still standing around, mostly at attention as before. "Okay men, I will say it then. Abandon ship."

PROLOGUE (SCENE 2)

Same Day
50 miles South of
Stuttgart, Germany

HANS ZANDER WAS RIDING NORTHWEST ON A DESERTED ROAD bordered by thick pine trees, feeling rather desperate. About an hour ago, he had dismissed the remaining SS guards at the camp and commandeered the Kubelwagen, before anyone else got the idea to nab it for themselves. His last view of the men was through the rearview mirror, as they stood around in utter confusion muttering to each other.

It was sad to see. Men wholly unfamiliar with the concept of thinking for themselves.

They had been that way since the moment they had donned the Nazi uniform, many since their first days with the Hitler Youth. Now they had nowhere to go. No one to tell them where to go or what to do. No matter. They were not Zander's concern any longer. Already — a mere one hundred kilometers behind him — and his mind had already dismissed them. For two years, they had served together, but now they belonged to the past. He would never see any of them again. No fond memories to retain, because none had been made.

He must focus now on the present and the future. Like the road ahead of him, straight and narrow.

But the truth was, if he didn't come across any regular German soldiers soon before running into an American patrol, his plans would be ruined. Worse, since he still wore his SS officer's uniform, it could be the end of his life. He wasn't exaggerating with the men. He and Heydrich really had heard reliable reports of SS officers being summarily executed when captured. It was becoming readily apparent to the Allies as they conquered more and more territory, the SS were responsible for all the atrocities they were uncovering.

Another confirmed report...just over a week ago, was that the Allies had made it all the way south to Stuttgart and now occupied the city, which meant Zander had less than eighty kilometers to locate his targets. If he didn't find some Wehrmacht soldiers soon, he'd have to turn around and head the other way until he did. He knew here in western Germany, tens of thousands of them had surrendered to the Allies over the last month. Of course, Hitler and Goebbels were keeping information like that from the public to avoid an all-out panic. But it was true. Commandant Heydrich feared the number could be far higher than that.

Zander could only shake his head in disbelief as he recalled the conversation. It really was over then. The glorious, thousand-year Reich had barely lasted more than a decade.

Zander remembered another moment that involved hundreds of thousands of German soldiers. It was an amazing day ten years ago when he'd attended one of the Nuremberg rallies. He'd stood there proudly holding his banner in the midst of a sea of humanity, all gathered in hundreds of perfectly formed rows, watching the Fuhrer and his inner circle walk by. An unimaginable spectacle. After hearing Hitler's phenomenal speech, the place went wild. Zander knew with certainty that everything Hitler had prophesied about the future of the Fatherland was destined to become true.

And for the next several years, it had.

Everything Hitler had promised unfolded just as he'd predicted. Germany was on a course to conquer and rule the world. Every country was falling beneath their feet. Those that had not yet done so, soon would be. And Hans Zander was an integral part of it all. Rising quickly through the SS ranks, doing anything and everything he'd been asked to do. And far beyond his duty. Zander had excelled in every task. In his last official review, Commandant Heydrich felt certain Zander would soon be named as the new camp commander upon his next promotion.

But now look. Look at how far things had fallen.

Zander was fleeing from that very camp, hoping to shed every connection to it he had ever made. He was on the hunt for a regular German soldier, so that he might forever rid himself of his SS officer's uniform. His reputation, which he'd crafted with such passion and precision these last several years, even his very identity, was about to be erased forever. As if it had never existed.

As if *he* had never existed.

His musings were suddenly interrupted by a sight up ahead. From this distance, it looked like people walking just off the right side of the road. He couldn't tell how many. As he got closer, he saw the gray clothing. A few blocks more confirmed they were indeed German soldiers. Three young men walking slowly without weapons or helmets. So bedraggled, if they weren't wearing Wehrmacht uniforms they could easily be mistaken for hobos.

One heard his car approaching before the others and turned around. Seeing who was driving, and no doubt, Zander's SS uniform, a look of panic came over his face. He yelled something to the others. They turned to look, then all three ran toward the trees. Zander floored it and quickly closed the gap, but they kept running. If he didn't do something quickly, he'd lose them in the woods. He pulled his car off the road, headed right toward them, and fired his pistol, aiming just a few yards in front of the one in the lead.

All three stopped, and so did he.

He brought the Kubelwagen to a stop, put it in neutral, and pulled on the brake. As he stood on the seat, he kept the pistol pointed at the men. "What do we have here, gentlemen?"

"It is nothing, Herr Obersturmbanfuhrer," one of them said, the one who saw Zander's vehicle first. "We were in a battle earlier this morning and got separated from our unit. We've been trying to find them ever since."

"Do you take me for a fool, Soldier? I have been in this general area for days. The bullet from my gun just now is the only battle sounds I've heard. You think I don't know what you men are doing? You are deserting. It's plain to see."

"Oh, no, sir. We are not—"

"Silence," he yelled. "Of course you are deserting. Where are your helmets? Where are your guns? And look at how you wear your uniforms...not like proud Wehrmacht soldiers. Like men who've surrendered, who've quit the fight."

Zander found it amusing how forceful and convincing he sounded, considering he was about to do the very same thing. "You men are cowards!"

That seemed to end their charade. Their shoulders slumped and they began to look toward the ground. The one who spoke first looked up and said, "Sir, I'm sure you know what's been going on around here...for well over a month now. The war is lost. Our entire regiment has already surrendered, including our commanders. They are miles ahead of us heading the same way, toward the Allied lines. We are only here because our truck broke down yesterday, several miles south. Perhaps you saw it as you drove here."

"What you're saying may be the truth. But Germany is still in this war. We have not yet surrendered." He looked around and got a thought. It was entirely possible with the Americans being so close, a patrol could come by here at any time. He had to take this conversation into the woods. He kept his gun in his hand but lowered it to his side. "Let's continue our conversation out of sight from the road. I want to talk with you some more before I decide what must be done. Continue walking toward the woods, but slowly. If anyone runs, I will shoot them."

Zander got out of the car and followed the men as they

walked deeper into the trees. Several times, he had to tell them to keep going, until he was sure they could not be seen from the road. Then he ordered them to stop. He spent the next ten minutes talking to them in a more casual, nonthreatening tone, as if taking an interest in their situations. Most of his questions had to do with things like what unit were they from and what battles had they fought in, what part of Germany they were from, what did they expect to go back to after the war, had any of them lost loved ones in the massive bombing raids in recent years?

One of the men, a young corporal, was from Hamburg, the same city as Zander. And like Zander, he had lost everyone in the Allied bombing raids that had leveled the city. There was no one waiting for him back home.

That was all Zander needed to hear. He promptly raised his pistol before anyone had a chance to think and shot each of the men in the forehead. They dropped dead where they stood. As fortune would have it, he and the young corporal were about the same size. Quickly, he undressed, took off the corporal's uniform, and put it on himself. He pulled the young man's papers out of his pocket to find out his name.

Karl Dietrich from Hamburg. Karl was four years younger than Hans and one inch shorter. But apparently, there was no one left back in Hamburg who could verify this information. So, he took out a lighter and set fire to Karl's papers. When they had thoroughly burned up, he stomped out the fire, tossed his gun into the woods, and calmly headed back toward the road.

Although it was tempting to drive the Kubelwagen the rest of the way to Stuttgart, he decided to leave it where it sat. Should he run into an American patrol, it would be more convincing if he was merely a lone corporal walking along the side of the road, looking for Allied troops to surrender to. He did go back to the car to get his canteen, but that was all.

He started walking down the road mentally preparing himself to face the next chapter of his life as Karl Dietrich, a young Wehrmacht corporal who had fought bravely and valiantly for the Fatherland, but who now was ready to concede defeat to the Americans. Hans Zander, the SS officer who had served as second-in-command at a Nazi concentration camp, and who'd personally killed dozens of Jews, starving hundreds more who'd worked in his labor crews...well, he must've died near the end of the war.

In any event, Hans Zander was no longer his concern.

From this point on, he would forever be known as Karl Dietrich. An honorable German soldier and soon to be a POW.

1

JOE BOYD WAS LOVING THIS.

He couldn't remember the last time he and his good friend, Jack Turner, had gotten to hang out together like this, just the two of them. It was really more on Jack's end than Joe's. In recent months, Jack had his hands full; not just with his growing family but as the Dean of the military history department at the University, Jack had been asked to lead his department through a series of major upgrades this year.

Joe's world hadn't changed too dramatically. In fact, the already-low crime rate in Culpepper had dipped even lower for a change. And fortunately, they had been spared the anti-police riots and protests bigger cities had faced. Joe figured it had something to do with the fact their town hadn't had any controversial incidents, really, since he'd come here several years ago. But he also thought it had something to do with the university itself, since it was a private school that leaned heavily conservative. Whatever the case, he was grateful.

"You do see the credits are rolling, right?"

Jack's voice interrupted Joe's thoughts. "What? Oh, yeah. Sorry." Joe was in charge of the remote. He reached for it, clicked on the button to play the next episode. They were at Jack's place watching *Band of Brothers* together. Jack had a huge flat screen TV, and since it was just the two of them, they had turned the volume way up.

"So, where'd you go?" Jack said. "You miss the end of that episode?"

"No, I caught it. I was just thinking about how nice this is getting to do this. You and me just hanging out, watching World War II flick. It's finally starting to feel like old times."

"Yeah. Rachel was so happy she could finally take Jack Junior to Charlotte to see her folks. Over the phone, her mom burst into tears when Rachel said they were coming to stay for a week. They hadn't seen him except on video for almost a year."

Joe hit the pause button, since the next episode was starting. "Maybe before we start this one, we can start snacking. Didn't you say Rachel left a pan of that buffalo chicken cheese dip she's famous for?"

"She did. I could go for some of that, too," Jack said. "I need to reheat it in the microwave first." He got out of his recliner but stood behind it a moment looking at the frozen image on screen. "That was an amazing episode." They had just finished Episode Two, the one called *Day of Days*. It depicted Easy Company during the D-Day landings and the events that followed after. "This is probably my fourth time watching this miniseries since it came out. But the realism still takes my breath away."

"Know what you mean," Joe said. "Think it's my third time. But it's the kind of thing you could watch every few years, and it wouldn't get old. Read an article a few years back, some guy interviewing some D-Day vets about this show and that other one Spielberg did, *Saving Private Ryan*. The vets said they were the closest thing to being there. No other World War II movies took them back to those days better than Spielberg's did."

"Think I read that article, too," Jack said. "Because of that, I make sure all my military history students watch both of them. And the one they did on the Pacific is pretty good, too."

"Maybe we could watch that series the next time we get together." Joe got up to stretch. He watched Jack walk out to the kitchen. Man, he had a nice place. Big open spaces, high vaulted ceilings with lots of wood beams.

"Sounds like a plan," Jack said. "Although Rachel might prefer it if we start doing things that get us off our butts. Like maybe doing some metal detecting again."

"I think Kate would agree with that. I only did it once or twice in the last year, with Joe Junior. Got him his own detector last Christmas."

Jack put the buffalo dip in the microwave and turned it on.

Just then Joe's cell phone rang. It was by the table where he'd been sitting. He looked down at the screen. "I better get this. It's Kate. She usually doesn't call when we're hanging out. Something must be up."

"Go ahead," Jack said. "This'll be done in a couple of

minutes. Feel free to head out into the veranda if you want some privacy."

Joe's instincts prompted him to do that. After walking through the French doors, he answered his phone. "Hey, Kate. What's up? Everything okay?"

He could hear her crying on the other end.

2

JOE HUNG UP, PUT HIS CELL PHONE IN HIS POCKET AS HE stepped back into the house.

"Is everything okay, Joe?" Jack came in from the kitchen.

"I don't know. Tell you the truth, I'm not sure. Kate's pretty upset, but she wouldn't tell me why."

"Was she hurt? Is it one of the kids?"

"No. I asked her. She said it wasn't anything like that."

"Well, that's at least a good thing," Jack said. "Guess you have to go home, right?"

"Yeah, I can tell that's what she wants. Whatever it is, she didn't want to talk about it over the phone." He handed Jack the remote. "I'll give you back the scepter to your throne."

Jack laughed. "We can finish our *B-of-B* marathon another time. Let's just make sure we put it on the calendar, so it really happens."

"Don't give up on our day just yet, until I find out what's up. She must've got some bad news, or something. Maybe a death in the family, I don't know. Let me get home, see if I can do any good. If it turns out, she needs me for more than just a little bit, I'll let you know."

"Yeah, you go ahead," Jack said. "Rachel and Jack Junior won't be home until tomorrow night, so if things settle down to where she's fine with you coming back, we'll just pick up where we left off."

"All right," Joe said. "Whatever the case, I'll let you know." He grabbed his keys and wallet from a table. "Save me some of that chicken dip," he said as he headed toward the front door.

WHEN JOE PULLED into his driveway, he was still totally perplexed.

He wished she'd have just told him over the phone, whatever it was. He was a homicide cop, had dealt with dozens of difficult and tragic situations for a whole lot of years. He could handle whatever it was. That's what he'd decided on the drive over, that this information had upset Kate but it must be something she was sure would *really* upset Joe, and she didn't want him to have to deal with it there with Jack. Couldn't have been about Joe's parents, since they had both passed away. Maybe it was his brother or one of his sisters.

He got out of the car. Whatever it was, the mystery would be solved in a few moments. He reached for the doorknob, paused, and braced himself before opening the door. As he stepped through the foyer and into the living room, Kate came walking out from the kitchen area. Her eyes were red, but it looked like she had stopped crying. When their eyes met, she made a face he couldn't interpret. But that wasn't unusual. He often couldn't read her faces. She walked toward him holding something out in her hand.

Was it a thermometer? "You okay?"

She nodded. "I'm doing better now that you're here. I feel so stupid getting so upset about this. And I really didn't want to mess up your time with Jack. But I just felt like I had to share this news with someone. Well, not just anyone. With you. And I didn't want to do it over the phone."

Joe walked toward her intending to give her a hug, but there was that white stick thing in her hand. She was still holding it out to him. "What's this?"

"Read it," she said. "Look at the little window in the middle. Don't you see it? There's two lines. Not one. Two. I couldn't believe it when I saw it."

Joe looked down at the thing in her hand. She handed it to him, so he took it. It wasn't a thermometer. Whatever it was, she was right. Two little red lines were showing in the window. "Okay, I see it. The two lines, I mean. But what's it mean, and why's it got you so upset?"

She got another look on her face. Joe needed some words here, not a look.

"Joe, it's a pregnancy test. You're looking at the results. Two red lines mean..."

"A pregnancy test?" Joe repeated. "A pregnancy test? That's what this is?"

"Yes. What did you think it was?"

"I don't know. I've been racking my brain trying to figure out what's going on since you called. A pregnancy test never came up in my head." He looked down at the little window again. "So, these two red lines mean—"

"I'm pregnant!"

"Really? You're pregnant?" He couldn't help it. His eyes suddenly filled with tears. "We're gonna have a baby? Again?"

Now her eyes filled with tears, seeing his. "What do you mean, *again*?" She said. "Joey's almost eleven. Been a while since I've been pregnant."

"Yeah, you're right." He wiped his eyes. "I don't know what I'm saying. But Kate, this is why you were so upset? This is great news." He grabbed her and hugged her tight. "We're going to have another kid. I can't believe it."

"I'm so glad you're happy," she said, still in the hug. "I was afraid you might be upset. We haven't talked about it in a while, but I figured we were done."

He released her from the hug but still held her hands. "I thought so, too. I mean, it's been you, me, Kristin, and Joey for so long, I figure that's who we are. That's the Boyd's."

"I know," she said. "Guess we've got another little Boyd about to join the club."

Joe couldn't stop smiling, even though this news was so crazy. "How sure are you this test is accurate?"

"I'm still going to the doctor, but it says it's ninety-nine percent accurate. It's got hundreds of five-star reviews. I did everything the instructions said."

Joe took a deep breath. "Guess it's for real then. Man, this is not what I expected."

"So, you're totally okay with this?"

"Of course, I'm okay. I mean, it's a bit of a shock. But the good kind. The kids are going to go nuts. They don't know yet, right?"

"I'd never tell them before you. But I agree. They will totally freak out."

"Do you know how it happened? Aren't you still taking those pills?"

"I was." She sighed. "But I messed up, a little. Well, maybe more than a little."

"How's that?"

"It was our anniversary trip, our little getaway. Couldn't believe it when I unpacked the bathroom bag. I'd left the pills at home. I didn't panic, because it had been so long since Joey was born, I half-wondered if I even needed to take them anymore. Guess I got my answer on that one."

Joe laughed. "Guess you did."

"I'm so glad you're happy about this. I don't know why I was worried you might be upset."

He put his arms around her again. "Kate, I'm the opposite of upset. Obviously, we didn't plan this. But it looks like the Lord wants another little Boyd running around this place. So, if that's what God wants, who am I to argue?"

"I love you, Joe Boyd." They kissed.

"Okay if I call Jack, let him know what's going on? He's over there probably still wondering who died?"

"That's what you told him?"

"No, but I'm sure he's like me and figured something bad must've happened."

"No, I don't mind if you call him," she said. "In fact, I'm okay if you want to head back over there and keep watching your war movies. I just couldn't imagine me sitting on something like this until you got home later this evening."

"You sure you're okay with me heading over there again?"

She nodded.

"Okay then," Joe said, "but do me a favor. Don't tell the kids until I get back." Then a thought. "I'll tell you what, let's wait until after church tomorrow. We'll all go out to a nice restaurant and tell them the news then."

"I'd really like that, Joe. That'll make a great memory."

"Then that's what we'll do. I'll just give Jack a quick call." He pulled out his phone, pressed the send button next to Jack's number. "Hey Jack, you're not gonna believe what Kate's phone call was about. No, it wasn't bad news. Not at all. Really, just the opposite."

3

Two Days Later
Culpepper Police Department

JOE HAD JUST ARRIVED AT HIS OFFICE A FEW MINUTES AGO. SET down on his desk what was left of his large half–caff. He'd given up getting doughnuts with his coffee years ago. In exchange, he allowed himself a nice dose of Irish cream half-and-half, which made it really yummy. Almost didn't miss the doughnuts. Almost.

His partner, Hank Jensen, wasn't in yet. Normally, Hank beat him into the office. Joe sat down and turned on his computer. As it booted up, he wondered what Hank would say about he and Kate's baby news. Joe had called him about it, because he didn't want Hank finding out about it on social media first, but Hank didn't answer. So, Joe had left him a voicemail.

He was pretty sure Hank would have listened to it, even though Hank hated voicemails. They'd had this discussion some time ago, the pros and cons of leaving voicemails. Hank preferred Joe not leave any messages, insisting it must be some kind of age thing, since he was at least ten years younger than Joe. He said he, his wife, and his friends never used voicemail. It was too much of a hassle. Their understanding was, you simply check your missed phone calls and call back the people you recognize as soon as you got the chance. It was so much easier and less time-consuming.

Joe's reply was, "You think listening to voicemails on a smartphone is inconvenient? No, inconvenient is having to come home and listen to voice messages on an answering machine, where you have to rewind a cassette tape to the beginning, then listen to each one — even the boring duds — to get to the ones that matter." In the end, Joe simply pulled rank on Hank. "I'm gonna leave you voicemails, Hank, so you're gonna listen to them. At least the ones you get from me."

Their office door opened, and in walked Hank, carrying something besides his laptop bag. Was it a shoebox?

"Sorry I'm late, Joe. Had to make a stop on the way in." Hank laid his laptop bag on the desk then handed Joe the little box. "Congratulations, Papa. Heard your voicemail last night, about you and Kate having a new baby. I could tell how excited you were on the phone. I know you used to like to smoke cigars. Don't know if you do anymore, but this seemed like the perfect gift to celebrate."

Joe looked down at the brand. Hank remembered the ones he smoked. "Wow, Hank. I don't know what to say. I'm overwhelmed."

"Don't gotta say anything." Hank sat down. "Me and

Wendy were just so happy for you guys. We didn't even know you were trying."

"That's the thing," Joe said. "We weren't. This was totally unplanned. Like you said, I'm super happy about it, but... definitely didn't see this coming."

"How did Kristin and Joe Junior take the news?"

"Took them out for dinner after church yesterday, told them then. They went absolutely nuts. Especially Kristin. She said she's gonna be the best big sister in the history of the world."

Hank laughed. "That's a pretty big commitment."

"I know, right?"

"So, when's it due?"

"Kate's still got to go to the doctor, has an appointment on Wednesday. But should be about six months from now."

"Well," Hank said. "It's a surprise, but at least it's a good one. Could be worse."

"What do you mean?"

"I don't know...what if this happened ten years from now? You'd be too old to even play ball with him, or her."

Joe shook his head. "Yeah, that might be the only downside to this. I'm like, just the right age energy-wise for Joey and Kristin now. I'm a little worried when this baby gets their age, what kind of shape I'll be in."

"I don't know," Hank said, "maybe you'll get lucky, and the baby's favorite thing will be reading books. That's something you could pull off even if you do let yourself go."

Joe laughed. "I've got no plans of letting myself go. But Father Time wins every game. I think that's a saying."

Their phone buzzed. Joe was closer, he picked it up. "Cold Case Squad, Lieutenant Joe Boyd speaking."

"Joe, it's Pendleton. I don't know where my secretary got off to, so I'm calling myself. Could you come to my office right away? Just been made aware of a situation that needs your attention. It's not a homicide or a cold case. But after I heard what's going on, I instantly thought you'd be the right man for the job. I'll explain when you get here."

"Should I bring Hank?"

"No, just you. You can brief him later."

"Okay, Cap. Be right there."

Joe hung up and explained things to Hank.

"Wonder what it is," Hank said. "I'll just sit here till you get back. Mind if I open one of these cigars?"

"You better not. Probably set off the smoke alarm in here."

"I was just kidding. You go on. I'll check my email till you get back."

JOE KNOCKED TWICE and stepped through Captain Pendleton's doorway. Pendleton was just hanging up the phone. He waved for Joe to take a seat.

"Come on in, Joe. You ever heard of a guy named Samuel Clemens?"

"Sounds familiar," Joe said, "though I'm not sure why. Was he a baseball player?"

"No, that's Roger Clemens," Pendleton said. "I'm talking about a criminal case, not somebody famous."

"Okay then. So, no. Don't think I've ever heard of a case with a guy named Samuel Clemens." But Joe was sure he'd heard that name somewhere before. "What did he do?"

"First-degree murder," Pendleton said. "Back in 1985, right

here in Culpepper. But it did make the national news for a week or so. Guess it didn't make its way up there in Pittsburgh, where you're from."

"If it did, got by me. So, 1985. That's over thirty-five years ago. But you said this wasn't a cold case situation."

"That's right, I did. The case got solved pretty early on. In fact, the killer—this Samuel Clemens—has been in prison since then. Served most of his years at Georgia State. The thing is, he just got paroled."

"Paroled?" Joe repeated. "After all these years? Who did he kill?" Joe knew in Georgia, certainly back in those days, most serious killers got death row. Those that got life usually got paroled way before now.

"It's not some Charles Manson-like thing," Pendleton said. "Not downplaying how serious it was, but the reason his parole's just happening now doesn't have anything to do with how vicious the killing was. Kind of a long story. I can tell you more about it later. The point is, I just got the heads up from a friend at Georgia State...Clemens was released this morning. The more important point is, he's on his way back here. May already be here now. Culpepper is where he's from, and it's also where the murder took place. Like I said, made the national news for a week, but it was the biggest thing in the local news for several months. I'm afraid there's going to be a big stir when it gets out that Clemens is back in town. Especially from the victim's family."

"A lot of them still left alive in this town, I guess," Joe said.

"A few are. Some of the main ones, who were all over the news when it happened, have died. But I checked, and there's a handful still alive and kicking. A couple of them are what you'd call known troublemakers. Several arrests apiece. Mostly small stuff, like drunk-and-disorderly and bar fights. I anticipate once they hear about Clemens getting freed and coming back here, we could have some trouble."

"You're probably right," Joe said. "You said something about me being the right man for the job. What kind of job you have in mind?"

Pendleton sat back in his chair. "Maybe I could say it this way...ever seen those old westerns where the sheriff makes a visit to a stranger who's just come into town, someone he thinks is going to cause trouble. And the sheriff tries to talk the stranger into leaving town before any trouble starts?"

Joe smiled. "Think I might've seen a few of those. So, you're wanting me to pay this Clemens fellow a visit and, basically, ask him to get out of town?"

Pendleton laughed. "Put that way, sounds a bit harsh. But that's the general idea. I was just hoping you could use your gift of persuasion to help him see coming back here's not a good idea. From what I gather, he doesn't have any family here. Besides that, you can use the leverage of him violating his parole. He may not have plans to start trouble, but the trouble that could erupt if he stays, might be enough to get him sent back to prison for good. You could go at it like that." He handed Joe a slip of paper. "He's supposed to be staying at this address. I don't know if it's a halfway house, or what."

Joe stood, seemed like the assignment was pretty clear. He took the note from Pendleton. "I can certainly give it a try, Captain. But there's no guarantee here. It's not like he's breaking any laws moving back."

"No, not when you put it that way. But if laws do get broke, even if he's not the one breaking them, he could very easily find himself right in the middle of it all. That's the thing you've got to stress with him."

"I'll see what I can do, sir." Pendleton's phone rang. He picked up the receiver and waved to Joe, so he left and headed back to his office to brief Hank.

His initial thought was...this is probably no big deal.

4

"So," Hank said, "what did Pendleton want? Anything interesting?"

Joe closed their shared office door behind him and walked to his desk. "Interesting is one way to describe it." He told Hank everything he understood about their task with this Clemens fellow.

"Yeah, that's something I'm pretty sure I've never done as a cop before," Hank said, "ask some guy to get out of town."

Joe handed Hank the slip of paper with the guy's address on it. "He's supposed to be staying at that place. That's if he's even back in town yet. If he's not there, he will be soon."

"The guy's name sounds familiar to me," Hank said. "But I don't know why."

"I thought so, too," Joe said. "Obviously, it's not because I got any memory of the case. Happened decades before I moved here."

"Happened before I was born," Hank said. "But you know, we live in this miracle age where we never have to wonder about anything. You got a question, no matter how small, just Google it. Or if Alexa's nearby, just yell it out. You'll have your answer in a few seconds." Hank turned around and started typing on his keyboard.

Joe laughed. "Yeah, that's definitely one of the differences between you and me. When I grew up, the internet was still years off. We didn't know the answer to something, we just shrugged our shoulders and somebody changed the subject."

"Okay," Hank said. "Mystery solved. It's Mark Twain."

"Who is?"

"Samuel Clemens. That's why the name sounds familiar. That's the real name of Mark Twain, the famous author. You know, Tom Sawyer, Huckleberry Finn."

"Yeah, I know," Joe said. "Read both books as a kid. That must be it then. Maybe while you're googling stuff, let's dig up anything we can find on *our* Samuel Clemens. Pendleton said this was a pretty big story back in '85 when it happened. See what you can find."

Hank added the words *murder* and *1985* to Clemens' name. Sure enough, several articles quickly appeared. "This beats having to go over to the library and dig up old news stories on microfilm. Glad they got all these old stories uploaded."

"I know," Joe said. "Let's skip the big national papers and click on the local ones. Probably get more useful info from those."

"Looks like the articles are in chronological order," Hank said. "Where do you want to start?"

"Click on the third one," Joe said. "The one where it says, *Culpepper Grad Arrested in Sanchez Slaying*." On the second line of the entry, Joe could see the *grad* they were talking about was Samuel Clemens.

"Guess our vic's name was Sanchez," Hank said as he clicked on the link.

The two men read the article silently for a few minutes, Joe looking over Hank's shoulder. At one point, as Hank scrolled down to continue reading, a picture appeared of the victim, Roberto Sanchez, and the accused, Clemens, as they appeared in 1985. A credit line below the photos mentioned they were taken from the Culpepper University's 1983 year-book, the year both men graduated.

"Gives some good background info," Hank said, "but very little on why the police arrested Clemens for the killing."

"You see that bit about this guy Sanchez being an up-and-coming TV reporter?" Joe said.

"Yeah. Sounds like he was modeling his career after Geraldo Rivera. That's who people were starting to compare him to."

"Rivera was huge back then," Joe said. "You couldn't turn on the national news without seeing him going after some cutting-edge story."

"It says both these guys graduated from Culpepper with degrees in journalism," Hank said. "I didn't even know Culpepper had a School of Journalism."

"I don't think they do," Joe said. "Not anymore. Maybe Jack will know more about it. There at the end of the article it says both men were working on some kind of documentary together. Maybe that had something to do with Clemens' arrest. Back out of this story and let's look for one about the trial. Maybe the one where the jury finds him guilty. That should have better details about the crime."

Hank did what Joe asked and found an article written on the day Clemens was found guilty. He clicked on it and they started to read some more. A few minutes later, Hank asked, "You finished?"

"Yeah, think I've read enough. So, they think Clemens felt like Sanchez had ripped him off and stolen some of his work?"

"That's my take on it, too," Hank said. "They said Clemens confronted Sanchez at his house, demanding his video footage back or the money he was owed. I mean, Joe, the police found him fleeing the scene shortly after Sanchez was killed. Him, just him, and no one else. And he had the vic's blood on his shoes. That's motive, means, and opportunity."

"Yeah, I suppose. But did you see he was killed with a dumbbell that belonged to the vic? He didn't bring a weapon with him. That seems more like a crime of passion, to me. Not premeditation. Seems like they should have gotten him for Murder 2, not 1st Degree. I mean, the jury took three days to reach a verdict. Not very slamdunk, you ask me."

"Maybe not, but it's not that unusual for juries to take that long when the case is entirely circumstantial, right? I've heard you say that."

"Yeah, guess so. Not that any of this matters anyway. We weren't there. Maybe I'd feel differently if I was. Anyway, think we've got enough to go visit this guy and do what Pendleton asked us to do. Why don't you type that address into your phone, get the GPS to tell us how to get there?" He stood up and grabbed his coat, headed for the office door. Hank did the same.

Another thing that seemed a little off to Joe about this guy Clemens' situation...how does a guy found guilty on a purely circumstantial case get stuck in prison for thirty-six years before getting paroled? He'd never heard of something like that. Pendleton had said he was going to explain why that happened, but Joe left his office before finding out.

"Let's go have a talk with Clemens."

5

SAMUEL CLEMENS PULLED INTO THE LITTLE LAKESIDE CABIN he'd rented for the next two months. Should be enough time for him to get done what needed doing. He'd followed the directions written down on paper at the real estate office in town. Fortunately, the young lady who'd worked there and had helped him find this place didn't seem to know who he was. She'd told him he could put the address into his smartphone, let the GPS app take him there.

He had no idea what a GPS was, or an app, for that matter. Not wanting to appear stupid, he'd told the real estate gal he'd lost his GPS thing and could she write out the directions to the cabin the old-fashioned way. She made a face like he was talking some foreign language until he'd explained the old-fashioned way was just using paper and pen. Thankfully, she knew what those two things were.

Clemens had heard of smartphones, had seen them on some of the movies he'd watched in prison. Could hardly believe all the crazy things people had invented over the last thirty-six years. According to his community supervision officer — the fancy name parole officers went by these days —Clemens had better get himself one of these smartphones if he expected to survive in this new modern world. The first evidence that the officer might not be exaggerating came when the real estate gal informed him the cabin he was renting "did have Wi-Fi but did not have a landline."

Now it was her turn to be talking a foreign language. What in the world was Wi-Fi, why was that a good thing, what was a landline, and why was its absence a bad thing? After a few more minutes explaining, he got the idea. The cabin had no phone, not one he could use. But if he got himself a smartphone, this Wi-Fi thing would make it easier for him to connect to the internet. Clemens didn't know how to use the internet. But she explained getting a smartphone would still allow him to call people, and for other people to call him.

Which was kinda important. Mainly, for one reason.

His parole officer had said he needed to be able to reach him at any time of the day, so Clemens better get one of these smartphones pretty quick. He mentioned some government programs available that could get him one for almost next to nothing, but Clemens didn't qualify on account of that inheritance he'd gotten a couple years back from his Uncle Joel...the only relative Clemens had who'd made some effort to stay connected with him all those years he'd spent behind bars.

This inheritance didn't make Clemens a rich man, but it was a decent sum. Gave him enough to avoid having to go to some halfway house. And right after getting his driver's license renewed, he was able to splurge a little on transportation. Bought himself a refurbished '65 Dodge pickup. Saw it for sale on one of the side roads that led out here from town. Not exactly like the one he'd lost when he got arrested back in '85. But it was close enough, almost the same color of red. Paid cash for it. That was a good feeling. Clemens hadn't felt anything close to a good feeling in years. Almost brought a tear to his eye as he drove the truck down the road the first time.

And now, here he was getting out of his truck and gazing at the front door of this cozy little cabin out in the woods by Lake Sampson. The same lake he used to fish in and water ski on in his youth. Not likely he'd ever water ski again but fishing at some point was at least a possibility.

But not for a while. Clemens had work to do. Really, it was more of a mission. A mission with two parts.

Part one, clear his name. Part two, payback.

He'd picked this place because it was still inside the city limits, technically—a requirement for his parole—but far enough away that folks weren't likely to bother him; the way they'd most certainly do if he'd stayed in town.

He walked around the back and opened the trunk lid, grabbed hold of the grocery bags containing all the cold stuff first. As he walked to the front door, he couldn't believe how quiet it was. Prison life was so noisy. And except for the occasional bouts in solitary confinement, it was anything but private. But here he was, all alone. No one to bother him. No one to tell him what to do. No danger. Could almost entice him to entertain a fantasy of giving up his mission. Just live out here like an old hermit, spend the rest of his days doing nothing but this.

But that fantasy had dissipated by the time he'd

unlocked the front door. He couldn't let this thing go. He'd hate himself if he did. Someone had stolen the last thirty-six years of his life. They had deliberately and without any regard for the suffering it would put him through, had destroyed any chances for Clemens to ever meet the right girl, fall in love, get married, and have a family. Here he was, a few months from sixty, with no photos to hang on his walls. No family memories to cherish. No woman to grow old with, no grandkids to spoil.

The man who'd done that, who'd taken all that away from him — if Clemens had figured things correctly — did get to experience all those things, and he was living right here in Culpepper, and had been the entire time Clemens had been locked up for a crime he did not commit.

Of course, no one else believed that.

Clemens had been let out on parole, he hadn't been exonerated. As far as this world was concerned, he was still guilty. Clemens and Clemens alone had brutally murdered Roberto Sanchez on that day thirty-six years ago. So, they locked him up and threw away the key. Out of sight, out of mind. Life goes on. And it did for almost everyone else.

But not for Samuel Clemens. To everyone else, he was still a felon. A convicted murderer. Wherever he went, for however many days he had left on this earth, that's who he'd be. That's all he'd ever be.

Unless Clemens did something about it. It was up to him and him alone to right this wrong. And to make the man who had done this murder pay for what he did. The only question Clemens hadn't yet resolved in his heart was...how far was he willing to go to bring about justice? In the end, would he be able to do to this man what his treacherous deeds deserved? Clemens had hurt — even badly — a number of men in prison, especially in those early years. But only in self-defense.

He had never actually killed someone before. When the moment came, he wondered...could he really do it?

6

IT WAS MIDMORNING.

Joe felt like he and Hank had done enough research on this Clemens fellow to accomplish their assignment. For the last ten minutes, they had been driving through Culpepper towards the edge of town. To satisfy Hank's craving to utilize all the technology the department provided, Joe had let him key in the address into the car's GPS. But he rarely glanced down at the screen. Joe recognized the street address on the slip of paper Captain Pendleton had given him.

"Guess you were right," Hank said. "This place is just outside of town." Hank *was* looking down at the screen.

"The screen tell you that, or did you just look out the windows?" He smiled at Hank. "You forget how many times I've driven through this area metal detecting with Jack. Pretty familiar with all the main roads in the lake area. We even camped out this way, but in a campground on the far side of the lake. Pretty sure this isn't gonna be some kind halfway house. Think it's one of the private cabins on the lake, the ones on the side closer to town."

"How's an ex-con afford a cabin on the lake?" Hank said. "Hasn't he been locked up for, like, thirty years?"

"Thirty-six. Guess we'll have to ask him."

"Maybe he had some stash hiding somewhere, waiting for him when he got out," Hank said.

"Maybe. But he wasn't a bank robber. He and the guy he killed were just two years out of college. Didn't that article say their conflict had to do with him trying to get paid for some video work he'd done? Felt the vic' had ripped him off?"

"Yeah," Hank said. "Doesn't sound like a man of means. You're supposed to turn left up here."

"The GPS lady gonna yell at me if I don't? I know a quicker route. Why don't you just look out the window, enjoy the scenery? I promise, we won't get lost."

Five minutes later, Joe turned down the dirt road that led to Clemens' address. Very familiar territory. Like all the places out here on Lake Samson. Covered with trees, mostly pines and other evergreens. Made every property feel more isolated and private.

CLEMENS COULDN'T BE SURE, but it sounded like a car had just pulled up outside. He had been sitting at a little rustic dinette table scribbling down some notes. Mainly, trying to come up with some kind of outline or plan he could follow in the weeks ahead. He got up from his chair, opened the curtain slightly, and peeked out the front window.

It was a shiny black sedan, parked right next to his truck.

Two guys got out dressed in cheap suits. Definitely not Feds, and he didn't know anybody from the Mafia. So, who were they? They were talking, but he couldn't hear what they said. One looked like early forties, the other late twenties. Their faces looked pleasant enough, but still he wished he had a gun. Made him feel so helpless being stuck out here with no way to defend himself. He had stopped at a Walmart and picked up a bat. Pretty hard to hide a bat, though, when greeting someone at the door.

He waited for them to knock then counted to five before opening it. When he did, he just opened it a crack. "Help you gentlemen? Pardon me for not being more hospitable, but a man can't be too careful these days. Especially out here."

"That's okay," the older of the two men said. "Not offended."

Definitely not a Southerner. Sounded like a Yank. Couldn't tell from where yet. Both men took out ID badges from their coat lapels.

"I'm Lieutenant Joe Boyd, and this is my partner, Sergeant Hank Jensen. We're from the Culpepper PD."

"We're the hospitality committee," Hank said. "Might you be Samuel Clemens, not the famous author?"

This kid was definitely from around here. Been a long time since anyone connected him with Mark Twain, he'd almost forgotten the connection himself. Most of the inmates he'd met weren't into reading childhood classics. "I am Sam Clemens," he said, opening the door wider.

"We understand you've been let out of prison very recently on parole," Joe said. "After more than thirty years, is that correct?"

"Yep. Thirty-six years. Hard to fathom at times, even for me. More than half my life."

"Okay if we come in for a chat?" Joe said.

Hank added, "I'm sure you know the conditions of your parole include members of law enforcement checking in on you at any time they please."

Clemens sighed. "Read that in the pamphlet. But I would've let you in even if you neglected to point out that fact." He opened the door fully and backed off to the side. "Sit anywhere you like. Haven't been here long enough to pick out a favorite chair."

The older man, Joe, sat in the chair Clemens felt sure would soon become his favorite. The younger fellow sat on the edge of the couch. Clemens picked the only chair not taken in the small living area. "I have some water bottles chilling in the fridge. Don't know how cold they are yet. Planning on making some iced tea shortly. Can I get you any—"

"That's okay, Mr. Clemens," Joe said. "Appreciate the offer, but this isn't really a social visit."

"Guess you got my address out here from my parole officer, or whatever they call them these days."

"Actually, no," Hank said. "We got it from our captain. He's the one who asked us to pay you this visit."

"Your captain? Don't see how a nobody like me rates that kind of attention."

Joe smiled. "Come now, Mr. Clemens."

"Please, call me Sam."

"Okay...*Sam*. I think we all know you are way more than a nobody. If you were, we wouldn't be here. And as my partner already said, our captain asked us to come out here to talk with you. He only gets involved in things that are pretty important."

Clemens was sincerely puzzled. "If you say so. For the last several decades I've pretty much felt like a nobody, pretty much been treated like a nobody. So, I came by that assessment honestly. Help me understand how I suddenly became somebody's top priority?"

"I'd be happy to explain," Joe said. "Really, it's the main reason we're here."

"Before we get into that," Hank interrupted, "mind if I ask a question? As you said, you've been incarcerated for over thirty years. Usually when someone gets out of prison after all that time, they don't..." Hank looked around the place. "They don't get to start off in a place like this. It's usually more like —"

"A halfway house for inmates?" Clemens said.

"Well, yeah."

"A fair question. And up until a couple of years ago, that's exactly what I would've expected should they ever let me out. Then an uncle died. The one relative who'd stayed in touch with me over the years. Shortly thereafter, I was informed by his attorney that he left everything to me. Didn't make me rich, and certainly didn't do me any good on the inside. But now that I'm out, it is giving me a better start than I had any reason to expect."

"That makes sense," Hank said. "But if you'll allow me to pry further, wouldn't the victim's family typically sue someone like you, as a means to obtain some financial restitution for the losses they incurred when you killed their loved one?"

That stung a bit. Clemens tried not to let it show.

"Another fair question. I suppose the answer has to do with timing. Turns out, my uncle outlived all the main kinfolk from my so-called victim's family, so there wasn't anyone left to come after my inheritance."

"So-called," Joe said. "That's how you referred to the man you killed, Roberto Sanchez. As your *so-called* victim. You claiming that you're not guilty of that crime?"

"Well," Clemens said. "I am. But for only one reason."

"What's that?" Hank said.

"Because I didn't kill the man."

7

HE DIDN'T KILL HIM. WHERE HAD JOE HEARD THAT BEFORE?

"No disrespect, but you do know," Hank said to Clemens, "every convicted murderer says that? It's almost a cliché."

Clemens smiled. "Yeah, think I heard that a few times inside, too. Only thing is, with me, happens to be the truth. Don't expect you to believe me. Didn't say it thinking you would. It's just...what it is. I mean, think about it. Why would I come back here to Culpepper, of all places? Got no family left here. Certainly, no old friends to reconnect with."

"As it turns out," Joe said, "that's one of the items on my agenda—for us coming out here, I mean—to answer that question. Why *did* you come back here?"

"Because I —" Clemens stopped himself. "Well, let's just say I've got...unfinished business."

"Not sure I like the sound of that," Hank said, before Joe could say the same thing.

"Nothing sinister," Clemens said. "Like I said, from what I

gather, the main family members of the guy I was supposed to have killed have all died."

"Did you read about that on the internet in prison?" Hank said.

Clemens shook his head no. "Never even been on the internet. They had it inside, in some special designated areas. Some guys were on it all the time. But it got invented years after I went in. Never saw any reason to learn how to use it."

"I thought you said you were innocent?" Hank said. "That's one of the main reasons guys in prison go on the internet, to do research about their case. See if they can dig up new evidence or maybe email organizations that work with the wrongly-accused, help them get their case overturned on appeal."

Joe wasn't sure where Hank was going with this.

"Know of some guys that did that, too," Clemens said. "Never saw any good come of it. Some of them spent years trying. A total waste of time. Besides, don't know how much you men looked into my record, but the few appeals my attorney tried in the beginning — halfheartedly, you ask me — went nowhere. And since my family pretty much believed I was guilty, they ditched me. After about a year, they moved to another town. Said they couldn't take all the dirty looks they were getting on account of what I did. So, I had nobody on the outside even caring about my case." He sat up in his chair. "Tell you what, whoever set me up covered all the bases. I'll give him that."

The look in Clemens' eyes almost made Joe believe him. He said this like he really believed it. "A moment ago, you said you were aware that most of the family members of your victim had died. How did you find out about this?"

"Well, one by one, they stopped showing up for my parole hearings. The first few, they all came. Man, did they hate my guts. And they made sure everyone on the panel knew how thoroughly I had ruined their lives. Didn't matter how hard I tried to behave in prison. There was no way they'd ever let me out. Over the last ten years or so, I'd see one or the other family members hadn't shown up. One of the guards that treated me decent told me why. They died. But the few who did show up made just as much of a fuss, so the board rejected me again. This last time, I wasn't even going to show up to the hearing. Figured, what's the point? But that same guard told me none of the family were left. None of the original ones anyway. So, I went. And what do you know? They approved it. They let me out. And here I am." He leaned back in his chair again, like saying all that had exhausted him.

What Clemens had just said explained another thing Joe had wondered about. How someone with Clemens' kind of case had *not* gotten paroled long before now. Of course, based on what Pendleton had told him, not all the family members had died. If they had, he and Hank wouldn't have needed to drive out here in the first place.

Clemens stood. "Don't know about you fellas, but I'm getting thirsty. Think I will grab me one of them water bottles. Care for one?"

"Sure," Hank said. "All this yakking's made me thirsty, too."

"Okay, I'll have one," Joe said. He wasn't sure he should.

The tone of this conversation seemed to be moving away from the getting-him-to-leave-town theme. He was finding Clemens to be a more sympathetic character than he'd expected.

Clemens came back with the water bottles, handed them each one, started to swig on his own.

"Thank you for the water, Mr. Clemens."

"Please, Sam."

"Sorry," Joe said, "Sam. You helped clear up some confusion I had about why you weren't let out on parole until now. But you still haven't explained why you decided to come back here to Culpepper seeing, as you said, you have no family, no real ties to this area anymore. I'm going to need a little bit more than you just saying you have some *unfinished business*."

Clemens set his water bottle on the table. "I figured you might. I know it's your job to be nosy, and I've lost the right to tell you to mind your own business." He took a deep breath, eyes roaming around like he was trying to figure out how to say as little as possible.

"You wouldn't be here trying to figure out who's really responsible for putting you in prison?" Hank said.

Clemens smiled. "Well, Sergeant Jenkins, I appreciate you saying that. Might be the nicest thing anybody's said to me in years."

Hank looked totally puzzled.

But Joe got it. The man's mind was certainly still firing on all cylinders.

"I don't follow," Hank said.

"You wouldn't ask me a question like that if you thought I

was guilty. What changed your mind? What made you think I'm innocent after all?"

"I don't think you're innocent. Nothing changed my mind. Why are you saying that?"

"Because Hank," Joe said, "if you thought he was guilty, you'd know he'd have zero motivation to come back here to find and confront the real killer, because he would know there was no one else."

Now, Hank got it. Joe felt sorry for how stupid he felt. But Clemens had a point. Joe had actually been thinking the same thing...that this was Clemens' motivation for returning to Culpepper now. It was about the only thing that made any sense.

Clemens broke the moment of silence. "Well, let me help you out, Sergeant. I'd be lying if I denied it. It's one of the main reasons I've come back. As I said at the beginning of our little chat here, I didn't kill this guy, Roberto Sanchez. Sure, I was angry at him for ripping me off. But not enough to kill the man. The thought of doing that never even entered my mind. But someone did kill him. And they thought it through so carefully they were able to set me up to take the fall. And when I fell, there was no getting up. This man — the real killer — stole two lives that day. Sanchez's and mine. I may not know how to use the internet, but I've had years to think about what happened. And I feel like I've narrowed down the possibilities considerably. The one that fits best is why I'm back here. In Culpepper."

Joe had always been a great judge of character, especially with perps. This man really did believe he'd been set up. He looked at Hank. He could see Hank was also affected by what Clemens had said. But it didn't matter. It didn't change the reason he and Hank had been sent there to visit Clemens. If anything, what Clemens had just said made Pendleton's concerns even more valid than when they'd started this conversation.

8

JOE LOOKED OVER AT HANK, COULDN'T QUITE READ THE LOOK on his face. "Mr. Clemens, Sam, we have a few more things to discuss with you, but I need to confer with my partner first. We're going to step outside a moment."

"Fine with me," Clemens said. "Give me a chance to use the john. Forgot how nice it is to use a bathroom that has a door."

Joe stood up and walked to the front door. Hank followed right behind.

When they got outside, Hank said, "Glad you suggested this. Wasn't sure how you wanted to get things to where they need to go."

"So, how are you reading this situation?" Joe said.

"You mean what do I think about this guy? I don't know, Joe. I'm starting to like him. I know that's not why we're here. We've only been talking a few minutes, and he could just be a first-class con, but he's making me at least wonder whether or not he really did this. What's your take?"

"Pretty much same as you," Joe said. "That's why I wanted to call this little pow-wow. Make sure we're singing from the same sheet music. What you and I think about this guy — in terms of his actual guilt or innocence — can't matter. Cap' sent us here with a job to do."

"Chase him out of town, you mean?"

Joe nodded. "We go back in there, that's gotta remain the goal. We can't allow our hunches — gained from a ten-minute chat — to override a year-long jury trial by people who heard all the evidence, frontwards and backwards, who unanimously found him guilty beyond a reasonable doubt."

Hank hesitated with his reply. "Yeah, Joe. I know you're right. But what if they didn't hear all the evidence? You know how many bad cases happened back then, especially with high profile media coverage like this one had. Lots of motivation to nail a guy to the wall, just to turn off the heat. If he was set up for this, maybe nobody cared enough to dig deeper, see if there was more going on."

"And maybe you're right," Joe said. "Still doesn't matter. Not today anyway. I admit...something about this thing doesn't sit right with me. If he killed the guy, then he knows he did, and there's no reason to come back here. With no family or friends left, what kind of unfinished business could he be talking about?"

"Proving who really did it?" Hank said. "Maybe make him pay?"

That was the only thing that made sense to Joe, too. He looked toward the front door. "I know. I'm thinking the same thing. But even if that's true, that's not our job today. I told you what the captain said. This victim has some remaining family members left in Culpepper. He doesn't know how to use the internet, which means he'll be digging things up the old-fashioned way. Asking lots of questions from lots of people all over town. Word is bound to get back to the family. That happens and this whole thing blows up in his face. That's the message he needs to hear today. Nothing else."

"Okay, Joe. I'll follow your lead."

They headed back inside.

CLEMENS HAD BEEN PEEKING through a slit in the front curtain at the two detectives talking, trying to figure out what they might be up to. He hoped he hadn't said too much. They didn't seem upset with him, but he felt vulnerable, knowing as a parolee he had barely any more rights now than he had back in prison. And he certainly didn't want to give the police any reason to send him back.

Looked like they were done and heading back toward the door. He hurried to his chair and sat back down, tried to act like he'd been there a while.

The door opened, and the two men returned to the same places they had been sitting. The younger one took a long swallow from his water bottle.

"Don't want to put you in too much suspense, Sam, about our little huddle outside. The thing is, based on some of the things you said, we have a real concern that you might be planning something that will — even if it's not your intent — get you put back in prison for the rest of your days."

"Well, I can assure you, that's the last thing I want. And I paid very close attention to what my parole officer said could get me sent back, even read the brochure he gave me several times. Paid particular attention to that part. So, you don't have to worry —"

"Sam," Joe interrupted, rather forcefully. "You know what instincts are, don't you? I don't think you get to be a man your age, who's been through what you've been through, who hasn't developed some."

"I think I know what they are," Clemens said. "Not sure I know what you mean, but I'm listening."

"Well, our instincts tell us — for whatever your reasons — you're not out here to fish, or just to commune with nature. You haven't told us the nature of your unfinished business, as you put it, but we're thinking what you're planning will likely not go the way you think. You go digging up the past, asking all kinds of questions all over town, you will unleash a hornet's nest that'll only wind up coming down on your own head."

Clemens took a deep breath. He needed to tread carefully. "I appreciate your concern, Lieutenant. I mean that. But even though I didn't spend any time on the internet, because of the internet being available to so many others, it left the prison library mostly empty. And I read lots of books, the old-fashioned ones with real pages that turn. Read quite a few books on how private detectives go about solving cases. Found a few good ones written before the internet got popular, so all their methods were the old school kind. Ones old-timers like me could follow. I have no intention of asking questions all over town. I plan to be very discreet in the way I pursue my...unfinished business. As I said, the last thing I want is to be sent back to prison."

"Even so, Sam," Joe said. "This plan of yours can't work. I know you think it can. I don't doubt, even if you are as quiet as a mouse about it, word of what you're doing will get out. And when it does —"

"But how can that be? All the family members, the ones who hated my guts, are all dead. I bet there's hardly anybody left in town who knows me. And even if there is, they remember the handsome, younger me in my mid-twenties. Not this old flea-bitten bag of bones you see before you."

"Because Sam...all the family members *aren't* dead. The ones you remember are. But some of the ones who didn't come to your parole hearings are alive and well. And they're not nice people, from what my captain tells me. They're not the live-and-let-live kind of folks. They won't just sit back and let you pursue your little investigation in peace."

This piece of news was certainly disturbing. "Well, Lieutenant, that is discouraging. I hadn't heard that. But you have to understand, I can't let this go. I won't make trouble for anyone, but my whole life was ruined by a lie. Not just one lie, more than a dozen of them. And I think I may know who that liar — who that killer, the real killer — is. Can't prove it. Not yet anyway. But if I leave or just drop it altogether, then my whole life on this earth will have been pointless. I will just die with the whole world thinking I was nothing but a lowlife murderer. Could you be happy with that? Could either of you men? Wouldn't you at least try to right such a wrong as that?"

Joe looked at Hank, who shook his head. "I'm not saying I can't sympathize with your situation, Sam. But what good would all that effort be, if all it did was get you thrown back in prison for the rest of your life? Probably before you barely got started. Certainly before you got enough evidence to make any difference at all."

"Well, of course, I wouldn't like that at all."

"Well, I'm afraid that's what you're facing. That's closer to reality than the hope you have of solving this thing. And because it is, our advice...our firm advice, is to give this up and enjoy the remainder of your days in peace, preferably living somewhere else where no one would have any reason to get you to violate your parole and get you sent back."

Clemens sat back in his chair. He didn't know what to say to all this. "Do I have any choice here? If I don't do what you say, will that be enough to get me sent back?"

Joe stood, then so did Hank. "No," Joe said. "You're not breaking any law if you stay. We had to come here just the same and make you aware of what you'll most certainly be facing if you stay on this path."

Clemens stood. "Well, I can see you men are ready to go. I appreciate your concerns for my welfare. I really do. And I will give serious thought to what you've told me." He stepped ahead of them and opened the door. "You men have a good day."

He watched as they walked to their car, got inside, and drove away.

9

WHEN JOE AND HANK GOT BACK TO THE STATION, JOE SAID he'd stop in and brief Captain Pendleton, so Hank could head back to their office and get started on something else. Joe walked through the hallways till he reached Pendleton's door. He greeted Pendleton's secretary, quickly glanced down at the little sign on her desk. "Hi, Marsha. Is the Captain in?" Marsha had only been there a few months.

"He is, Lieutenant Boyd. I think he's just returning some emails. Want me to see if he can see you?"

"Please. Tell him I want to give him a brief update on the assignment he gave me and Hank this morning."

Marsha pressed the intercom button for Pendleton's office and told him what Joe said. He said to send Joe right in. Joe could hear him reply and nodded to Marsha that he'd gotten the message. He knocked twice, opened the door, and walked in.

"Come on in, Joe. How did it go with our aging parolee, Mr. Clemens?"

Joe wasn't too sure how much to say. Neither he nor Hank had a great deal of confidence that Clemens would heed their warning and leave town. "Pretty good, I guess."

"You guess? Then it doesn't sound like things went pretty good. The main thing is, were you able to convince him it's in his best interest to leave town?"

"Convince might be too strong a word. We certainly pressed all the angles pretty forcefully trying to get him to see."

"But he's not getting it?" Pendleton said.

"He said he'd certainly think about what we said. But both Hank and I got the feeling he's pretty set on staying."

"Did you tell him some of Sanchez's family is still in town? And these aren't the kind of guys who will react well to the news he's come back?"

"Cap', like I said, we pressed all the angles, including that one. Including how easy it would be for him, if he stays, to get sucked into the kind of trouble that could get him sent back to prison. Even if he didn't start the trouble."

"But he still didn't buy it?"

"Don't think so."

"He say why?"

Joe sighed. He hoped Pendleton wouldn't ask this. "We finally got him to tell us. I'm sure you'll find this hard to believe, but he says he's come back to, basically, clear his name."

"What?"

"Yeah, he wants to find out who really did what he went to prison for."

"You mean, murdering Sanchez? You're kidding, right?"

"That is what I mean, and I'm not kidding."

Pendleton let out an exasperated sigh. "He's the one who really did it. I was here then. Followed the whole case front to back. It wasn't open-shut, but darn near close. When it was over, I don't think anyone in town had any doubt, let alone a reasonable one." He massaged his temples. "This is just great."

"I don't know what else we could have said, Cap'. We really emphasized how easily digging all this up could backfire on him, wind up getting him sent back. But you know we don't have a legal basis to insist he comply."

"I know, I know. It's just...I don't know. Guess we'll just have to see how this plays out."

"He said he had no plans on making any kind of scene and would be very discreet as he looks into this."

Pendleton just shook his head. "This can't end well. It's only a matter of time before he does something and word gets out that he's back in town."

MARSHA HENDERSON, Pendleton's secretary, could tell his conversation with Lieutenant Boyd was wrapping up, so she quickly placed the phone back on its base before Boyd came out. It was a risky thing to do, but it might just have paid off. She had figured out that occasionally if she'd used the intercom to get a message to Pendleton, he sometimes forgot to hang up on the other end.

She had just heard his entire conversation with Lieutenant Boyd.

The door opened and out walked the Lieutenant. "Have a nice day," he said.

"You too, Lieutenant." When he left the office and was

well down the hall, she contacted Pendleton again. "I was going to take my midmorning break, sir. If that's okay with you?"

"Sure, go ahead Marsha. Think I could survive that long without you. I'll just let any phone calls go to voicemail. You check them when you get back."

"Sure will. Be back in a few minutes." She got her purse and headed out of the office toward the parking lot.

Once there, she got inside her car, turned the car on so the A/C would run, and pulled out her phone. She had already put his name and cell phone number into her contacts from the business card he'd given her that horrible night three weeks ago. The night she did one of the stupidest things she'd done since becoming an adult. Well, an adult who worked for a living and desperately needed her paycheck to survive. She had gone to a party at a cabin on Lake Samson and wound up drinking one too many margaritas. She should've called Uber or Lyft, had someone drive her home, but she felt like she could handle it. Halfway into town, she'd overcorrected when a rabbit ran across the road, and her car slid off into a drainage ditch. She wasn't hurt and, fortunately, didn't stop fast enough for the airbags to blow.

But she was definitely stuck, and there was no backing the car out without help. Just then, a large pickup truck had pulled in behind her. Her heart started beating. She'd prayed whoever this was wouldn't hurt her. Turned out, the man who had come to her aid was someone she instantly recognized. He'd come to Pendleton's office many times to interview the captain for the local newspaper. It was Tom Hazelton, a lead reporter for the Culpepper Gazette.

Hazelton had mostly treated her kindly and was even able to pull her car out of the ditch, using a chain and his pickup. But he also recognized her as the, "new gal who worked the front desk for Pendleton." He could also tell that she was still way too drunk to get back behind the wheel. He insisted she let him drive her home, then he'd drive her back out the next day to fetch her car.

Marsha had been so grateful, right up until Hazelton pulled into the parking lot of her apartment complex. That's when he'd made it clear that he expected a favor in return for the, "pretty big thing he had just done for her." For a moment, she'd worried things were going to get creepy, until he'd spelled out the kind of favor he'd wanted. As she listened, it wasn't something she thought would prove too difficult at all.

She was calling Hazelton now, there in the police parking lot, to return that favor. She heard his phone ring several times, then he picked up.

"Tom Hazelton, Culpepper Gazette."

"Mr. Hazelton, this is Marsha Henderson. Captain Pendleton's secretary. Remember me?"

"Marsha, Marsha. Yes, I do. Something about a car running off the road into a ditch, if I recall. I've been wondering if you remembered the deal we made there at the end."

"I remembered. It's just you made it clear you wanted the scoop on a story that had potential to be something big. Haven't had too many big things since then. But I might have one now."

"Really? I like the sound of that. Haven't had any big stories lately in the local section. What do you have for me?"

"Well, I overheard Captain Pendleton just going over something with Lieutenant Boyd a few minutes ago."

"Lieutenant Boyd? That sounds promising. I'm all ears."

"Okay, I don't know all the details of the situation, but I know they were talking about something that sounded pretty confidential, something Captain Pendleton wanted the Lieutenant to handle personally, involving some guy named Clemens who just got out of prison. From what I gathered, it happened a long time ago, and he just got out on parole. I guess this Clemens fellow killed someone named Sanchez. I wrote down the names as they talked."

"How did you hear all this?"

"I don't want to say. But you can't let anyone know you got this from me. I would get fired in a heartbeat."

"Marsha, I never reveal my sources. Your secret is safe with me. So, go on. Anything else?"

"Just something to do with Sanchez's family. If I understand it right, the Captain was trying to get the Lieutenant to talk this guy Clemens into leaving town, because he was concerned some of the victim's family members might get angry if they heard he'd come back here after getting out of prison. I don't really know too much more than that. I've lived here all my life, and I've never heard about this murder case, so it must be older than me."

"Oh, it definitely is," Hazelton said.

"So, you know about it?"

"Yeah, I do. I was just a kid when it went down, maybe ten or twelve. But it was a huge story. Went on for about a year."

"So," Marsha said, "is this the kind scoop that makes us

even? Is it big enough to match the...*favor* you did for me that night?"

"Marsha, you are in the clear, my dear. This is exactly the kind of thing I was talking about."

"And we don't have to do this thing anymore, right? After this, I'm all done doing—"

"Marsha, I'm not a blackmailer. I'm a reporter. Ever heard of quid pro quo? I do something for you, you do something for me. That's all this is. And you have more than held up your part. Of course, if you hear anything juicy there at the precinct, and you want to pass it on..."

"Goodbye, Mr. Hazelton." Marsha hung up.

10

SHORTLY AFTER THE TWO DETECTIVES HAD GONE, CLEMENS went ahead and made himself a batch of brewed tea and put it in the fridge, so it could start getting cold. It was certainly an unpleasant interruption to his morning, being confronted by those lawmen, but it still beat every morning he'd ever spent in prison. And as best as he could tell, no real damage was done by their visit. Like the Lieutenant had said, he wasn't breaking any laws being here, but it was going to add some fresh challenges to his little project, seeing that the local PD would now be keeping a close eye on him.

He decided to take a shower and get cleaned up for the day. As the water in the shower poured over his head, he found himself amazed at the sensation. He'd taken plenty of showers in prison, of course, but not like this. No one watching. No one even close by. In fact, no tension at all. Just him standing there, all by himself, the only sounds made by the running water as it splashed over his body.

Likely because of the conversations with the two detectives, Clemens found himself thinking back to that time in 1985 when he'd first confronted Roberto Sanchez about the money he was owed. If he had to do it again, he'd have dropped the whole thing. But back then, five hundred dollars was an enormous sum. And then there was the principle involved. It wasn't right what Sanchez had done to him, using him that way to further his own ambitions. And stealing Clemens' video work, which Sanchez had denied, but Clemens knew exactly what he was planning.

OCTOBER 10TH, 1985
  Gibraltar Road, Culpepper, Georgia

CLEMENS WAS FUMING.

He had just learned from a friend and fellow videographer that Roberto Sanchez had hired him to do the rest of the video work on his documentary. He had promised that work to Clemens. It was one of the main reasons Clemens had said yes to help him out with this project in the first place. That he would get to do all the close-up work, videotape all the one-on-one interviews. Not only had Sanchez reneged on his pledge, but he still hadn't paid him a dime for all the work Clemens had already done.

He pulled up onto the driveway of Sanchez's house. Even that, Sanchez could afford to buy a house, which he lived in by himself. It wasn't a big one, but Clemens and almost every other guy he knew that had graduated two years ago from Culpepper's journalism program, were either living at home with their parents or sharing a cheap apartment with several roommates.

Sanchez had the looks, the charm, and the voice to be in front of the camera. He'd already been hired by the local TV news to cover various stories around town, but he had set his sights on more. Much more. He was telling everybody he was gonna be the next Geraldo Rivera, and this documentary he was making was going to be just the thing to open up doors for him in major markets, maybe even the networks.

But he couldn't afford to pay Clemens the five hundred dollars for the work he'd already done?

Clemens wasn't buying it.

He got out of the pickup and headed for the front door. Deciding against ringing the doorbell, Clemens banged on the door with his fist. A few seconds later, he did it again. Then he heard the sound of footsteps coming from the other side.

"I'm coming, I'm coming," Sanchez yelled. "Would you stop banging, whoever you are?"

Clemens saw the peephole grow dark, figured Sanchez was trying to see who it was, so he took a step back.

It opened. "Sam, what are you doing here? And what gives with all the racket?"

Clemens didn't wait to be invited in. He walked past Sanchez into the living room. Sanchez closed the door behind him. "Just had an interesting conversation with Rutgers. Couldn't believe what he said." Aaron Rutgers was the other video guy.

Sanchez made a face. "Oh, you did? Well, I was gonna call you and—"

"Sure you were, Roberto. And when was that gonna be?

Rutgers said you gave him the rest of the work four days ago."

"Right, but I've been very busy since then. I've had to do three stories for the station. Haven't even had a minute to work on the documentary project."

Clemens looked over at the dining room table, saw abounding evidence that Sanchez had just lied. He walked over just to make sure. "No time to work on the documentary, eh? Then what's this?" Clemens pointed to the video camera set up on the table. *His* video camera, which he'd let Sanchez borrow, so he could practice his "visual style" in front of it. It was pointed right at a chair, presumably, the chair Sanchez had just been sitting in. The red record button was flashing, which meant it was just being used and was now on pause. Beside it on the table lay a mic, plugged into a recorder.

Sanchez looked at it all then back up at Clemens. "Okay, busted. I'm sorry. I was just dictating some notes about the project, figured it would be easier to record them than have to write them all down. But really, I was gonna call you and tell you about this...production decision."

Production decision," Clemens repeated. "That's what you're calling this? Wow, Roberto, that's rich. How about just plain old betrayal and backstabbing?"

"What? No, that's not what this is. Sam, I saw all the B-roll footage you shot. You did everything I asked for, and it looks great. I'm sure I'll wind up using most of it in the final cut. But for the rest of this project, I decided to go with Rutgers. You don't have any experience doing one-on-one interviews. He's got a ton. And besides that, he can edit his own work. I've seen several samples. It's as good as anything

I've seen done at the station. This documentary is way too important to cut corners on quality. The future of my career is riding on this. It's nothing personal."

Clemens couldn't believe this load of crap. "Cutting corners on quality? No experience with one-on-one interviews? I spent half a semester on doing interviews. Got an A in that class. In fact, I got an A in every one of my classes. I would never cut corners on anything I've ever done."

"I'm sorry, I shouldn't have said that. But Sam, doing a school project is not the same as working out in the field. Rutgers has done these things in the real world. And with a project as big as this, I need the very best. But I promise, when we're all done, your name will be in the credits at the end."

"Well, if that's how it's gonna be," Clemens said, "then I at least want to get my five hundred dollars...now. Shouldn't be too hard if this project is as big as you say it is."

Sanchez sighed. "Sam, I don't have the money now. I told you, I'd pay you when I sold this thing. But believe me, you will get the money. All of it. This thing I'm working on is getting very hot. Once I have it all put together, I have no doubt about getting it sold. Wouldn't be surprised if someone like *60 Minutes* or *20/20* doesn't make me an offer."

"Forgive me if I don't applaud. Maybe I might if I knew what this thing was about. Why are you being so secretive? What are you trying to hide?"

"I'm being secretive because I have to. For now. I've been gathering evidence about something. Something very serious. Guess it won't hurt to say that much. But this is a small town, and I can't take the chance anything leaks out before I've confirmed everything beyond any doubt. I'm getting close. Believe me. But I don't want to say anymore right now."

Clemens looked at the table. "Well, if I can't get my money now, I at least want my video equipment back."

"Aw, c'mon Sam. Just give me a few more days with it. I'm almost done what I'm working on."

"Doesn't Rutgers have any cameras you can borrow?"

"No, he doesn't. But really, just a few more days."

"All right. But what day? Not just gonna leave it here indefinitely. How about Saturday?"

"Saturday would be fine," Sanchez said. "I should be all done with it by then."

THE PRESENT

THAT ENTIRE CONVERSATION played back in Clemens' mind as he stood there in the shower. That's when he remembered.

He had gone back to Sanchez's house that next Saturday to pick up his camera equipment. When he got there, he'd found Sanchez's car parked in his driveway, and his front door slightly open. He'd called out Sanchez's name, over and over, but there had been no reply.

It took some effort to push the door open enough to walk through. That's because Sanchez's bloody, lifeless body was lying there on the floor in the foyer. blocking the door.

That Saturday in October, 1985, was the day that had changed Clemens' life forever.

11

Two Days Later
Culpepper, PD

JOE WALKED DOWN THE HALL SIPPING HIS COFFEE THINKING about his breakfast conversation with Kate. Of course, it was all about the new baby. It was official now. Kate had been to the doctors, and he'd confirmed the results of the pregnancy test. Over waffles, she and the kids were already trying out baby names. Joe had tried to join in, but his level of zeal was just not quite there yet. He was still warming up to the idea that in a few months from now their whole world would be turned upside down. In a good way. He believed that.

He just didn't feel it inside yet the way the others did. Kate knew he'd get there eventually. She gently scolded the kids along those lines when they'd given him a hard time for not coming up with any names.

He opened the office door to find Hank had beaten him

in again this morning. "Morning, Hank. I'm liking this new punctual you."

Hank turned around to face him, an unhappy look on his face.

"What's the matter?"

He handed Joe his iPad, already turned on, and opened up to something. "Looks like our day just got a little messy. Read this."

Joe set his things down on this desk, took a seat, and lifted the tablet close enough to see the words on the screen. He knew what Hank was getting at as soon as he read the headline: NOTORIOUS CONVICTED KILLER FROM THE 80'S BACK IN TOWN. Joe looked down at the byline, saw that Tom Hazelton had written the story. "Man, how did he find out about this?"

"Read it, Joe," Hank said. "Read the whole thing."

So, Joe did. As he scrolled to keep reading, he saw it even included a mugshot of Clemens. It was old enough that Joe didn't realize it was him at first. The article didn't reveal anything about the case that he and Hank hadn't already learned, but it left Joe wondering why Hazelton had written the story at all. Did anyone in Culpepper really care about a thirty-six-year-old murder case? It's not like some unsolved mystery, not in the minds of almost anyone who'd read it.

"I thought you and Hazelton were buds," Hank said. "Did he contact you about this?"

"I thought we were buds, too. And no, he didn't check in with me on this. My guess is, he knew if he did I'd try to talk him out of writing it. What good does a story like this do?"

"I don't think a guy like Hazelton cares very much about serving the public good," Hank said. "Since we're sharing guesses, mine would be he's desperate for staying relevant in a medium that is quickly fading. Other than baby boomers and folks older than that, not a whole lot of people reading local newspapers anymore. Even online."

"You might be right. Maybe that'll be a good thing here. Maybe nobody will read it."

"Wouldn't get my hopes up on that, Joe. The thing is, a guy like Hazelton would already know these things. He's probably hooked up to the major social media platforms. I would be surprised if he hasn't already posted about the story on places like Facebook and Twitter, maybe some others, linking the post to his story in the online version of the Gazette. Which means, by the end of the day it'll reach a much wider audience in town. I don't know if that's going to matter. Like you said, it's such an old case. Most of the people angered by it back in the 80s have passed away."

"Most have," Joe said, "but not all. The one good thing is this picture. Clemens doesn't look like this guy in the photo very much anymore. In any case, I'm going to give Hazelton a quick call, see if I can stop him from blasting this on the internet." He handed Hank's iPad back to him.

Hank stood. "I'll give you some space. I'm gonna head out and interview a witness who called us about that hardware store robbery last week. I was waiting just to make sure you saw that article."

"Thanks, Hank. I'll catch up with you later." He pulled out his phone, found Hazelton's info in his contacts, and pressed the button. A few rings later, Hazelton answered.

"Tom Hazelton of the Gazette. How can I help you?"

"Tom, Joe Boyd here."

"Lieutenant Boyd. Let me guess. You read your local

paper today and caught that riveting story I wrote about an infamous ex-con from the 1980s."

"Something like that. Not sure riveting is the word I'd use to describe what I read. But, yeah. That's what I'm calling about."

"You didn't like it? I'm disappointed."

"Really, because I'm disappointed you wrote it. At least, that you wrote it before checking in with me."

"You think I should've contacted you first? That's interesting. I'm not totally sure that's how the Founding Fathers intended the First Amendment to work."

"Nobody's talking about the First Amendment here, Tom. I'm talking about professional courtesy? I've given you a lot of stories over the years, exclusive stories."

"You have. And I've appreciated every one of them. I think, though, the operative phrase there is...*over the years*. It's been months, if not a full year since the last time you sent anything decent my way. This story came across my desk, and I could instantly see it was newsworthy. So, I confirmed the facts, did a little research on the back story, and let 'er rip."

"You wouldn't mind telling me how you found out about this?"

"Of course I would, Joe. You know I'd never divulge my sources. I did, and no one would ever come to me with anything."

Joe didn't expect that one to fly. "Well, if you can't tell me that, maybe you'll do something else for me? Hank tells me you'll probably be going on all the social media sites today to drum up more interest in your story in the Gazette."

"Hank would be right. I was already starting on that little project."

"Well, glad I caught you in time."

"What do you mean?"

"Therein lies the favor," Joe said. "I'm asking you to *not* do that, to not take it any further than the Gazette website."

"And why would I do that?"

"Why? How about to keep a lonely old man who's paid his debt to society, and is now finally out of prison after thirty-six years, from possibly being sent back for the rest of his life?"

"What? I don't follow. How could my story cause that much trouble?"

Joe wondered if guys like Hazelton ever thought through the consequences of their actions. "Well, for starters — and this next part is off the record — understood?"

"Understood."

"Certain members of the victim's family," Joe continued, "still live in Culpepper. And these family members aren't, let's say, the churchgoing forgiving types. You keep stirring the pot, and they will find out about Clemens' getting out and coming back. Do you really want to be responsible for what might happen if they decide to take matters in their own hands?"

Hazelton didn't immediately reply. Then he said, "That would be most unfortunate. And it certainly wouldn't be my intention to cause this Mr. Clemens any physical harm. But I don't see how you can put the responsibility on me for the choices others make — the wrong, illegal choices others make. My job is to report the news. I'm at least part of the old school bunch who strive to report it accurately and without any personal bias. But news is news, Joe. And this story is news. If I worried about what crazy people might do with the information contained in my stories — if any journalists did — we'd never write a thing."

Joe was disappointed to hear this, but not really surprised. He thought of a verse he'd read in the Book of Proverbs that morning: *Every way is right in a man's own eyes...* "Okay, Tom. I think I follow your logic. I'll keep this in mind the next time a real story comes my way."

"Come on, Joe. Don't be that way. I gotta make a living here. It's not like we live in a town with big stories happening every day. Cut me some slack."

"Okay, Tom. I had to try. You have a nice day." He hung up before Hazelton could answer.

He wondered if anything would come of this "breaking" news story, if maybe he should drive out there to see Clemens and warn him about this new development. He'd forgotten to get Clemens' phone number, didn't even know if Clemens owned a phone. At the very least, he could advise Clemens not to shave off that beard he'd begun to grow, or get a haircut.

So, he wouldn't look a thing like that picture of him that would soon be circulating all over the place on social media.

12

Next Day, Just Before Noon
Little River Saloon
Outskirts of Culpepper

ALONZO SANCHEZ PULLED HIS HARLEY STREET 750 INTO THE bar parking lot and scanned the cars until he found his Uncle Juan's at the far end in the corner. All the other motorcycles were parked in a special section near the front door, but Alonzo chose a regular parking slot next to his uncle's car. Main reason was, he was tired of getting hassled by other bikers for riding a "Baby Harley." Alonzo wasn't a biker at heart, but he got this smaller Harley for a great price. It was fun to ride and cheap to keep.

Inside, he hoped to find his Uncle Juan still sober, at least enough to appreciate the info Alonzo had come to share. He took his black leather backpack off his shoulder and carried it in his right hand. Alonzo liked eating at the Little River, served pretty good barbecue and Tex-Mex. Uncle Juan mainly came here for the booze and to shoot the breeze with friends. Sure enough, he found him at the far end of the bar downing a beer, laughing at somebody's joke. An old boxing match played on the TV above their heads. Didn't seem like anyone cared. As Alonzo got closer, his uncle looked up, saw him.

"Look who it is, boys. Little Alonzo, my favorite nephew. How you been, boy?"

Little Alonzo. How much longer would Alonzo have to put up with that? Been hearing it since he was a kid. "Uncle Juan, I've been great. But maybe you haven't noticed, I'm almost as tall as you now. Can we finally drop the Little Alonzo?"

"Don't get sore, amigo. I'm just playing with you."

His friends nodded their hellos to Alonzo. He nodded back. "Say, Uncle Juan, can I speak with you for a few minutes? Maybe over at one of those tables? Got something to show you. Something I saw online a little while ago."

"You drove all the way out here to show me something you saw online? It some kinda big deal?"

"Think it might be. You'll know better than me."

"Okay, pick a table by the window. Gonna refill my beer, then I'll be right over. Get you one?"

"Yeah, I'll have whatever you're drinking. I might even order something to eat after we're done talking."

Alonzo found a table, set his backpack on the bench seat, and sat down beside it. He pulled out his tablet and turned it on. He'd been here enough times his tablet quickly recognized the bar's Wi-Fi. He clicked on the app for the Gazette, found the article he'd been reading earlier. A minute later, his uncle scooted into the seat across from him, set two fresh beers on the table.

"So Alonzo, what you got for me? Something on that gizmo? I have to read something this early in the day?"

"Uncle Juan, it's almost noon. If you want, I'll read it to you."

Juan took a swig of his beer. "Why don't you tell me first what all this fuss is about before anyone starts doing any reading?"

"Okay, here's the gist of it. I got a text from an old girlfriend a few hours ago, asking me if I had read an article in the Gazette yet this morning. I told her I don't usually read the Gazette. What am I...some old guy like you, reads the paper over coffee every day?"

"Old guy like me," Juan repeated. "Okay, wiseguy. I ain't read the paper every morning maybe ever. Go on with your story."

"So, she sends me a link to this article. Tells me I should look at it. Wonders if the guy the article's talking about is someone I'm related to, since we got the same last name. I click on it, and I see this headline." Alonzo held up the tablet, so his uncle could read it for himself:

NOTORIOUS CONVICTED KILLER FROM THE 80S BACK IN TOWN.

Juan's eyes bugged out as he read it.

"It talks about this old guy who's been in prison since 1985 for the cold-blooded killing of a popular, local television reporter named Roberto Sanchez. Isn't he the relative you were telling me about a few months ago when I asked you how you managed to get that nice house you live in? You told me you inherited it from your father, who got it from his brother when he got killed back in the 80s. Isn't this the guy, this Roberto Sanchez?"

Alonzo could tell by the look on his uncle's face that it was.

"Gimme that." Juan reached for the tablet, started reading the entire article. The more he read, the angrier he looked. When he finished, he handed it back to Alonzo. "Yeah, that's the guy. Roberto *was* my uncle, and the coolest dude I ever knew. I was only fourteen at the time, so we weren't that close. But he was like this super-handsome TV star. Everybody in town knew who he was, and we all knew he was headed for the big time. My whole family was so proud of him. He was already making more dough than our dads ever made, and he was the first Sanchez to graduate college. That is until this jerk here — the guy in this article — bashes his head in with a dumbbell over a measly five hundred bucks. Just kills him, right there in the living room of his own home. Which is my home now. I'm just glad I never saw what happened. Not sure I could've lived there, if I had seen it."

"So, this killer," Alonzo said, "gets out on parole after all these years and thinks he can come back here to Culpepper...like nothing ever happened?"

Juan shook his head no, bit his lip. "We can't let this happen, Alonzo. It ain't right. Don't matter how many years have passed. The state may say he's done his time, and maybe there's nothing we can do about that. But we sure got something to say about where he lives when they let him out."

"You mean, where he *doesn't* live?" Alonzo said.

"Right. Where he doesn't live," Juan repeated. "I can tell you right now, no way this guy's living here. Not in our town. Not after what he did."

"What are we gonna do?"

"I don't know yet. The first thing is, we need to find out where he's staying. Think you could dig that up?"

"Definitely," Alonzo said. "Might take me a day or two, but I'll give you a call as soon as I know."

13

IT WAS ABOUT MIDDAY. SAMUEL CLEMENS HAD DRIVEN BACK into town after getting directions at a convenience store for the nearest place to buy cell phones. He figured it had to be done, so he'd better get it done right off. He got out of his car and tensed up as he reached for the glass door. He had no idea what to say, didn't even know the right questions to ask. Through the windows, he could see everyone who worked here was less than half his age.

Once inside, his first thought was that this looked like no store he'd ever been to. Didn't have any aisles, just a handful of shelves around the perimeter with a couple dozen cell phones mounted on little stands. A few more counters in the center with more cell phones and electronic tablets. Not a single cash register in sight, just four desks, one in each corner, with office chairs in front of them. It put him more in mind of a bank lobby than a store. One desk was empty, three clean-cut young men wearing shirts and ties sat behind the others. Two were chatting with customers. The one who wasn't noticed him, smiled, and stood.

Sam smiled back, wasn't sure if he was being invited over. The young man walked his way, held out his hand. "Good afternoon, sir. My name's Reynolds. How can I help you?"

Sam shook his hand. "Good afternoon to you too, Mr. Reynolds. Guess I'm here to buy one of these cell phones."

"No need for the *Mister*. Reynolds is my first name. Come on over to my desk, have a seat. Unless you'd like to take a few minutes and check out our phones. That's fine. Some people do all their browsing online first and come in with their phone already picked out."

His first name was Reynolds? This was about the fifth young person he'd met since coming back to town with an oddball first name. "I better come over and sit with you for a while. I have no idea which phone I want."

"Fine," Reynolds said. "Hopefully, I can help you narrow down your choices, get you just the right one to best meet your needs."

He walked back to his desk and sat. Clemens sat in one of the chairs provided. "See, that's the thing with me. Hope you're a patient young man. I'm probably gonna need more help than most people who come in here." He tried to remember the phrase his parole officer suggested he use when describing his situation, to avoid having to reveal the decades he'd spent in prison. "You'll probably find this hard to believe, but I've never owned a cell phone before. Don't really even understand how they work. I am — or have been, I guess you could say — living off the grid for quite a long time now. Where I lived, we didn't have cell phones, or tablets, or any of these other electronic things people use these days. I've never actually even used the internet."

The young man's eyes widened like Sam had just confessed he'd come from outer space. "I see," he said. "Okay, so...I guess I'll need to explain some more basic things first before we get into looking at individual phones. Are you at all familiar with how the internet works, or what kind of things you can do with a modern cell phone?"

"Afraid not. I've seen other people use it, the internet I mean. And of course, as I get around town I can see...almost everyone seems to have one of these phones. Most of the people I see seem like they're looking down at them every chance they get. Was at a doctor's office a few days ago getting checked over. Maybe five or six others in the waiting room. Everyone but me were looking down at their phones. Don't know what they were seeing, but not a one of them rang the whole time I was there. Half of 'em were tapping on them something fierce, too. I'm thinking I probably don't need any of the fancier ones like they had. I just want one that lets me call people and gets phone calls from someone who needs to reach me."

Reynolds smiled. "Well, Mr. Clemens, even the most basic, least expensive smartphones do way more than function as a telephone. They can all go on the internet and come with Google already loaded. Know what Google is?"

"I've heard it talked about often enough. Can't say I'm totally sure what it is or how it works."

"Okay...then I guess I'll start there."

He spent the next ten minutes explaining how Google worked. Occasionally, he'd start getting into way more detail than Sam could follow, but he seemed able to read the confusion on Sam's face when that happened, and backed off. Eventually, the picture started to become clearer and what Sam understood were things he could hardly begin to fathom. How was it possible — as Reynolds explained it — that all the encyclopedias that had ever been written could be accessed by Google in seconds, not to mention all the articles and essays written on any topic. Anything a man was curious about, anything at all, he simply needed to "Google it," and just like that, pages of websites — even videos — on the very thing you were curious about would suddenly appear on your screen. And you didn't have to pay a thing for this information. You could just click on the links and read as much or as little as you pleased.

Then Reynolds said, "Besides being able to use the internet, with all smartphones you get the ability to text people, which is like sending and receiving little notes to people you want to connect with, without having to talk on the phone. They all have great cameras now, too. The resolution on these pics is ridiculous, really Hi-Def."

Sam decided not to ask what that meant. "Where do you take your phone to get these pictures developed? How many pictures can you take at a time?"

Reynolds laughed. "I'm sorry, I'm not making fun. I guess when you said you've been living life off the grid you weren't kidding. See, you don't have to take your phone anywhere. The photos are digital. They don't have to be developed. You just click on the camera app button, point your phone, and click. Here, I'll show you." He picked up his phone, tapped on it, pointed it at Sam, and tapped on it again. He turned it around to show him.

"My goodness," Sam said. There he was, big as life, right on the guy's telephone.

He set his phone back on the desk. "And if I push the video button, I can actually take a pretty high-quality video. The storage capability of these phones — especially when connected to the cloud, which we'll set up for you — is pretty much limitless. I mean, literally, you could take hundreds and hundreds of pictures and not run out of space."

Clemens could scarcely comprehend what he was being told. "I'm guessing when you say cloud, you don't mean... actual clouds."

"No, sorry." He spent a couple more minutes explaining the concept of cloud storage. Then he went on to talk about several more apps that come with most smartphones, including GPS, which he had to explain, and emails, which he had to explain, and apps that told you exactly what was going on with the weather, including actual radar of the weather in your area at any moment of the day.

After a while, Sam's mind was spinning. It was almost too much to comprehend. How could all of these things have been invented while he was inside? It was like listening to a science fiction movie. He couldn't imagine ever using even a fraction of the things these smartphones could do. "Listen, Reynolds, I appreciate all the time you've taken with me here. It's been really helpful. But if I'm being honest, I probably don't need to buy a smartphone. How much for a dumb one? Do they make those anymore?"

Reynolds laughed again, then apologized again. "They really don't, Mr. Clemens. But I will sell you one of our most basic and least expensive smartphones. And I can show you how to just use the phone functions. And if you'd like, I'll show you how to use Google. That way when you get home, you can search it for videos on how to use the other apps when you get ready to try them out. Or you can call me, and I'll see if I can help. I'll put my name and phone number in your contacts folder. How's that sound?"

"That sounds great, Reynolds. Let's do that. How about I just sit here and you go pick out a phone for me? And I'll probably need some extra batteries. Do you have any that recharge?"

Reynolds smiled. "You don't need any batteries, Mr. Clemens. All the phones are rechargeable and, once charged, they last for hours. I'll grab one of our new chargers. You aren't going to believe how easy they are to use and how quickly they work."

Clemens doubted that. At this point, he wouldn't be surprised if Reynolds told him these smartphones could even talk.

14

SAM WALKED OUT TO HIS TRUCK STILL TRYING TO PROCESS THE shocking price he'd paid for his telephone and gear. And that's with him getting the least expensive phone set up the store offered. But then, as the young man had explained, he was getting much more than just a telephone. He was getting ready-access to all the information in the world at his finger-tips, not to mention an app that would literally direct him to any address he typed in, and a camera that took profes-sional-quality pictures and could hold thousands of them in storage.

Of course, the only thing Sam cared about was the phone.

So, he got in the pickup, turned it on to get the A/C running, and took out his phone. He pulled out the business card his parole officer had given him and typed the informa-tion into his contacts. Now he had two people in his phone he could call. He tapped on the parole officer's name and then the little telephone icon, and just like that, it was dialing his number. His parole officer was delighted that Sam had gotten the phone and took down his information. He must have been very busy, because he quickly said he had to go.

Then Sam decided he should give his number to this Lieutenant Boyd, so he typed *Culpepper Police Department* into the little Google box and, just like that, it appeared on screen. He clicked on the little Call button, and the screen switched over to the phone. It was dialing. This was crazy how easy it was. He asked the woman who answered to put him through to the Lieutenant, which she did. After a few rings, he heard the Lieutenant's voice on the other end.

"Hello, Lieutenant. I bet you can't guess who this is."

"Well, I was never very good at guessing but, you're right, can't say I recognize the voice."

"It's Samuel Clemens. I decided it was time to take my first step into the modern world. I'm calling you from my new cell phone. Do you remember —"

"I certainly do remember you, Sam," Joe said. "In fact, I was about to head out to my car to come see you. You calling me saved me the trip."

"You were coming out to see me? I'm actually still in town, still over here at the cell phone store. Know where that is?"

"Well, I don't actually need to see you. Just needed to talk with you but didn't have your phone number. Well, guess you didn't have one."

"Now I do. Let me give it to you, so you can have it if you need to reach me again."

"Okay, then I'll hang up and call you on my cell phone.

So, you'll have my personal number instead of the department's."

"What do you mean? How?"

"See, when I call you back on my cell phone, you'll have my number on your phone. All we need to do then is—when we're done talking—you tap on the Recent Calls tab and the first number at the top will be mine. Hold your finger down on that and a box will open up giving you a chance to add me to your Contacts. Just type in my name and it'll match that number to me. I'll do the same on my end, and from then on, we're all set."

"I don't know if I'll ever get over how nuts this stuff is," Sam said. "Okay, think I can manage that."

They did what Joe suggested, and moments later they were talking again.

"So," Sam said, "what did you need to see me about?"

"Afraid it's not good news."

"Okay, what's the bad news?"

"Guessing you haven't read the morning paper?"

"No, but the young man who sold me the phone said I could actually read the news on this thing. Not sure how to find it, the newspaper app I mean."

"Did he show you how to use the text features?"

"He did. Again, I've never used it though."

"It's super simple," Joe said. "I'll text you the link for the article. After we hang up, you can click on the link and your phone should take you right to it."

This all sounded so crazy. "Okay, I'll give it a try. What does the article say? And why is it bad news?"

"Somehow, I don't know how, but word leaked out about you being back in town. A local reporter featured your return as the main article in the local section. It's got a summary of the crime and, pretty much, the whole story."

Sam's heart sank. This wasn't good.

"It was going to get out sooner or later," Joe said. "I just hoped we had a bit more time before it did. The main thing right now is, they got this picture of you in the article, looks about fifteen to twenty years old. You haven't been to the barbers yet, have you?"

Sam laughed. "Not hardly. And it's not high on my list."

"Good, that's good. How are you for groceries?"

"Got about enough to last me a week, I guess."

"That's good, too. If we're lucky this thing fades away by then. That is, of course, you do like we talked and don't poke any hornets' nests."

"I think I can manage that," Sam said. "Now that I got this here phone, sounds like I'm pretty connected to the world, the way this young fella explained things."

"Yeah, they're pretty amazing. Used to hate them, but now, don't know how I could even function without it. All right, you head back up to your place by the lake, we'll see if any buzz about this story goes away on its own."

"You got my number, and I got yours," Sam said. "And Lieutenant, thanks for the heads up here. Not used to anybody giving two hoots about how I'm doing. Really appreciate it."

"No problem, Sam. We'll be in touch."

"How about that?" Sam muttered aloud as he pulled out of the store parking lot and headed home.

ALONZO SANCHEZ HURRIED to his motorcycle before the guy

got away. He could hardly believe what he had just seen. Twenty minutes ago, he'd ridden to this little shopping center near his apartment, because it had a decent smoke shop. When he came out, he saw this old, bearded white guy coming out of the phone store next door. For some reason, he looked familiar. Then it dawned on him why.

Alonzo quickly pulled out his phone and clicked on some of the pics he'd saved last night while messing with this new app. It was like a photo editor, but it let you change people's ages, so you could see what they'd have looked like years ago or years from now when they got old. Since meeting with Uncle Juan about the ex-con who killed his cousin, Alonzo had been working on trying to find out where he might be staying. But he decided he needed to know what the guy looked like first. Doing the math, the ex-con had to be close to sixty, but the pic of the guy in the article couldn't have been more than forty. Alonzo used the app to get an idea of what the guy might look like now.

THAT guy just walked out of the phone store. Looked just like one of the pics he'd made on the app.

He followed behind the guy's red pickup truck, three cars back. Figured he needed to keep his distance, seeing that he was on his bike. He wished he was driving a car right now. It would be a lot easier for the guy to notice a motorcycle following him than a car.

Alonzo couldn't believe his luck, like the man upstairs was looking out for him. After he'd created those aged pics of the ex-con, he'd made a list of all the halfway houses in town where ex-cons might stay when they got out of prison. He was thinking he might have to spend hours staking out these places, try to get a glimpse of the guy in the photo. But look? He was almost positive he was following the guy right now.

It was like a gift.

The guy's truck continued making its way down the same main road for about a mile, but then he turned left when Alonzo thought he should have turned right. Maybe this wasn't the guy after all. He was taking the road that led out of town toward the lake. Alonzo knew where all the halfway houses were, all of them solidly in town. Still, he kept following. But it was even harder now. A mile down this winding road, and there were way less cars, so he had to stay even further back. Of course, the upside was, with less cars, it was easier to keep the ex-con's red pickup in his sights.

He continued on for about five minutes, then Alonzo noticed a traffic stop up ahead at an intersection with a convenience store. The light was green, and the ex-con turned left. Alonzo raced toward the light trying to make it before it turned red, but he missed it by a few seconds. He slammed on his brakes and barely stopped in time. Looking left, he saw the pickup moving further and further away. There wasn't anyone else at the intersection but him, so he ignored the red light and turned left. Then he hurried as fast as he dared to close the gap between the two vehicles. He looked back to make sure no one had seen him at the convenience store. It seemed like he was in the clear.

BUT SOMEONE *HAD* SEEN HIM.

Sam had noticed back in town this motorcycle that seemed to be tracking with him. Twice as a test, he had changed lanes and noticed in his rearview mirror, the biker did too. Then again when Sam had turned left taking the road out toward the lake, the biker turned left also. He was hanging way back, but it definitely got Sam's attention, especially after Lieutenant Boyd's warning. And now look, the biker missed the light and had just run through it. There could only be one reason...he didn't want to lose sight of Sam's truck.

"Well," Sam muttered aloud. "Since you're following me..."

He decided not to take the roads that lead back to his cabin. Instead, he picked some of the roads in the vicinity. They all led to different cabins situated around the lake. Sure enough, although quite a ways back, the biker was always there. Sam took a chance the guy meant him no harm, at least not now, since there were several times when it was just the two of them on the road. If the guy wanted to take him out, he could've just zipped that bike right up to Sam's pickup and plugged him through the side window.

So, he kept driving till he saw a dirt road that didn't have any fresh tire tracks and turned in there. After a couple hundred yards, it led to a clearing with a lone cabin facing the lake. The place looked deserted. It was actually a really nice piece of property. Sam stayed in his truck, looking through the rearview mirror, until he saw the biker way down the road behind him. The biker had stopped.

Sam got out, grabbed his bag with his phone and gear, and walked to the front door. Then he took out his keys and pretended to try and unlock the door. He stayed there longer than it should take to open it, but apparently, he had stayed long enough.

When he glanced down the road, the biker was gone.

He breathed a sigh of relief as he headed back to his truck. Figured his next purchase had just been made for him, and he couldn't wait a week to get it.

Tomorrow, he'd have to carefully drive into a certain part of town and buy himself a gun.

15

Same Day
Culpepper Gazette Newsroom

TOM HAZELTON HEARD HIS PHONE CHIME, THE SOUND IT MADE when he had a text. Used to be when he was working on something, he'd ignore his text messages till he was done. Couldn't do that anymore. The latest round of cutbacks at the paper had eliminated his editor's secretary. Poor thing had been at the job for over twenty years. Her removal resulted in Hazelton's editor now contacting him by text whenever he wanted to talk, even though his office was less than fifty yards away.

Tom picked up the phone and, sure enough, it was his boss, Andrew Barton. His texts always used as few words as possible. *Need to talk.* Tom knew the other words Barton had neglected to include. *I want you to stop whatever you're doing — no matter how important it is — and come to my office now.*

Tom got up and headed there. He knocked twice and let himself in.

Barton looked up. "Hey, Tom. Got a story I need you to get working on. And before I tell you what it is, I don't want any grief from you about it being a puff piece and why can't I give it to somebody else."

"That means it must be a puff piece," Tom said.

"Maybe it is," Barton said, "but it's an important puff piece, and you're still my top guy."

This was flattery, not an actual compliment. He sighed. "Okay, what is it?"

"Just got off the phone with the principal of Culpepper High. They've got a pretty significant event coming up this weekend and wondered if we would do a featured piece on it in the local section on Friday. Front page, lead story kind of thing. You know, take up the same space in the paper as your big feature on that murderer getting out of prison after thirty years. Have a feeling, even though this one's nothing sensational, it'll get a bigger reaction than your big crime story did. Have you looked at the comments section on that story lately?"

Tom had. It was dismal. Apparently, no one cared. Not even his mother. "I know. Really thought that one would stir the pot. I don't get it. It was such a big story back in the 80s. You remember it, don't you?"

"I do," Barton said, "which is why I let you talk me into letting it be the lead feature story. Guess we both read that wrong."

"It wasn't just you and me," Tom said. "I even got a phone call from that detective, Lieutenant Boyd, when he read the story. He asked me to please not promote it on our social media sites, afraid it would cause all kinds of trouble for the ex-con. Of course, I didn't listen."

"Well," Barton said, "our website guy told me we did get several hundred people who read it. That's something anyway. Just no one cared enough to leave a comment. But, I don't think that's gonna happen with this new story. You write this one the way I know you can, and I wouldn't be surprised if we got tons of comments from the public."

"Okay, what's it about?"

"There's this school teacher who's being awarded Teacher-of-the-Year this Friday for the fifth time. No other teacher has won it more than twice. But there's more, he's let them know he's going to be announcing his retirement on Friday. The guy's been there for thirty years. The principal said they're planning to make a big deal of it, give him a banquet when the school year ends in a couple of weeks. He said people from all over town will come to this thing. I guess this guy's like everybody's favorite teacher. For ten years, he was the tennis coach. Got them to the state championship three times."

"What subject did he teach?"

"I didn't even ask. You can find out. I'm sure you ask the principal, he'll give you some names of students you could interview about this teacher. You know, even some students from his early years. They've gotta be in, like, their forties now I guess. Get a smattering of different age groups, including a few from his current class. Maybe interview some of his fellow teachers. Again, let the principal tell you which ones would actually say something favorable. And of course, you'll need to interview the teacher himself. Maybe him and his wife. They've been together the whole time. A real family man. Got two married kids, five grandkids."

"Sounds like the man's a saint," Tom said.

"Yeah, it does. And that's how the story should go. Anybody says something negative, leave it out. We do this right, we could get hundreds of people leaving comments on the website. Oh, that part about him announcing his retirement, they want that to be kept as a surprise. He's going to announce it that night, but they don't want it to show up in the story during the day. Just say something about him having a surprise announcement to make that they won't want to miss."

"All right, Chief," Tom said. "I'll get right on this. What's the guy's name anyway?"

"It's Albert Dietrich," Barton said. "But apparently, everybody calls him Al."

"Dietrich," Tom said. "Sounds German."

16

It was just a little more than twenty-four hours since Sam had spotted that kid on the motorcycle following him. He'd just gotten back from his trip to the section of town where he was most likely to find a gun, one he could buy with cash, no questions asked. All the way there and back, he kept looking in the rearview mirror but, thankfully, saw no sign of that biker.

And his mission had been successful. Actually, it couldn't have gone better. The first guy he'd talked to put him in touch with another guy who actually had the guns. He had to pay the first guy fifty dollars for the tip, which seemed fair. The guy with the guns was just a kid. Sam figured he couldn't have been more than sixteen years old. He had six handguns to choose from, including "this really old one." Clemens couldn't believe what he was looking at, the kid had no idea. It was old but also likely worth more than the other five guns combined.

Sitting there at the dinette table in the cabin, Clemens

was cleaning up the gun, admiring it the whole while. It was a classic Colt M1911 .45, semi-automatic and he was pretty sure it was vintage World War II. Easily worth $2,500, likely more. He'd gotten it for $300, including a box of ammo and an extra clip. It was heavier than he'd expected but felt very solid and balanced in his hand.

One thing was certain, this gun had one-shot stopping power.

It had been so long since he'd held a gun. As he finished putting it back together, he wondered who the kid on the motorcycle was. Obviously, he was too young to have been around when Sanchez was murdered in '85. The Lieutenant had said some of Sanchez's other relatives were still alive, ones that hadn't been a part of the trial or all the probation hearings that followed. But Sam also wondered if it could be someone connected with the real killer. The guy who'd gotten away with committing the crime. Seemed to Sam, those were the only two groups of people who might have a motive to do him harm.

At least, now he was ready for trouble, if any came.

All this got him thinking about the guy who actually killed Sanchez. The only thing that made sense to Sam was that he must have had something to gain from keeping Sanchez from finishing his documentary. Sanchez wouldn't tell him what it was about, and it sounded like no one else knew either. It had never come up at the trial. Sam's defense attorney tried to plant reasonable doubt in the jury's mind by bringing up Sanchez's reputation as a ladies' man. He was supposed to have been sleeping around with a number of different women, some of them married. The idea was,

Sanchez was probably killed by a jealous husband or boyfriend, not Sam.

But these were all just rumors, and the jury didn't buy it.

Really, the only plausible scenario that surfaced during the trial came from the prosecutor. Sam had done it, by himself, because he was angry about being dropped from the film project and not getting paid his five hundred dollars. But Sam was sure the real killer's motive had to be about shutting down that documentary. There had to be a way to find out what it was about, and that's where he planned to put the focus of his own investigation.

He also remembered something he'd forgotten about that first day when he'd confronted Sanchez about dropping him from the project. He remembered seeing some guy in a parked car across the street. A blond guy about their age, who looked vaguely familiar. He'd watched Sam as he walked toward Sanchez's house. But he was gone by the time Sam had come back out, and he never saw him again after that.

JUAN SANCHEZ and his nephew Alonzo had spent the last fifteen minutes driving out from town to the Lake Samson area, following Alonzo's directions toward the cabin where this Clemens fellow was staying. They had just turned onto the dirt road that led directly to the cabin and the lake itself.

"There's the cabin up ahead," Alonzo said. "You can just see the corner of it past the trees. This is as far as I got yesterday. Didn't want to take a chance on him seeing me. But I know this has to be the place. When I got back into town, I went on Google Earth and found this road. There's only one cabin at the end of it, and that one's it."

"Okay," Juan said. "Here's the plan. For starters, we leave the clips out of the guns. Don't want to take any chance either one of us wind up shooting the guy. We're only here to scare him, convince him he needs to leave town."

"What if he has a gun?"

"Alonzo, the guy just got out of the joint. He knows he gets caught with a gun, he goes back in for the duration. Besides, even if he did have one, the way I got this figured, he's not gonna even have a chance to go after it."

"Okay, what are you thinking?"

"We drive down there and park, like we're there on purpose. We knock on the door, our unloaded guns in our waistband behind our backs. We're just two guys meeting a buddy at his cabin to fish. He answers the door, and we act surprised, like we realize we must be at the wrong place. Let me do the talking. I'll ask him does he know Jeb Hodgins, cause that's who we were supposed to meet, and we thought this was his cabin."

"Who is Jeb Hodgins?" Alonzo said.

"Don't know. Just made him up. Of course, he'll say he doesn't. But everything's cool. I apologize for bothering him. I must've got the address down wrong. That'll be the cue."

"For what?" Alonzo asked.

"To make our move. We both rush him, shoving him back through the door. We do some ground and pound on his face, but not too much. Just enough that he knows we mean business. Then I tell him we know who he is, and tell him who we are, and that there's no way he's moving back into this town. If he does anything other than cooperate and agree to leave, we pull out our guns and shove them in his face. If the beating doesn't do it, I guarantee that'll get his attention."

"Should we give him some kind of deadline?" Alonzo said. "You know, for getting out of town."

"I'll tell him we'll be back in three days. He's not gone, and we'll make sure he's gone for good."

"That's a good line," Alonzo said. "So, you ready to do this?"

"I was born ready, my boy. Let's go."

They drove down the dirt road until it opened to a clearing. There was the cabin and the lake. But no red pickup.

"Shoot," Juan said. "He's not here. You sure this is the place?"

"Yeah, I'm sure. Look around. There's no other cabins here. This is definitely the road he drove down."

Juan walked over and peeked in the front window. "I don't know, man. This doesn't look right. All the furniture have sheets over them, like people do when they're gone for months."

Alonzo walked over and looked inside. "I don't know what to tell you. This is definitely where he went yesterday."

Juan walked back to the front door, looked around then shook his head in disgust. "Look up there, Alonzo." He pointed to the upper right corner of the front door. "What do you see?"

Alonzo looked up. Took him a few seconds to see it. "A spiderweb."

"A massive spiderweb," Juan said. "The kind that takes weeks to make. Which means, the front door hasn't been open for that long. Which means, Clemens didn't come here yesterday and walk through this door. Which means, you got played."

Alonzo swore. "I'm sorry Uncle Juan. I did my best to stay far enough back that he wouldn't see me. I guess just being on a motorcycle with so few cars on the road...he somehow figured out he was being followed."

Juan stepped back from the door. "It's all right. That's probably what happened. But you said he was driving a red pickup?"

"Yeah. It was an old one but looked like it was in good shape. Had those old-timey fenders."

"You mean a stepside?"

"Yeah, think that's what they call 'em. Might have been a Ford or a Dodge, but I wasn't close enough to tell which one."

"Good, that's good. We might still be in business. There's a chance he didn't spot you in town. Probably happened like you said, when he started riding out here in these mostly-empty lake roads. Let's head back in the car. He's probably staying at another cabin on one of these other nearby roads. It might take a while, but we'll just start driving down each one till we see an old red pickup. Come on, let's get back in the car."

17

JOE BOYD WAS SITTING AT HIS DESK FINISHING UP AN EMAIL when his cell phone rang. Glancing at it, he noticed it was Sam Clemens. Figured he'd better answer it, since Clemens wasn't much of a talker. Something must be up. "Hey Sam, what's going on?"

"Is this Lieutenant Boyd?"

"It is."

"How'd you know it was me?" Clemens said.

"Says so, right on my phone. If I called you, you'd know it was me, too. You'd see my name pop right up on the screen. Doesn't work with everybody, just those in your contact list." Boyd couldn't believe he was tutoring someone on the basics of cell phone use. "Mind if I put this on speaker, so my partner Hank can listen in?"

"Fine with me."

"So, what are you calling about?"

"Well, it may be nothing. But I've been thinking on it a while and figured I should call. Because it may be something, too. Anyway, yesterday I called you from my truck right after buying my phone. On the way home, once I got away from town, I started noticing a motorcycle trailing me about a hundred yards back or so. Turned everywhere I turned, even ran a red light to keep up with me. That's when I knew it wasn't my imagination anymore."

Joe didn't like the sound of this. "So, what happened?"

"Well, once I figured it was something real, I decided not to head back to my cabin. I drove past it then kept driving around the lake till I found a dirt road that hadn't been used in a while. Pretended it was my place and drove down to it. Even got out with my keys, pretending to unlock the door. When I looked down the road, he'd taken off."

"Looks like your ruse worked," Joe said.

"Yeah, but for how long? Whoever it was, knows what my truck looks like."

"Good point."

"So, what would you like me—hold on, Lieutenant. Sounds like someone just pulled up in front of the house."

Joe's instincts kicked in. He stood up.

"A car just pulled up next to my pickup outside," Clemens said. "I don't have any friends, so I'm not expecting any visitors."

Joe turned to Hank, who'd heard everything that was said. He quickly stood, nodded to Joe. "Sit tight, Sam. We'll be right out there."

"Yeah, think you better," Clemens said. "They're out of the car now, an older guy and a younger guy. The younger guy resembles the kid on the bike yesterday. Not a hundred percent sure, but pretty sure."

"Do your best not to get into anything," Joe said. "Just keep them talking, and we'll be there in a few minutes."

"I'll try."

SAM'S INSTINCTS told him this had to be trouble. He hurried over and grabbed his Colt .45, tucked it in his waistband. Someone knocked on the door. "Be right there." He opened it slow, looked up at the two guys. The older, bigger guy was maybe fifty. The younger one maybe thirty. Both had dark hair, looked Hispanic. "You gentlemen lost? Wasn't expecting any company."

The older one acted surprised. "I'm sorry. My name's Juan. This is my nephew, Alonzo. We thought this was the cabin of our friend, Jeb Hodgins."

"Don't know anyone by that name," Sam said.

"Well," Juan said. "Sorry to have bothered you. I must've got the wrong address."

"That's okay, you men have a nice —"

Suddenly, the two men rushed forward, shoving Sam backward into the living room. He almost tripped over the coffee table.

"Our last name is Sanchez, old man," the younger one yelled. "That name ring a bell?"

The bigger one, Juan, grabbed hold of Sam's shirt, pulled his arm back ready to punch Sam in the face. It wasn't hard to spot, so Sam shifted his head to the right just enough that he missed. The missed punch threw him off-balance. Sam took advantage and shoved his left knee up into the guy's face. He screamed in pain and dropped to his knees. Sam smacked both of his fists down on the back of the guy's head, like an angry chimp might do. He collapsed to the floor.

The kid, Alonzo, swore at Sam and ran full into him, driving them both against the living room wall. He quickly began to pummel Sam's abdomen with his fists. Sam tightened his muscles, so the blows only hurt half as much. But the kid was strong, and he had to think fast. He kicked his right leg upwards, full force, between Alonzo's legs, right into his groin.

That did it. The punches stopped. He doubled over on the floor in agony. For good measure, and to make sure he wasn't getting up, Sam grabbed him by the hair lifted his head, and punched him square on the jaw. That put the kid out, at least for a few minutes. That's when Sam saw the pistol in his waistband. He pulled it out, as the bigger man Juan was rolling over to face him. Juan pulled the pistol from behind his back and pointed it at Sam.

Sam realized then the gun he was holding had no clip.

"Stop right there, old man," Juan said. "Or I'll blow you away."

Sam looked at the grip of Juan's pistol. "You'll blow me away? Kinda hard to do that without any bullets, don't you think?" These guys came in here with unloaded guns. They probably figured the two of them could beat up an old man like him, no sweat.

Juan looked at his gun as if he just realized it was unloaded. He started to get up. Sam grabbed hold of the barrel of the kid's gun and threatened to smack Juan in the head with it. "Ever been pistol-whipped before? You make one move in my direction, and you'll find out just how bad it hurts."

Juan looked down at his nephew on the floor, still out cold, and backed away.

"He'll be fine in a minute or so," Sam said. He thought about taking out his Colt .45, which was loaded, but decided it wasn't necessary. Besides, the Lieutenant and his partner were on their way. Wouldn't do for them to know he had an illegal firearm in his possession. "So, your nephew said your last name was Sanchez. He knew I'd recognize the name. Guess you're relatives of Roberto, the guy I was supposed to have murdered back in '85."

Juan wiped the blood from his fat lip on his sleeve. "He was my cousin. I was fourteen when you killed him."

"You were fourteen when he died. When he was murdered. But I'm not the one who killed him. I'm just the one who paid for it. About the only good thing I got from being inside was learning how to defend myself."

"Well, the courts said you did it. The jury said you did it. You lost every appeal."

"Fair enough," Sam said. "Doesn't make it so. But I did the time. Now I'm out. If I was guilty, and I knew I was, give me one good reason why I would come back here, to this town? Got no family here. No friends. Obviously, a few enemies. But why would I come back here when I could go anywhere else, try to start over."

"I don't know. Why did you come back? No one wants you here. We sure don't. All the pain you caused my family. You got no idea all the sorrow and heartache you caused."

"Juan, I can't even begin to imagine you and your family's pain. But can you imagine the pain of being arrested and put in prison for thirty-six years for doing something you never did? My whole life got taken away from me. Look at me. I was younger than Alonzo here when they put me away. Now I'm an old man. But your gripe ain't with me. It's with the guy who caused all that pain for the both of us. That's the reason I came back. The only reason. To figure out who that guy is, make him pay for what he did. Try to clear my name, because I ain't no murderer. There's no way I would've killed Roberto over five hundred dollars. Or any amount of money. I just graduated college, had my whole life in front of me. Why would I kill your cousin over nothing?"

Juan didn't say anything for a moment, then, "You really didn't do it?"

Sam shook his head no. "I really didn't ."

Alonzo came to, started to get up. He looked at Sam, face filled with rage, moved toward him.

"Hold on, Alonzo," Juan said.

"What? Why?" He reached for the gun in his waistband.

"Looking for this?" Sam said, holding it up.

Juan took a step toward Alonzo. "You asked why? Because while you were out on the floor, he and I been talking. And I'm starting to wonder, maybe this guy didn't kill Roberto. Maybe we got this whole thing wrong."

"You're kidding," Alonzo said.

"No. I wish I was. But I'm not."

Just then they all heard police sirens coming down the dirt road.

18

As he whipped the car behind the other two and came to a stop, Joe said, "The front door's open. That ain't right." He shut the car off and both men got out, pulled out their weapons.

Just then, Sam appeared in the doorway looking unhurt. He held up his hands. "Come on in, gentlemen. Think you can put your guns down, though. Had a bit of trouble. May need your help to sort it out." He stepped back into the cabin.

Joe and Hank lowered their guns but didn't put them away yet. They walked through the doorway, found an unusual scene. Sam was standing off to the side. Two pistols were laying on the coffee table, turned in such a way that Joe could see they had no clips. Two men he didn't know were sitting in the living room, one on the couch, the other in the chair. Both looked pretty beat up. Sam didn't have a mark on him.

"Lieutenant Boyd, Sergeant Jensen? Think that's what your name is, son?"

"It is," Hank said.

"Meet Juan and Alonzo Sanchez." Sam looked at the reaction on Joe and Hank's faces. "Yes, they are related to the man I was accused of killing, Roberto Sanchez. Juan was Roberto's cousin, and Alonzo is Juan's nephew."

Joe shook his head. He'd already figured out what went down. "So, these two men came here uninvited, not just to this property but even into this room."

"That is correct," Sam said. "They were not invited, but —"

"And let me guess," Hank said, "Alonzo, you own a motorcycle?"

Alonzo looked down. "Yes sir, I do."

"I'm gonna guess, Juan, that's your car out there parked next to Sam's truck."

"Yes, Sergeant. It is."

"And more importantly," Joe said, "these two pistols on the coffee table belong to you two men, correct?"

The two men nodded, obvious regret on their faces. "But Lieutenant, you can see the guns had no bullets. Either one. We didn't come here to shoot anyone."

"We just came to scare him," Alonzo said.

"Oh," Hank said. "Then we got no problem here. You leaving the clips out makes everything all better."

"I'm not saying that," Juan said. "We done wrong here. I know that now."

"Mr. Sanchez," Joe said, "I'm glad you see that, but I'm not your priest, and this isn't church. You didn't just do wrong. You both committed serious crimes. For starters, Alonzo, we can probably get you for stalking. Following Mr. Clemens yesterday on your motorcycle, then coming back here today intending to bust in here like you did. Clearly premeditated." He looked at Sam. "Let me guess, Sam. You opened the door, and they strong-armed you, meaning, they shoved their way in here intending to beat the crap out of you."

"Yeah," Sam said. "Pretty sure that was the plan. But Lieutenant—"

Joe looked at Juan and Alonzo. "Just because something happened, and Sam here got the better of you two, doesn't change the fact that you guys broke in here to assault him and cause him serious bodily harm."

Hank laughed. "Man, would I have liked to see that go down. The two of you getting your butt kicked by a sixty-year-old man."

"Sergeant Jensen," Sam said. "Everything you said is true. And I'm not making any excuses for what these two men did, and what they'd hoped to do to me. But if it's okay with you, I'd rather not press charges. I'm not hurt. Nothing's broke. They came here for one reason, but might be leaving with their minds in a better place than when they came in. In an odd way, that almost makes it worth it to me."

"What do you mean, Sam?" Joe said.

"What he means," Juan answered, "is that we did come in here convinced Mr. Clemens killed Roberto. I mean, I've believed that every day since the trial. I wound up inheriting the house where Roberto was murdered. I left there this morning and looked up, told my cousin, today we'd be dishing out some justice to the man who killed him. But after Mr. Clemens here beat the crap out of us, as you said, we got to talking. And I heard him out, heard his side of things. Now that I have, I'm not sure he's the one who done it. In fact, I'm thinking the one who did might still be out there walking free as a bird."

"Come on, Sam," Hank said. "You don't believe that. Tell me you're not buying what this guy's selling. He's only saying this to get you to drop the charges."

"I am not," Juan said. "Obviously, I don't want to go to jail. But this thing's bigger than that to me. I want justice for Roberto. I thought we'd had it, but I'm not so sure anymore. Have you heard Sam explain why he came back here? It really doesn't make any sense, unless it's for the reason he's saying, to find the real killer and clear his own name."

Joe and Hank looked at each other. They couldn't argue against that. "So, you really don't want to press charges, Sam?" Joe said.

"No, I really don't. I don't think Juan is trying to con me to get off easy. Besides, I've got another reason for not pressing charges besides mercy."

"Which is," Hank said.

"You press charges, and this thing will get in the news. Could generate all kinds of negative stuff in people's minds about me. Relatives of the guy they think I killed breaking into my place, and me getting the better of them. Could get hundreds of people in town thinking about me who aren't thinking about me now. Make it really hard for me to go back to town and start talking to the people I need to see to help me get at the truth. What I'd prefer — if you two fellows agree — is to drop this whole thing. I'll stay up here, like you suggested, for the next week. See if interest in that story goes away. Then I'll slip back into town, start pulling on some threads."

"I guess we can do that, Sam," Joe said. "What about these two guns on the table?"

"They're both legal, Lieutenant," Juan said. "You can check on them."

"We plan to," Hank said.

"Well, for now," Joe said, "you two can leave. And I do mean now. Without your guns. Give Hank your phone numbers, and your drivers' license info. We'll give you a call if and when the guns check out as legit." He waited as Juan and Alonzo got up and made their way over to Hank.

Juan turned to Sam. "I am sorry, Mr. Clemens. For coming here like this. I ain't never been beat by someone as small and as old as you." He smiled. "But in a way, I'm glad it happened. If there's anything Alonzo and I can do to help you with your investigation into my cousin's—"

"Hold on there, Mr. Sanchez," Joe said. "How about you let the police handle any investigation that needs to be done?"

"You plan on reopening the case?" Juan said. "Cause I thought it was considered closed and solved."

He had a point there. Hank made a face at Joe, suggesting he was thinking the same thing. "We'll have to see," Joe said. "Point is, best the two of you just go back to living life, whatever your life was before you read about Mr. Clemens coming back to Culpepper. He's keeping us in the loop on what he's doing. We don't need any more hands in this situation right now."

"Okay, Lieutenant," Juan said. "And thanks...for letting us go."

Joe nodded as the two men headed out the door. He

turned to Sam. "You good now? Anything you need us to do?"

Sam shook his head no. "Unless you want to do as the young man suggested...and get someone down at your place to reopen this case. I sure wouldn't mind the help."

Joe didn't know what to say. But he was pretty sure Captain Pendleton would blow his stack if he and Hank went back to the station and got that conversation started.

19

Same Day,
Culpepper High School

TOM HAZELTON OF THE GAZETTE WAS WALKING THROUGH VERY familiar halls toward what he hoped was his final interview for this story. He was following directions to the office of Albert Dietrich, the celebrated math teacher who'd been named Teacher of the Year for the fifth time. Tom had attended and then graduated from this high school so many years ago. Little had changed. They'd torn down and totally rebuilt the high school gym, added another wing on the east side to accommodate some modest growth. But other than that, it was pretty much as he'd remembered.

He came into the building where math and science were taught, trying to recall the teachers he'd had for those subjects. He could remember their faces, but not their names. That might've had something to do with the fact that it was in this very building that he'd faced the realization that he sucked at math and science. This wasn't altogether a bad thing, because he'd discovered at the same time, he had an above-average ability to write. Got all A's in English and Composition. And because he had, he was allowed to choose journalism as an elective in his senior year.

And, of course, that one class had set him on the path that would later become his lifelong career.

Thinking about all this, though, didn't stir wonderful feelings of nostalgia or fond memories. Because what he was doing now totally confirmed in Tom's mind that his career was, as they say, circling the drain. Look at what he was doing now, for crying out loud? A stinking puff piece about some local teacher getting some local award. This was the kind of assignment he used to get back in his twenties when he'd first started at the paper. He knew he'd been given this assignment, because all the young, freshly-graduated journalists who should be sent out on stories like this didn't exist anymore.

The Gazette hadn't hired any in five years. No one read their newspapers anymore except very old people. And any young person who might be interested in a career in journalism wouldn't pursue working at a local newspaper. He wouldn't have either if he was just starting out. He'd have gone where the action was, where the opportunities were growing and expanding, not fading into oblivion.

That's where Tom was now. The Wasteland of Journalistic Oblivion.

Say, that had a nice ring to it.

He smiled. Still had a knack for turning a phrase. Maybe he could turn it into a book, about the demise of old-fashioned, newspaper reporters.

Like him.

"Excuse me, sir, can I help you find something? You look a little lost."

"What?" Tom said. The young woman's voice jarred him from his thoughts. It was after school hours, but she looked young enough to be a student.

"My name's Marsha Manning. I'm one of the science teachers here. Are you one of the parents or grandparents of a student? Maybe need to meet with their teacher?"

Did she say grandparent? "No, actually. Marsha, my name is Tom Hazelton." He paused, then realized it was ridiculous to think she might have heard of him. "I'm a reporter with the Gazette."

"Oh, are you here to interview Mr. Dietrich, about being named Teacher of the Year again?"

"That's exactly why I'm here. Am I close to his office?"

"Very close. Just continue down the hall. It will be the second door on your left."

"Thank you very much."

Tom found the door with Dietrich's name on the front, knocked and heard someone tell him to come in. He already knew what Dietrich looked like after looking him up on the internet. The man he found sitting at a desk in a moderately sized office looked very similar. "Hi, Mr. Dietrich. Tom Hazelton from the Gazette. Hopefully, you were expecting me."

Dietrich half-stood to shake hands, then sat down again. "I am, Tom. Please call me Al. Mr. Dietrich is what the kids call me. Or Mr. D."

"As it turns out, quite a few adults do, too. Spent the last day or so interviewing several of your former students — the ones I could find who still live in town, that is — and every single one of them still referred to you as either Mr. Dietrich or Mr. D. Even the ones in their early forties."

Dietrich laughed. "I know what you're saying. I still bump into some of the older ones in town from time to time. I tell them they can call me Al now, but they insist it can't be done."

"Well, it was obvious they all think quite highly of you. I'm interviewing you last just in case I needed to give you a chance to respond to anything any of the others might've said that you might disagree with, or be concerned about."

"Well, fire away," Dietrich said. "I'll do the best I can with—"

"No need, Al. No one said anything that could even remotely be considered challenging or controversial. Seems like they are awarding the right person for the Teacher of the Year. For the fifth time. And I'm not just talking about former students. I interviewed several of your colleagues, both the teachers and some in administration. Nothing but good stuff all around."

"Well, that's nice to hear. I'm certainly going to miss this place, and especially the people. I've had a great run."

"Well," Tom said, "maybe we'll start there. What are you going to miss most, the teaching, the coaching, or...what?"

"Don't think I'll miss the teaching all that much," he said. "Math is math, and it doesn't get more exciting every year, if you get my drift."

Tom laughed. "Math was never exciting in any year of my life."

Dietrich laughed. "So, you get what I mean. I do love when the lights come on for my kids. When they haven't been able to get something, and I explain it again in a different way, and they get it. The biggest smile comes over their face. That part is really fun. But see, that's the part I'll miss most, the people. Both the kids and the other teachers I work with."

"How many of them know you're planning to retire?" Tom said.

"Not many. In fact, probably just the principal. You know with social media these days, you tell one person, then they tell one person, next thing you know everyone is posting or texting about it."

Tom sighed. "Yeah, social media has its good parts, but in many ways it's really ruined my profession. In fact, I've actually begun to think about retiring."

"You have?"

"Yeah. And it's largely due to the impact of social media. For example, you may have read that story I wrote a few days ago about this murderer coming back to town after more than thirty-five years. An ex-con who got paroled. You've lived here long enough. You probably remember it. The guy's name is Sam Clemens, killed this young TV reporter named Roberto Sanchez." Tom noticed this strange expression come over Dietrich's face. For just a few seconds, then he snapped out of it.

"Yeah, I read that story," he said. "I vaguely remember reading about it back when it happened. It was quite a shocking thing. I went to school with both of those guys, graduated from Culpepper the year after them. The University, I mean. Didn't really know either one of them well. So, this guy...Clemens...is back in Culpepper after all these years. Why do you think he came back? He have any family here?"

"Don't think he does," Tom said. "Not sure he has any connections. Who knows why he came back? Maybe—like all guys in prison—he's convinced himself he's innocent, so he's pulling an OJ."

"An OJ?" Dietrich said.

"Yeah, you know, he's come back to search for the *real* killer. I don't know. Maybe he just wants to finish out his life in someplace familiar."

"Yeah, maybe. So...what did that Clemens story have to do with social media impacting your career?"

"Oh, it's just, you'd think a story like that would generate a good deal of interest. But we got very few comments from readers on our website about it. Nowadays, getting comments matters. Like, really matters. Not too many years ago we couldn't care less if readers responded to our stories. Now everybody tracks everything. Like this story we're doing about you. My editor's all excited. You're so popular in town, he's expecting hundreds of comments once I write this thing. Anyway, enough talking about me and my woes. Maybe next, it'll help if we can get some background on you. Since you've been teaching for so long and have lived in the area all your life. Tell me a little bit about your family history. I'm guessing Dietrich is German, right? When did the first Dietrich come to the states from Germany? When did the first one come to Culpepper?"

There was that strange look again. Tom wasn't sure how to read it.

"Well," he said, "we are German. I mean, of German descent. The family tree, well, not much to tell there. My father was the first one to come to the US. He started out in New York but came down here to go to the University. That's where he met my mom. After he graduated, he decided this was a pretty nice place to raise a family. So, this is where we stayed. And this is where I grew up."

"That's interesting," Tom said. "So, your father came over from Germany. Was that before or after the war?" Again, that look on Dietrich's face. Tom got the distinct impression he didn't want to talk about this, which only made the reporter-side of Tom more curious.

"It was after the war. He was just a regular German soldier, got no higher in rank than a corporal. He never liked to talk about his war years, understandably. But it was obvious, by the end he came to hate Hitler and all he stood for. He'd gone back to his hometown after Germany surrendered to find his entire family had been wiped out. So, he decided there wasn't any reason to stay. Found a way to come here, went to college, got a decent job, became a citizen as quickly as he could, and pretty much raised us to love America. Other than putting sauerkraut on our hot dogs, growing up, we never even ate German food. That's pretty much all there is to know about our family history."

"I see," Tom said. "Okay, that should be enough on that. Let's see what else do I need to ask you." He flipped open his list of questions. He glanced up quickly at Dietrich's face and was almost certain he saw a look of relief.

20

JOE PULLED INTO THE PARKING SLOT THAT HAD BECOME THEIR
unofficial reserved space at the station. He and Hank got out
of the car at the same time and headed for the side entrance,
which was closer to Captain Pendleton's office. On the way
there, Joe had called his secretary saying they needed to
brief him on the Clemens-Sanchez case. She had called back
with the message he'd be able to see them as soon as they
got in.

"You want to handle this without me, Joe?" Hank said.

"I don't think so. Not this time. I'm anticipating some
pushback from the captain on this, might help for him to see
we're both at the same spot. We *are* both at the same spot,
right?"

"Yeah, Joe. Not so sure Pendleton cares what I think but,
yeah. What are you going in there hoping to get him to do?
Reopen the Sanchez case?"

They got to the door. Joe opened it and let Hank go
through first. "I don't know. That would be like a mega can of

worms, so maybe I won't aim so high. We'll just give it to him straight, see where we end up when we're through."

When they got to Pendleton's door, Hank returned the favor. The secretary smiled and notified Pendleton that they had arrived. He told her to send them right in. When they were standing in front of his desk, he said, "So, tell me more about this Clemens-Sanchez case. I wasn't even aware there was such a thing. Last I heard that case was closed over thirty years ago. I am aware of an assignment you were given to persuade Mr. Clemens to leave our fair city for other environs. Tell me that's what you're really here for. To say, *Mission Accomplished*. He'll be leaving very soon."

Joe looked at Hank, who gave him a look back that said, *you first.* "Well, Cap, things didn't go exactly as we planned."

"Okay, how far off are we from our stated goal?"

"A good ways, sir," Hank said. "Probably fair to say, we're not even in the ballpark of that...stated goal."

Pendleton sighed. "You're kidding me, right?"

Both shook their heads no. "This might take a few minutes to explain, Cap," Joe said. "But if you hear us out, I think it'll make sense." They spent the next ten minutes bringing him up to date on the situation. Not just their initial visit with Sam but the incident that just happened out at the cabin, the confrontation between Sam, Juan, and Alonzo Sanchez. And what it all seemed to mean to them...that none of them were thinking now that Sam had likely killed Roberto Sanchez, including Juan and Alonzo.

"Guys," Pendleton said. "This was supposed to be easy. You were supposed to make this go away. Now we've gone from chasing the guy out of town, to what, rolling out the red carpet? You want to give him the key to the city?"

Joe hated this part of Pendleton's personality. He knew it kinda came with the territory, the pressures of running the whole show. He had to worry about the politics of things, balancing the budget, keeping the mayor and city council happy. "Captain, we don't have to make a big deal out of this. Right now, I don't see why anyone else has to know anything we've said. Clemens certainly isn't going to blab to anyone. He's trying to keep as invisible as possible while he tries to figure out who really did this. Who stole his life. And the two Sanchez relatives have no reason to do anything with this. Before they left, they actually offered to help Clemens find the real killer. I mean, think about that. They went in there to beat the crap out of him and came out asking how they could help. Of course, Hank and I told them they needed to let it go, completely. I said we'd handle it."

"So, do you think they will?" Pendleton said. "Let it go?"

"I think so, Captain," Hank said. "But I don't think it would hurt to keep them in the loop on this, at least in part. You know how families get with these kind of situations. They just want to know we're on it. They only get tempted to get involved when they feel like no one's doing anything. I mean, up until a little while ago, I'm sure they thought the whole thing was settled decades ago. Now they're pretty convinced the real killer is still out there, walking scot-free. I think if we don't do anything about this, eventually, they might hook up with Clemens, try to help him figure out what really happened."

"We definitely don't want that," Pendleton said.

"No, we don't," Joe said. "And Cap, don't tell me that the list of reasons we gave for why we think there's something here didn't affect you. You're too good a cop to not see some-thing isn't adding up."

Another big sigh from Pendleton. He leaned back in his chair. Joe could tell they were winning him over.

"You really think this guy might be innocent?" he said.

"I really do," Joe said.

"I agree with Joe," Hank said. "It just doesn't add up. Besides Captain, aren't we your cold case squad? You asked us to focus our attention on unsolved murders in this town, starting with the eighties. Well, that's what we might have here. An unsolved murder from 1985. You give Joe and I the green light on this, and we're right on point."

"He's right, Cap," Joe said. "I wasn't thinking about it that way but, that's really what this is. It wasn't in our murder box of unsolved cases downstairs, but it's starting to look more like maybe it should have been."

Pendleton didn't say anything for a few moments. Joe knew he'd never verbally admit defeat. He would just casu-ally give in and start playing along as though he was never really against it.

"So, this guy Clemens have any idea who did it? Who he thinks did it? He have any leads at all?"

"I don't know," Joe said. "We didn't get into anything like that with him. And we wouldn't, not until we ran everything by you. So, that mean we can start looking into this?"

"Don't see how I could stop you," he said. "But listen to me good on this point...you guys need to treat this almost like an undercover operation. I want zero publicity on this. The public thinks justice has been served. Until we know better, I want to keep it that way. We don't know who the real killer is, whether he's been walking around Culpepper the last thirty-six years with a big smile on his face, or if he moved away to some other place. For all we know, he could be dead. But on the off chance that he is, and has been, living in this town, we would be wise not to show him our hand."

"Totally agree with that, Captain," Joe said.

Hank nodded. "Me, too."

"Okay gentlemen, go to it. Quietly. Keep me in the loop."

21

AFTER THE MEETING WITH PENDLETON, JOE AND HANK headed back to their office. Just before stepping inside, Joe looked at his watch. "Tell you what, Hank, think I'll take a drive out there to Clemens' cabin. Make that my last stop before heading home. You know, try to do a little winning hearts and minds with the guy. See if I can get him to start viewing us as allies."

"All right, Joe. Have a feeling that process has already started. Think he can kinda tell we're mostly on his side."

"I suppose so. But I want to make it official, maybe set some boundaries on this thing, see if I can get him to share any of the things he's already figured out about who the real killer might be. Because other than thinking it's not him, we haven't got a lot to go on here."

"Okay," Hank said. "I've got plenty to do to finish out the day here."

Joe turned around and headed for the parking lot. He reached for his phone, thinking to call Sam, give him a heads up. Then decided to wait until he was just a few minutes from his place. Didn't want the guy having too much time to think or fret about the reason for his visit.

SAM WOKE up from an unexpected nap, to find himself safely laying on the sofa in his cabin, not surrounded by three inmate thugs ready to pounce on him. Which is where he'd been in his dream. As he sat up and stretched, he wondered how long he'd have to be out before dreams like these stopped happening. This one was probably generated by the confrontation with Juan and Alonzo. He was glad to find he was still pretty handy with his fists and feet but hoped that might be the last such incident for a very long time.

He woke up feeling a little hungry, decided to look over the ready-made frozen dinners he'd loaded in the freezer. See if one caught his eye. Just then, his phone rang. It startled him, even though it sounded like an old-time telephone ring. Reynolds, the young tech, helped him set it up like that before he'd left the store. But not before he'd played fifteen or twenty oddball samples for Sam to pick from when someone called. They were all so much nonsense, like weird sound effects from some bad sci-fi movie.

He'd told the lad, "I'll just take the normal-sounding one." And Reynolds replied, "Which one is that?"

Can you imagine? He didn't know, and he wasn't kidding.

The screen said it was Lieutenant Boyd, just like the Lieutenant said it would. What a crazy thing. "Hello, Lieutenant. Sam here."

"Hey, Sam. Hope I didn't catch you in the middle of

something, but I'm just a few minutes away from your place, thought I'd stop in and talk with you about something."

"Okay, I guess that would be fine. Not doing anything too important at the moment. Is everything...okay?"

"Everything's fine. Actually, wanted to share something of a positive development but figured it might be better to share it in person rather than over the phone."

"I like positive developments," Sam said. "Should I put on some coffee?"

"No, thanks. Had my limit of caffeine for the day. Feel free to make some for yourself if you want. I'll be there before you know it."

Sam wondered what was up. He didn't have to wait long to find out. As the Lieutenant had said, a few minutes later a car pulled up outside. He walked to the front door and opened it to welcome his guest. When the Lieutenant got out of his car, he actually smiled at him. Maybe this really was going to be something positive.

We'll see.

Sam stepped back to let the Lieutenant come through the doorway. He walked right over to the very same spot he sat in when he was here last. Sam walked over and sat in the chair. "So, what is this positive development you came all the way out here to discuss?"

"Well Sam, I'll get right to it. After hearing you out, both Hank and I feel —and coupling that, I should add, with more than ten years as a homicide detective — we feel like you might actually be innocent of the Sanchez murder. It certainly didn't hurt to see how quickly the two Sanchez relatives got turned around after talking with you. Anyway, we are now officially inclined, guess you could say, to believe you were probably framed. Haven't read the transcripts of the trial, just the newspaper accounts, but we also think you had a pretty lousy defense attorney. So, we talked it over confidentially with our captain, and he's given us the green light to start looking into your case."

Sam could hardly believe what he was hearing. "I...I don't know what to say. Most I was hoping for was not getting put back in jail over this."

"Now you understand," Joe said, "this doesn't mean anything has changed legally for you. We don't have the authority to declare you innocent. In the eyes of the law, you're still guilty of this crime. And it's not going to be an easy road to get that overturned. In fact, about the only thing that might work is if we can dig up sufficient evidence to prove either you couldn't have done it, prove someone else did, or both."

"I understand," Sam said. "That's pretty much what the road has always looked like for me coming back here. Given all the years gone by, I'm not even totally sure that's a possibility. All I knew coming here was, I had to give it a try. Of course, I didn't figure I'd be getting any help. What's that gonna look like, if you don't mind me asking? Going forward from here?"

"Don't mind at all. It's pretty simple. You keep doing whatever you had in mind. And we'll start coming at this — Hank and me — the way we go about these sorts of things. Believe it or not, we've gotten pretty good at this. We actually run — well, I do — the cold case squad in our department. That's essentially what this thing is, a cold case. Only thing is, we're the only ones that think it's still unsolved. Virtually everyone else out there..." Joe pointed toward the front door.

"...Thinks you're guilty as sin. So, they're not likely to be as helpful as they might be if this were a normal cold case investigation."

"Well," Sam said, "wouldn't that be a little different now with you and your partner getting involved? Folks around here know who you are and know it's your job to look into these old cases."

Joe sighed. "See, that's the thing about this. Our captain isn't giving us a blank check to work with. Since this is officially a closed case, and since we don't have any real evidence to say otherwise at this point, he's not giving us permission to talk plainly about this with people. We have to be very discreet. Not just us, but you, too. Especially you, Sam. We've got to do the best we can not to stir up any publicity about this. Not until we come up with something concrete in terms of evidence we can take to court. All we've really got right now are hunches and suppositions. That's not enough to make a difference. Are you following me here?"

"Yeah, I am. I think I understand what you're getting at. I'm guessing I'll keep digging — discreetly — and so will you and Hank. And we'll compare notes as we go? That about the size of it?"

"Yep," Joe said. "So, for starters, since you've had all this time to think about these things, have you come up with any hunches about who the real killer might be?"

Sam suddenly found himself involuntarily pulling back. It only took him a moment to realize why. While he was extremely glad to learn the Lieutenant and his partner were now officially on his side, it was something he hadn't counted on. And he wasn't entirely comfortable sharing anything he had come up with. Mainly because, they didn't really have the same agenda here. In a way they did, in terms of both wanting to catch who really did it. But not in terms of the consequences the real killer would face when that moment arrived.

They'd want to put him in handcuffs in the back of their police car.

Sam would want to see him dead and buried in a shallow grave.

"Sam," Joe said. "Did you hear me? It would help to hear any initial thoughts you have about who did this. Help point our nose in the right direction."

"Yeah, I heard you. I was just thinking about it. See, the problem is, it's not like I could do anything much behind bars. Except think about it. Even if I had some strong ideas, wasn't too much I could do with them until I got out."

"Okay, now you're out. What are you thinking?" Joe said.

"About all I know or...what I believe, is that whoever killed Roberto Sanchez did it to stop that documentary he was making from ever getting made. That's the only thing that makes sense to me." Sam figured it wouldn't do any harm to share that much.

"So, that's what you figure the real motive of the killer was?"

Sam nodded, decided to share one other thing. "And I remembered something else, that day when I confronted Sanchez about taking me off the project and about paying me what he owed me. I saw a guy in a car parked across the street from Sanchez's house. Young guy, about our age. Blonde hair. He was just staring at me as I got out of my car and went inside Sanchez's house. When I came back out, he was gone."

"Don't know who he was?" Joe said.

Sam shook his head no. "Have no idea. He did look vaguely familiar, but I couldn't even tell you why."

"You got anything else?"

"No. Told my lawyer about the guy in the car back in '85, but he didn't think there was anything to it. That wasn't the day Sanchez was killed, he said. Could've been just somebody visiting another house on the block."

"So, don't have a whole lot to go on here, do we?" Joe said.

"No, we really don't," Clemens said.

22

Joe went home after his meeting with Sam. His mostly unfruitful meeting. He tried to put it out of his mind till the morning. Over the years, he'd gotten better at doing that, so he could give Kate and the kids most of his attention. After dinner, they'd spent the evening eating popcorn and watching a new family movie on the streaming Disney Channel. The kids had gone to bed making their strongest case for the next family visit to Disney World. They hadn't gone in several years and they pointed out, once the baby came it would likely be several more years before they went again.

Of course, he and Kate gave the perennial "We'll see" response followed by the conversation-killing, "Now go to bed."

When Joe woke up the next morning, his mind kept replaying certain parts of the conversation with Sam. His instincts told him Sam wasn't being totally straight on this thing. He'd thought about pressing him on that but didn't want to start things off on the wrong foot. It was really important to keep Sam on board and cooperating. Joe could always play hardball if any concrete examples came up where it became clear Sam was holding things back.

After eating breakfast with Kate and the kids, he kissed them all goodbye and headed for the station. Once there, he briefed Hank on things, then they started brainstorming ways to generate some new leads to follow on this case.

SAM WOKE up feeling pretty good. Slept better than he had in a long while. No prison dreams and only got up twice to go the bathroom. Both times he was able to go right back to sleep. He figured it must have something to do with how much his circumstances had improved in the past few days. He hadn't anticipated getting the local cops on his side and would never have imagined the turnaround with the victim's remaining family, Juan and Alonzo. He could actually start looking into this thing without any big hindrances blocking his way.

After making himself some coffee and a nice hot bowl of instant apple-and-cinnamon oatmeal, he started using his miracle machine, his new smartphone. The first idea he'd come up with was to contact the TV station where Roberto Sanchez had worked, see if anyone had been working at the station during the time Sanchez was there. That prompted another task. He couldn't likely call there and say, "Hi, I'm the guy who just got out of prison for killing Roberto Sanchez in '85. Wonder if you could help me prove some-body else did it?"

He thought on it some more and right about the time his coffee mug was half-empty, something clicked. He scribbled down some notes on a pad then looked up the telephone number for the local TV station. Using Google. He just typed it in, and there was the number. Guess nobody used the Yellow Pages anymore. Seeing how easy this was, why would they?

After a few rings, a nice girl answered and asked how she could help him. "Hi, my name's Bill Evers from the Atlanta Journal-Constitution. I write human interest stories for them. Read where a long-time inmate named Samuel Clemens had recently been paroled for a murder committed there in your town back in 1985. Judging by the sound of your voice, I'm guessing you might not have been working at the station then."

The girl laughed. "Well, Mr. Evers. I wasn't even born then."

"I'm not surprised. It was a very long time ago," Sam said. "We're doing a follow-up story, guess you could say, on this situation. Reason I'm calling you folks is, the fellow this guy Clemens killed was a reporter for your station at the time."

"Oh, my. That's awful. Sorry to say, I've never heard about it until just now."

"Again, not surprised. What I'm really hoping for is to find someone who might be working at your station who does remember. They'd be pretty old at this point, seeing that it was thirty-six years ago. Do you know of anyone there, maybe in their late fifties, early sixties, who's been working at your station this whole time?"

She paused a moment. "I don't. I'm sorry. Two people come to mind who are about that age, but I know both of them have just started working here in the last five years. But I'll tell you what, if you let me put you on hold for a moment, I can put in a call to our general manager. He's been here for at least twenty years, and he'd probably know if there was someone else you could talk to who might be able to help. Like, maybe someone who'd retired already but they worked here back then."

"Well, young lady, that's a fabulous idea. I'd be happy to hold if you want to give that a try."

"Great. I'll be back with you in just a moment. May take a little longer if I can't get hold of him right away."

He heard a click, then some pleasant music.

A few minutes later, she got back on the phone. "Mr. Evers, I was able to talk with Mr. Edwards, our GM. I explained what you said, and he gave me the name of a man who he said actually worked with Mr. Sanchez—the one who was killed—back in '85. He spent his whole career here until he retired a few years ago. You got something to write this down?"

"Sure do," Sam said.

"Okay, it's Barry Carmichael. I don't have his number, but he still lives here in Culpepper, and we're a pretty small town. Probably not too many men with that name living here would be my guess."

"Great, that's great. You've been so helpful, my dear. I'll look this fellow up, see if he'll chat with me a few minutes. You have a great rest of the day now." She said goodbye and they both hung up.

"Well," Sam said aloud. "Barry Carmichael. Guess I'll see if Google knows who you are, Mr. Carmichael."

In just a few minutes, he was dialing the one-and-only Barry Carmichael living in Culpepper. A man answered who sounded about his age, or older. "Hello, Mr. Carmichael. This is Bill Evers here from the Atlanta Journal-Constitution. Got a few minutes you can talk with me?"

"So, you're really a person?" Carmichael said. "Was almost not gonna pick up, since I didn't see a name or recognize the number. Usually, it's some sales call. I get so sick of those."

"I know," Sam said, even though he didn't. Maybe he'd understand after he had his phone a while longer. "But I'm a real person. Got your phone number from some kind folks over at the TV station where you used to work. From a Mr. Edwards, the general manager over there."

"Oh, yeah. Worked there the better part of my life. I was never on the air, though. Mostly did work in production. Editing mostly. You say you're with the Constitution? Can't imagine why someone at Georgia's largest newspaper would want to talk to me."

"Well, just trying to get some background on a story I'm working on. Happened back in 1985. I understand you worked at the station then?"

"I did, as a matter fact. Only about two years at that point. Boy, were things so much different back then."

Tell me about it, Sam thought. "Then maybe you can help me with my research here. I'm sure you must recall when a young reporter was killed, murdered, named Roberto Sanchez."

"Oh, yeah. Roberto. What a terrible thing. He and I were almost the same age. Of course, he was becoming quite the celebrity, so we really didn't hang out much. But I did edit a number of the stories he reported on. I even knew the fellow that killed him, Sam Clemens."

That surprised Sam. He was pretty sure he'd never heard of this guy before.

"Well, I knew who he was," Carmichael said. "He was a video guy, a cameraman. Didn't work at the station, mostly freelance I think. But after he'd been arrested, I recognized him. Think I saw him working with Roberto on some projects. Not ones for the station, mind you. But Roberto was always setting his sights high. Had different things going on the side, as I recall."

"Actually," Sam said, "you just talked about something I was going to ask about. Some of Sanchez's side work, I guess you could say. Were you aware he was working on some big documentary at the time of his death?"

A pause. "A documentary?" Carmichael repeated. "Yeah, now that you mention it. I do recall him talking about that in the weeks before he died. Talked about it with me, as a matter of fact. Asked me if I ever did any editing work on the side. I told him I wish I could, but I didn't own any of my own equipment. He suggested maybe I could use the station's equipment. You know, after-hours sort of thing."

"Really?" Sam said.

"Of course, I shut that down right away. No way I was gonna lose my job over some side work. Especially after hearing Roberto say he was willing to pay me serious money, but it would have to wait until *after* he sold the story. I thanked him for asking, but said I wasn't interested. That pretty much ended anymore conversation on the subject."

"Do you recall Sanchez ever telling you what the documentary was about?"

Another pause. "No, don't think he did. Actually, I just remembered. I did ask him when we first started talking, before that part came out about me using the station's equipment. The thing is, he wouldn't tell me. Acted like the whole thing was top-secret. I don't know if that was just to try and stir my interest, or if it was actually true. Roberto had a way of embellishing things, if you know what I mean."

Sadly, Sam did. "So, you don't have any idea at all? He never gave you any clue?"

"No, don't think so. I got the impression though — can't recall exactly why now — that it was some kind of biography piece, but not about somebody famous. Actually, I remember now. He was the one that gave me the impression. At first, he started telling me a little bit about it, but then stopped. He said, *It's not about somebody famous, more like somebody infamous.* I know he wanted to be some hot shot investigative reporter, like Geraldo Rivera. I figured he was doing some kind of hit piece on somebody but didn't want to let anyone know the details yet. Course, shortly after that he was killed. The whole documentary thing evaporated. I never gave it another thought till you just asked. It never came up in the murder trial."

No, it didn't. "Well, thank you, Mr. Carmichael. This has been very helpful."

"If you say so. I tell you anything you can use in your story?"

"Very possibly," Sam said. "You got my number now on your phone, right? Feel free to call me if anything else comes to mind about this."

"I do, and I will," Carmichael said.

They exchanged further pleasantries and hung up. Then quickly before he forgot, Sam added Carmichael's name to his contact list, so if he ever did call, Sam would remember to answer with, "Hi, this is Bill Evers from the Atlanta Journal-Constitution."

23

JOE AND HANK HAD HAMMERED OUT A BASIC STRATEGY TO make some headway on this Sanchez case, when a call came in from a witness to an earlier case they had worked on. The witness had just remembered something possibly important and wanted to talk to a detective. In person. Hank said he'd go see the guy, so Joe took out their worksheet and started in on the first item. Which was, calling the local TV station where Sanchez had worked at the time of his death, see if anyone there remembered working with him.

If so, maybe he'd talked with them about that documentary he was making. He looked up the number and dialed. Moments later, he was introducing himself to a young receptionist and explaining why he called. Before he finished, she interrupted him.

"It's so funny you calling and asking about Roberto Sanchez. I've never even heard his name before today, and now you're the second person calling about him — right out of the blue."

That got Joe's attention. "Really? Who was the other call from?"

"Let me see," she said, "I wrote it down right here. It was a reporter from that big Atlanta newspaper, named Bill Evers. He was asking the very same thing. Wanted to know if anybody still worked here who worked back when Mr. Sanchez was killed. Is there some big thing going on about this case all of a sudden?"

"No, no," Joe said. "Not really. It's just the guy who went to prison for killing him got out on parole recently, after thirty-six years. Not sure what that reporter's fishing for, but there's no big story brewing here. I'm just following up on some loose details." He tried to sound as nonchalant as possible.

"Oh, okay. Well, I can tell you the same thing I told Mr. Evers a little while ago. Turns out, no one works here now who worked here back in 1985. But I was able to find someone who did who retired recently. His name's Barry Carmichael. I don't have his phone number but—."

"That's okay. Name like that should be pretty easy to find," Joe said, "thanks so much for your help. I'll give Mr. Carmichael a call."

He hung up wondering what the heck? Why would a reporter from the Atlanta Journal-Constitution be interested in this case? Not a good development. Pendleton wanted to keep this thing as quiet as possible. Joe better call this guy Evers, see if he could extinguish his interest in the story before calling Barry Carmichael. He went online and got on the newspaper's website. To his surprise, they didn't appear to have any reporters named Bill Evers. He searched the site every way he could with no luck.

He was just about to call them directly to see if he was

someone new, who hadn't made it on the website yet, when an idea hit him. He smiled as he thought about it. Maybe there was no Bill Evers at the paper, because Bill Evers didn't exist. Maybe Bill Evers was really Sam Clemens, using this as a ploy to get some free info. The more he thought about it, the more likely this scenario seemed. So, he found his number and called Barry Carmichael instead.

"Hello?"

Carmichael had a pleasant-sounding voice. "Is this Barry Carmichael?"

"It is. Who might this be? You sound human, and I don't detect any foreign accent."

Joe laughed. "Right on both counts."

"I wasn't going to pick up, since I didn't recognize the number but decided to take a chance it might be real."

Joe figured he was talking about sales or robo-calls. "Well, I'm glad you did. Saved me from having to leave a voicemail then us playing phone tag the next few days. My name's Lieutenant Joe Boyd. I'm with the Culpepper —"

"I know who you are, Lieutenant," Carmichael interrupted. "I've seen you on the local news a few times. Think I might've edited a couple of the early ones. I was still at the station then. You mainly work homicides, as I recall. I think the last few have been old cases, am I right?"

"You are, sir. They call them cold cases."

"Working on another one now?"

Man, Joe wasn't expecting this. He was supposed to be the one asking questions. "Not sure just yet. Maybe. Doing some preliminary research, I guess you could say. Involving a case from 1985. Think you might've already been contacted about this once today, by a reporter from an Atlanta paper?"

"How'd you know that? You're correct, but how did you know?"

"The receptionist at the TV station told me when I called her just a few minutes ago. And I wouldn't be surprised if Mr. Evers was asking you the same questions I'm about to."

"Evers," Carmichael repeated. "That's his name. You two know each other?"

"Possibly," Joe said. "You wouldn't have his telephone number there, would you?"

"I do. Put him in my Contacts after he called, in case I remembered anything else about the Sanchez situation. Got it right here." He paused to find it then read it aloud to Joe.

Joe wrote it down, quickly compared it to Sam Clemens' phone number on his contact list. Then he got the biggest smile. "You know, I'm almost positive I know this reporter you spoke with. Bill Evers, you said?"

"That's his name. Funny thing is, I did remember something else. Not sure it would be any help for the story he's writing."

"Well," Joe said, "how about this? How about you answer a few of my questions then you can tell me the new thing you remembered. I'll give Bill a call and give him your new information."

"That would be just great, Lieutenant. I haven't had this much excitement in quite a while. Being interviewed by a big time reporter and a famous homicide detective in one day."

Got one of those right, Joe thought.

"Okay, fire away. But let me guess, would your first question be about the documentary Roberto Sanchez was working on when he died?"

"It would be," Joe said. "I know nothing about it came out

in the trial, but perhaps you heard the man accused of killing him, Samuel Clemens, was recently let out on parole?"

"I did read about that in the Gazette."

"Can I share something with you in confidence?" Joe said.

"By all means. I heard things all the time at the station I could never talk about. Pretty good at that."

"Well, I've spoken with Mr. Clemens since his release on parole. Of course, like most folks in prison, they're not guilty of the crime they were accused of. Anyway, he's insisting he didn't do it, even after all these years. He believes Sanchez was killed because of some documentary he was making at the time. I don't even know if this documentary was —"

"Oh, it's real," Carmichael said. "I know that for a fact. Roberto was definitely working on a documentary. Seemed to me it took up all his spare time. He even tried to get me to edit it when it was done. I turned him down, but I know it was a big deal to him. Sadly, don't know what it was about, as I said to Mr. Evers. He was always so hush-hush about it. He did say one time — now, I'm paraphrasing here — it wasn't about somebody famous, but infamous. Don't know how much weight to put on that. Roberto had a way of exaggerating things at times. You know, overstating their importance."

"Definitely know a few people like that," Joe said. "So, were these all the things you shared with Bill Evers?"

"Pretty much."

"Was there anything else? You said you had remembered something new?"

"Yes, that's right. The new thing is — and again, not saying this will make an ounce of difference to anyone — I remembered after he died, the TV station was a bit smaller then. Guys on the low-end of the totem pole like me often wound up wearing a lot of hats. I got tasked with cleaning out all the stuff from his office and getting it to his surviving family. Wasn't much, just a couple of boxes. But I remember in one of those boxes putting a number of books about World War II in there. They weren't novels but decent hard-back books. You know, history books about the war."

This could definitely be something. "Interesting," Joe said. "You don't happen to recall any of the titles? Don't need the exact words but maybe what they were about?"

Carmichael sighed. "I don't think I do. But they were nice ones. Wait a minute...I do remember one book. Not the title, but it was about the SS and the Nuremberg trials. I remember because I was tempted to steal it. I had just watched a documentary about the Nuremberg trials, I think. Anyway, I behaved and left it in the box. There were three or four other World War II books, but I can't recall anything else about them. Not sure if that helps any."

Joe wasn't sure, either. But his instincts told him...it just might. "Thanks, Mr. Carmichael. Really appreciate this. I'll definitely pass this onto Bill Evers the next time I speak with him."

24

After jotting down some notes from his phone call with Barry Carmichael, Joe spent the next hour doing online research from ideas generated by the call. As he finished up, Hank came back to his desk.

"Get anywhere with that first item on the list?"

Joe turned around in his chair. "I did. Nothing groundbreaking but something real, I think. There's no one left at the TV station from the time Sanchez was killed. But they connected me with a retired guy named Carmichael who remembered something useful. Learned two things from that call, actually."

Hank sat. "Like what?"

"Well, got a little more insight into Roberto Sanchez. Kind of a showboater, very ambitious. Got the impression, not very well-liked. You know the type, extremely talented but knows it. According to this Carmichael fella, this documentary was a very big deal to him. Treated it like a state secret, but he'd said enough for Carmichael to think it was about *somebody*, more than something. Like a hit piece about somebody he described as *infamous*."

"Infamous," Hank repeated. "Kind of got a sinister connotation to it."

"Yeah, it does."

"Anything more than that?"

"Not a lot. But there was one other thing that might be a clue about the documentary's theme. He said after Sanchez was killed, he got the assignment to clear out his things and deliver them to the family, which he did. Filled up two boxes. In one, there were four or five books about World War II. He only remembered what one was about. It was on the SS and the Nuremberg trials. Know anything about that?"

"Pretty sure not as much as you," Hank said. "Definitely not as much as Jack." He was referring to their mutual friend, Professor Jack Turner, the Dean of Military History at Culpepper. "I know the SS were the very worst of the bad dudes among the Nazis. And the Nuremberg trials were where they exposed all the Nazi atrocities, like the Holocaust and the camps. And they hanged most of the main guys."

"That's a pretty good summary," Joe said. "I'm sure better than most millennials can manage. The real question is... what's an ambitious, showboating, twenty-four-year-old TV reporter doing with a bunch of World War II history books? Especially one about the SS and Nuremberg? Not exactly fun reading for a guy that age. World War II ended thirty years before this."

"You think he was doing research for his documentary?" Hank said.

Joe nodded. "Carmichael didn't mention any other books in those boxes. And he said Sanchez spent all his spare time on this documentary. Put those two ideas together — a hit piece on somebody infamous and a bunch of research books on World War II —and what do you come up with?"

Hank thought a moment. "A Nazi war criminal."

"Bingo. You really have been paying attention."

"Guess you're rubbing off on me. So, think that might've been what Sanchez's documentary was about? He was working on exposing a Nazi war criminal?"

"Leaning that way," Joe said. "I was looking some things up before you walked in. Turns out, finding Nazi war criminals was still a pretty big deal in the 1980s. Two big fish made the national news a short while before Sanchez's murder. One was Klaus Barbie, known as the Butcher of Lyon. He was captured in Bolivia then extradited to France in 1983. That made national headlines. The other one was Dr. Josef Mengele, nicknamed the Angel of Death. This was a seriously warped individual, did all kinds of horrible experiments on Jews, including kids. He died in Brazil in 1979 but made the news again in 1985. That was the year his remains were found and identified."

"So," Hank said, "if somehow Sanchez had discovered a Nazi war criminal living here in the US, and he could prove it —"

"And unveil his proof," Joe said, "in his very own documentary —"

"Yeah," Hank said, "that would pretty much launch his career into the big leagues."

They both looked at each other a moment.

"You think that might be it?" Hank said. "We just figure out the *why* question here?"

"Don't know. Maybe we have. It's definitely a scenario

that fits the few things we've uncovered so far. But we're a thousand miles away from proving any of it. But if you think about it, if this was what Sanchez was working on, it would definitely provide a serious motive for someone to want to stop him from completing it."

"A much stronger motive for murder," Hank said, "than throwing your life away over five hundred bucks."

"I know, right?"

"Say, Joe, you said there were two things you got from that call with the guy from the TV station. What was the other one?"

"Oh, yeah. Kind of humorous in a way. Looks like our friend Mr. Clemens is pretty clever and has some pretty good instincts."

"How so?"

"Guess what was the first item on *his* list to go after in this investigation?"

Hank thought. "Based on the look on your face, I'm going with the same thing you did...calling the TV station."

Joe nodded. "Yep."

"But how'd he pull that off? It's not like anybody down there would want to help him."

"Right, and he knew that. So, he calls down there masquerading as a reporter from the Atlanta Journal-Constitution. Like he's doing a follow-up story on him getting out of prison after thirty-six years. A story on himself, in other words. Completely pulls it off. Winds up talking to the same guy I did. The guy thinks he's talking to a big-name reporter. Even agrees to call him if he remembers anything else. Which he does but hasn't told him yet."

"That the thing you just told me?"

"Yeah, the part about Carmichael cleaning out Sanchez's desk and finding those World War II books."

"So, how did you figure out that it was Clemens masquerading as a reporter?"

Joe explained how.

"That *is* clever. So, you gonna call Clemens and give him the update about the books?"

"I don't know. I mean, it's not like we're two law enforcement agencies sharing the same turf. I don't owe it to him. But I can't think of a good reason not to tell him, can you?"

Hank thought a few moments. "I really can't. Like you said, he's clever and has good instincts. This time he just went for the same idea we came up with. Maybe you tell him the new bit and it stirs up something brand new in his head. And since you included him, maybe he does the same with us on anything new he digs up. I mean, it's not like we got a lot to go on here."

"Yeah," Joe says. "I'll tell him." Joe picked up his phone, looked up Sam's number. Then wondered how he was gonna let Sam know he'd uncovered his little gimmick with Barry Carmichael.

"Say, Joe," Hank said. "Maybe when you call him and he picks up, say, *Hey, this is the Atlanta Journal-Constitution. We hear you been pretending to be one of our reporters.*"

Joe smiled.

25

THE PHONE RANG A FEW TIMES AND SAM PICKED UP. "HELLO, Lieutenant."

"See," Joe said, "I knew you'd get used to this phone pretty quick."

"So, what's up?"

"How you coming with your investigation? Find anything useful yet?" There was a long pause. "Come on now, Sam. Don't hold back on me. I told you we need to compare notes."

"Remember you saying something about that. Did turn up something. But I had to do a little...role playing. Nothing wrong with that, right?"

"Depends, I guess. Wouldn't have anything to do with pretending you're a big-time reporter with an Atlanta newspaper?"

"Uh...yeah. It did. How'd you find out about that?"

Joe told him all about his phone call to the TV station then to Barry Carmichael.

"So, you know now I wasn't exaggerating about the documentary. It really was a big deal to Roberto. I've been racking my brain trying to figure out who this infamous person might be. Whoever it is, I'm pretty sure he lives here in Culpepper. Or at least he did at the time of the murder. That's the only thing that makes sense to me. I mean, the whole time Roberto was working on it he never left town. This was years before the internet. Back then when you want to investigate someone you had to go where they were. So, I'm thinking *Mr. Infamous* is a local."

Joe was impressed with Sam's logic.

"And all the footage I shot for the documentary was all local," Clemens continued. "You know what B-roll footage is?"

"Can't say as I do."

"You actually do. You just don't recognize the name. It's in every documentary ever made. It's the background stuff. You know the scenery, the set up stuff. He had this whole list of places in Culpepper he wanted video of. Places that showed off the town, help the viewer get a sense of where the story is taking place. All of it was in Culpepper."

"I agree, Sam. That's significant. Got something else to toss in the stew. Mr. Carmichael remembered something after your phone call. Told me what it was. I said I knew you and would pass on the message for him. This is for Bill Evers at the Atlanta Journal-Constitution."

Sam laughed. "That would be me. What did he remember?"

Joe told him all about the World War II books Carmichael had seen in the box of Sanchez's personal belongings. Including the book about the SS and Nuremberg trials. He didn't say anything about what he and Hank had discussed regarding what this new revelation meant. Turned out, he didn't have to.

"He was going after a war criminal," Sam blurted out. "Some Nazi SS guy. Has to be. Don't you think?"

"Kind of what we were thinking, too. Me and Hank."

"So, Sanchez must have found some information," Sam said, "that convinced him a Nazi war criminal was living here in town. Gotta be it. It would explain why he was being so hush-hush about it. Not the kind of thing you want leaking out until you had all your ducks lined up in a row. Maybe whoever it was, got wind of it at some point. And that's why he killed Roberto."

Joe couldn't have said it better himself. "It's a viable theory, Sam. Of course, that's all it is right now. A theory, an idea. Points our nose in a certain direction. Doesn't give us anything to act on."

"Not yet," Sam said. "But hey, this is some serious progress, don't you think? You've got to admit, makes a whole lot more sense why someone would want to kill Roberto. Stop a thing like that from going public."

"I agree." Joe released a sigh. "It's a good feeling to narrow the options a little, but we've got a long way to go here. It's a shame all Carmichael found in those boxes was a stack of books. Guess the killer must have gotten hold of the footage Sanchez had made so far, and destroyed it. You never heard anything more about it after you were arrested?"

"Not a peep."

Neither man said anything for a few moments.

"Well," Joe said, "we'll have to give it some more thought. Maybe the next logical step will present itself."

"I'm sure it will," Sam said. "But I feel good we're making some headway anyhow. And thanks for the call. Appreciate you keeping me in the loop."

"No problem, Sam. Thanks for sharing what you turned up. Let's stay in touch."

LATER THAT EVENING, Joe and Kate took their coffee mugs out on the wood deck behind their house. The sun had already set behind the row of trees that lined the backyard. The kids were watching episodes of *The Mandalorian* in the family room.

"So," Kate said, "want to talk about it?"

"Talk about what?"

"Talk about whatever's bugging you? You were obviously distracted all through dinner. Is it the new case you're working on?"

Joe often briefed Kate about his cases, usually only sparing her the sordid details when there were any. So far, in this case, that wasn't a problem. She had great instincts, and he never once worried that she'd share something with her friends. "Yeah, I guess it is. Remember that proverb, *Hope deferred makes the heart sick*?"

"I do."

"Guess that's what I'm struggling with a little." He filled her in on the latest details of the case, including the new stuff they'd come up with about the Nazi war criminal angle."

"You think we might have a Nazi war criminal here in Culpepper?"

"If we did, he's likely dead now. But if we're on the right

track, he could have easily been alive in 1985 when the Sanchez murder happened."

"From everything you said, sounds like you're on the right track to me. And it kinda confirms your hunch about Sam being wrongly imprisoned. A Nazi war criminal would definitely not want his identity exposed. Especially then. That's a serious motive for murder."

"I know," Joe said. "I'm good with all that."

"Then what's bugging you? How has your *hope been deferred*?"

"On the car ride home, I realized...as exciting as this development is, we got nothing to go on from here. The video footage Sanchez shot for the documentary was likely destroyed over thirty years ago by the perp. The perp himself — if it was this old Nazi — is almost certainly dead now. We don't have a single clue about his identity. It makes me sick to think after committing all the atrocities he probably did during the war, he winds up committing this horrific Sanchez murder, pins the thing on Clemens, and gets to live out the rest of his life in lovely little Culpepper. He gets away with it. Poor old Sam Clemens' whole life is ruined. And now he's got no way to clear his name. I mean, we've got a great theory here that, to me, probably explains the case. But I can't do anything with it."

Kate didn't say anything a few moments. Then said, "Yeah, that stinks. If that's the end of the story. Seems like you're giving up a little too soon, don't you think?"

"I'm not giving up. It's just...without that original video footage, I don't know where else we can go with this."

"Well, here's an idea. This case has got a World War II side to it. You are probably one of the only homicide detectives whose close friend is a World War II expert. Maybe you should run this all by Jack. You know, take him out to lunch, tell him everything you got. See what he says. Can't hurt, right?"

Joe smiled, took a sip of his coffee. "No, that wouldn't hurt one bit."

26

To Joe's great surprise, Jack was available for lunch the following day. In fact, he was happy to hear from Joe and said he had something he wanted to share with him also. They had agreed to meet at Shanghai Lane, a somewhat upscale Chinese place not far from the University. Joe had arrived a few minutes ago, tried to resist dipping too many fried wonton noodles in that sugary duck sauce. He looked up, saw Jack coming in through the front door, and waved him over.

When Jack got close, he held out his hand. "So good to see you, my friend. I was just talking about you with Rachel last night, thinking I should give you a call."

They shook hands and both men sat down. "Guess our wives know best," Joe said. "Kate is the one suggested I should call you."

"Glad you did."

A waiter came up and took their drink orders. Jack had been there before, asked the waiter to bring some tempura calamari. "It's my favorite appetizer here. Got this amazing dipping sauce."

"Sounds good to me," Joe said. "I've only had it with marinara. But I like most things Chinese. You're looking good, Jack."

"Started going back to the gym again. We'll see how long I last this time. Gonna have to work out twice as hard after this lunch."

Joe involuntarily sucked in his gut. Then gave up a few seconds later. "Couldn't believe you were able to get free so quick."

"Well, hired some new staff in my office. They're finally getting up to speed. I'm actually able to get home for dinner on time again."

"How's Jack Junior?"

"Growing like a weed. Saying all kinds of fun things. Almost every day. How's Kate doing? The pregnancy going well?"

"Yeah, she's doing fine."

"Well, that's a good segue into the reason I wanted to talk with you. Looks like our kids — at least our newest ones — might be on the same Little League team."

"What are you saying? You saying..."

"Rachel's pregnant. Number two is on its way. Looks like just a couple months behind you."

"That's great, Jack. Congratulations. Kate will be so excited."

"Rachel's beside herself," Jack said. "Of course, she's hoping it'll be a girl."

"What about you? You got a preference?"

"Nope, just that it's healthy, whether a he or a she."

"Same here."

The waiter came back, set down the drinks and a nice big plate of calamari. It looked and smelled wonderful. Then he took their orders for lunch.

After he left, they said a quick blessing over the food. Jack asked, "So, what do you want to talk about? You said it has something to do with the case you're working on."

"Yeah, you read about that guy who recently got paroled after a murder he committed back in 1985?"

"Did read something about that," Jack said. "The article said he was coming back here to Culpepper where the crime had been committed. I also remember they were both graduates at the school, the guy who got killed and the guy who killed him."

"That's what the paper said." Joe picked up one of the pieces of calamari, dipped it in the sauce. It was yellowish, nothing like marinara, had a bit of a kick. But he really liked it. "Man, good call on this."

"I know. My turn." Jack grabbed hold of one, the kind that looked like a small octopus. Dipped it in and started chomping down.

"Turns out," Joe said, "now that me and Hank been digging into this thing, the paper's got it all wrong. But it's worse than that. The paper's got it wrong because the courts did, thirty-six years ago."

Jack looked properly stunned. "You're saying the guy is innocent? They had the wrong guy in prison all this time?"

Joe nodded. Grabbed another piece of calamari. "Both Hank and I are convinced and, after sharing why with our Captain, he's inclined to agree. Gave us the green light to reopen the investigation. Course, until we have solid evidence to prove who really did it, we have to run this like a covert op. Can't do a thing that might leak this to the press."

"I understand, Joe. You know I am—"

"I'm not worried about you talking, Jack. I trust you as much as Hank. Thing is, just as we started to make a little headway, we ran into a brick wall." Joe spent the next ten minutes updating Jack on all the developments in the case, including the most recent details about the World War II angles. After laying all that out, he spelled out their dilemma. That even though they may have figured out what really happened, the evidence that could back it all up, including the true identity of the Nazi war criminal, may no longer exist.

"Wow," Jack said. "Fascinating stuff, but I see what you're saying. That's always a challenge with these cold cases. Digging up enough evidence to make it stick, when many of the people involved, even the forensic evidence itself, has been lost to the sands of time. That's crazy to think we had a Nazi war criminal living out his life here in Culpepper. Wonder what in the world brought him here, of all places."

"Didn't most of them wind up in Argentina or Brazil," Joe said, "or some other South American country?"

"Well," Jack said, "a ton of Nazis headed for South America after the war. Most of the surviving leadership it would seem. And that's where most of the more famous ones were later captured, in places like Argentina, Bolivia, and Brazil. But if we're talking actual Nazi war criminals — the kind who committed most of the horrific atrocities during the war — the overwhelming majority of them got away with it, scot-free. At least in this life."

"Why does that not surprise me?" Joe said. "I know a little

bit about the Nuremberg trials from some documentaries I watched. But those are just the top guys, right? Like Goering, Hess, and Himmler."

"Yeah, but not Himmler," Jack said. "He committed suicide before they could catch him. A bunch of them did. But you're right. Nuremberg was only about trying the bigwigs. Problem was, the trials took so long, by 1949 most of the world was ready to move on. People didn't want to keep hearing about the horrors of the war anymore. So only a hundred and ninety-nine defendants were tried. Of those, only thirty-seven were sentenced to death. Can you believe that? After being responsible for the death of tens of millions, six million Jews alone, only thirty-seven Nazis were executed."

Joe couldn't believe it. "How many do you think got away with it?"

"Over ten thousand, at least," Jack said.

"Really?"

"Yeah, really. Think about it, Joe. You had countless lower-level officers — especially in the SS — guys at the colonel, major, captain, and lieutenant levels, even sergeants and privates...shooting old people, women, and children for virtually no reason at all. You've seen the documentaries and the movies, I'm sure. Every time the French resistance killed a German soldier, the local German officer in the nearest town would line up ten innocent civilians and kill them all by firing squad. Stuff like that happened all the time, in every town the Nazis occupied. All the guards in all the concentration camps, most of them committed crimes against prisoners worthy of the death penalty in any justice system. Yet after the war, by the hundreds and thousands, these lower-level Nazis just snuck away, blended back into the general population. Except for some committed, mostly-Jewish Nazi hunters, no one ever came after them."

Joe was shocked. "I had no idea that happened. Guess I can see with how slow the wheels of justice turn, people getting tired of rehashing the horrors of the war."

"I've read estimates," Jack said, "that several thousand of these lower-level Nazis assumed new identities and migrated to the U.S. in the late 40s. So, guess it is possible one of them made their way here...into neighborly little Culpepper."

"I'm really starting to think one of them did," Joe said. "Only wish there was some way of figuring out who he was."

Jack got this look on his face.

"What is it, Jack?"

"I was just thinking. Maybe there is. Didn't you say that fellow from the TV station boxed up the belongings of that guy who was murdered...and delivered them to the guy's family, including those World War II books?"

"Yeah."

"Well, it may be nothing, but I know when I've done research, especially back in the days before the internet, I always underlined and wrote notes all over the books, in the margins and anyplace it would fit. Are any of the dead guy's family members still alive?"

Joe got the biggest smile. "Professor Turner, you are something else. You know that?"

27

SAMUEL CLEMENS SPENT THE BETTER PART OF THE MORNING trying to figure out how to reach Juan Sanchez, Roberto's cousin. Sam remembered him saying he had inherited his house. Back in the day, you would just look a guy's number up in the phone book, or dial 411 and ask the information lady for the number. Now with these cell phones, it was a bit more convoluted.

He was finally able to locate where the guy worked. He was a mechanic at a local car dealership. Sam called down there, got transferred to the service department and asked for Juan by name. The lady who answered sent someone to get him.

A few minutes later, Sam heard a click then a man's voice. "Hello, this is Juan Sanchez. Can I help you?"

"Hi, Juan. This is Sam, Sam Clemens. You remember, the guy you and your nephew Alonzo visited, out at my cabin?"

"Oh, yeah. Mr. Clemens, course I remember you."

Sam heard some muffled sounds then Juan's voice again, speaking much lower.

"We're not allowed to take personal calls on the company phone. Give me your number, and I'll call you back on my cell."

Sam did then said, "Will you be calling me back soon?"

"Yeah, just need to get to a place where I can talk. Gimme a sec." He hung up.

As he waited, Sam realized it was close to lunch. He wandered over to the fridge and was just about to open it up when his phone rang. "Okay, then. Guess he really meant it." He walked back and picked it up, saw an unfamiliar number, guessed it had to be Juan. "Hello, Sam Clemens."

"It's me, Juan."

"Thanks for calling back so soon. And please, call me Sam."

"Okay...Sam. I can only talk a couple of minutes. If we need to talk longer, I go on lunch break in fifteen."

"This won't take long."

"Good. How are things coming with your search? You know, for my cousin's killer. Made any progress?"

"Some. And that detective who came the day you were here, Lieutenant Boyd, he's working on it, too. We were just comparing notes yesterday."

"Good to hear. So...something you want me to do?"

"I remember you mentioning something about inheriting the house Roberto lived in at the time he died. Do you still live there?"

"Yeah, I do."

"Good. Think I may have mentioned he was working on a documentary when he was killed. I believe the man who killed your cousin did it to stop that film from getting made. Your cousin was borrowing some of my camera equipment for the project. That day, when I came to his house and found him murdered, I'd gone there to pick that equipment up. Course, that never happened because of the way I found him. Don't really care about the equipment anymore. I'm sure it's totally obsolete. But I am wondering if maybe Roberto left any information on that equipment that might help me figure out who the documentary was about. We have reason to believe, it could be about exposing a Nazi war criminal."

"Whoa," Juan said. "A Nazi criminal. You think Roberto was working on something like that?"

"Could be, yeah. But that's why I need to see what's in those boxes."

"Okay... I actually inherited the house from my older brother. Roberto left it to him. He lived there a long time, then he left it to me when he died two years ago. There's supposed to be some old boxes in the attic with Roberto's things. My brother told me so once, but said none of it was worth anything. So, I never went up there to look for myself."

Sam thought about the twelve-hundred bucks he'd paid for that camera and, for a moment, thought Juan's answer meant the camera couldn't be in those boxes. But then he realized, an old video camera from the early 80s probably *wasn't* worth anything anymore. "Juan, is there any way I could get a look at what's in those boxes? Might not be worth any money but there could be some valuable info in there that might help me crack this case."

"Sure, why not? When you want to see it?"

"As soon as I can."

"Like I said, I get an hour for lunch. Only live ten minutes from here. I get off in fifteen. Well, ten now. I'll text you the address. Can you meet me there in twenty minutes?"

"Sure. I'll be there. And thanks, Juan. Really appreciate you doing this."

"Well, I want to do anything I can do to help get this guy. See you soon."

THE FIRST THING Sam did after he hung up was to add Juan's name, phone number, and address to his contact list. He was starting to get the hang of this. He thought he remembered where Roberto's house was but after so many years, he didn't want to accidentally make a wrong turn and miss the chance to meet with Juan. Sam clicked on the Maps app and typed in Juan's address. Just like that, the route from his cabin to Juan's place appeared. It was eighteen minutes away. He got up to leave right away.

On the way there, he was feeling pretty hopeful. The idea to pull on this thread came after he'd talked with the Lieutenant yesterday, and they'd concluded *Mr. Infamous* was likely a local man — at least back in 1985 — and also likely, as a Nazi war criminal he'd be living here under an assumed name. That had to be the reason Sanchez had been killed, to keep what he'd uncovered from being exposed to the world.

Just then, Sam had a flashback of that blonde-haired guy he'd seen in the car by Roberto's house that day he'd confronted him about taking him off the project, and about the money. Maybe the guy wasn't connected, like the prosecutor argued during the trial. Just some kid waiting for one of Roberto's neighbors. But what if he was there spying on Roberto?

Maybe he was part of some secret Nazi network that the SS officer in Roberto's documentary belonged to. He'd seen Sam go into Roberto's house. And it was a nice, Fall day. Roberto's windows were open. Sam remembered that. Maybe the blond kid got out of the car, came up to the house, and heard the two men arguing. They had gotten pretty loud a few times. He wouldn't have needed to get too close to hear what they'd been talking about.

Someone beeped loudly at Sam's truck. He looked up, realized he'd been waiting in a left-turn lane and the green arrow had just come on. He waved apologetically at the man behind him and quickly turned left.

But that could be it.

The guy in the car was way too young to be the Nazi war criminal himself. But he was blonde, a perfect Aryan specimen, as Sam recalled. And he was just sitting there in the car, staring at Sam as he walked toward Roberto's house.

He could be connected to the scheme. It wasn't that far-fetched.

28

SAM FOLLOWED THE GPS INSTRUCTIONS AS HE DROVE INTO town. Still had a hard time believing this little thing he bought could do all this. It was showing this blue arrow running through the map on the streets he was supposed to take, and this pleasant lady's voice kept coming on telling him where to turn and when. The screen refreshed every few blocks like it knew where he was going. It even knew how fast he was driving and how much time he had left till he arrived at Juan's house.

This was crazy stuff.

He got there in twenty minutes, right on the money. Juan's car was in the driveway. It was the same car they used when they came to his cabin. He got out, looked around to make sure no one was looking. Not sure why he did that, probably just Joe warning him to stay in the cabin for a week, laying low till any buzz about that newspaper article died down. Wasn't sure that was necessary anymore.

Anyway, he rang the doorbell. Heard some footsteps then it opened. It was Juan, smiling like they were old friends.

"Come on in."

As he stepped into the foyer, he froze.

A flashback of the bloody scene from thirty-six years ago came at him like a slap in the face. He was looking down at the floor and saw Roberto's lifeless body lying there, his legs actually in the way. Sam knew instantly he was dead by the massive wound on his head. Off to the right a few feet was the bloodied dumbbell used to crush his skull. Sam had never seen anything so awful.

"Sam, you okay?"

Sam looked up, grateful for Juan's distracting voice. "Yeah, yeah. I'm fine."

"Wow," Juan said. "I forgot. This was where Roberto was killed. I never think about it anymore. When I come in the house, I mean. This the first time you been here since...you know, since the trial?"

Clemens nodded. "Really, since the day I discovered his body. I never came back here after that."

"Man, that's heavy. Why don't you come on in, get past the doorway? That's where it happened, right? Right there by the door?"

"That's what they said at the trial. That I hit him right here by the door. But I don't think that's what happened. That's where his body was, but I actually had to push it away — with the door — to get it open enough to walk in. Now that I'm standing here and remembering what happened, I think he was killed closer to the dining room table. I remember seeing a bloody drag mark a few feet in front of his body. I can see it in my mind as plain as day. But it never came up in the trial. If I had hit him as soon as I walked in the door, he would've fallen back away from the door. He wouldn't have been in the way when I tried to come in. Whoever did it, I think, hit him with dumbbell over there —" he pointed to a spot closer to the table. Then he dragged him to the front door, on purpose, so that whoever opened it would bump into his body, like I did."

He remembered something else. "The front door was open when I knocked, a couple of inches. I remember yelling Roberto's name into the opening a bunch of times, but of course he didn't answer. That's when I pushed the door open and found him." Now he understood — for the first time — why the killer set things up this way. "He wanted my feet to step into the blood as I came through the doorway."

"Who did?" Juan said.

"The killer. That has to be it. He killed Roberto before I got here, then dragged the body in front of the door and left it open, just a little. He must've gotten out another way, maybe through the kitchen door. Or a window."

"Man," Juan said, "you look like you're figuring all this out right now."

Sam looked up at Juan. "I am. I've thought about it so many times in prison. But now standing here – the very place where it all happened — I can see it all so clearly. Whoever it was, had to know, beforehand, that I would be coming to meet with Roberto then. That's the only thing that makes sense. And he set it all up so that I would get the blame. I'm in the house right around the time of the killing, and my footprints are right there in his blood."

"That really sucks," Juan said. "But who would do that? Who would know you were coming here at that time?"

"That's the big question, isn't it?" Sam instantly thought again about the blonde-haired guy in the car, the one who'd been there a few days earlier when Sam had confronted Roberto. If he had gotten out of the car and came close enough to listen to their conversation, he would've heard Roberto ask Sam to borrow the camera equipment for a few more days. And then heard Sam reluctantly agree and give him till that Saturday, when he'd be back to pick it up.

This made sense. He explained everything to Juan.

"So, you think this blonde fellow was the killer?"

"Could be," Sam said. "Or maybe he told this information to the Nazi war criminal, who then came and did it himself. I don't know."

Juan took a few steps back as Sam shut the door behind them. "Can't believe Roberto was working on a story about a Nazi war criminal. Are you sure about that? Seems like a crazy thing to do. But then, I remember my brother saying how bad Roberto wanted to get into the big leagues, as he called it."

"We're not positive. But all three of us are thinking the same thing...me, Lieutenant Boyd, and his partner Hank. That's why I need to look in those boxes, see if what's inside gives us the proof."

"Well, come on. I'll show you how to get into the attic. I'd go up there with you, but I'll be late getting back from my lunch break."

"You're going to leave me in your house by myself?"

"Sure, if you can't trust an ex-con, who can you trust?" He smiled. "Come on, the pull-down ladder is in the hallway."

Sam followed him through the living area and down the hall. He could see an attic panel in the ceiling at the end. Juan had to jump a few inches to reach the little rope handle. But when he pulled it, the ladder came right down.

"It's pretty sturdy, but please be careful. Especially coming down, since I won't be here. There's a light at the top. You just have to pull on that chain. They put boards down on top of the rafters, so you should be okay walking around. But watch your head. You can't stand up straight in there."

Sam started making his way up the ladder. He stopped to listen to Juan.

"There's all kind of crap up there. Stuff I stuck up there, stuff from my brother's time with the house, and then the boxes from Roberto. Those are going to be the furthest ones back. If I remember, they're all clearly marked."

"Thanks so much, Juan. Really hope this idea pays off."

"Me, too. I'm gonna go finish eating my leftover pizza, then head back to work. If you get hungry, feel free to get something out of the fridge." He walked down the hall toward the kitchen when his phone rang. "Wonder who this is?"

He answered it. "Lieutenant Boyd, yeah, course I remember you. We were just talking about you a few minutes ago. Who? Me and Sam, Mr. Clemens. Yeah, he's here now. So, what can I help you with? What? You're kidding? No, course you are not." He walked back toward the attic opening and looked up at Sam. "You want to know if I know about any boxes that might be here in the house that once belonged to Roberto?" He smiled at Sam. "As a matter fact, I do. You guys really need to coordinate your efforts a little bit better. I'm talking about you and Sam. He's here for the same thing. He's up in the attic now, came to look at the same boxes you're just asking about. Yeah, I'm serious. What? Sure, you can come over. Right now, if you want. Thing is, I gotta head back to work in a few minutes. But I'm leaving Sam here, and I'll leave the front door unlocked. One of you just lock up on your way out." He listened a little bit more, then said, "Sure, I'm okay with that."

"So, is he coming over now?" Sam said, still on the ladder.

"Says he is. Only thing he asked is that you don't leave before he gets here."

29

SAM FINISHED CLIMBING THE LADDER, FOUND THE STRING, AND pulled it. It was connected to a bare lightbulb that did a fairly good job of pushing back the darkness. He carefully reached for some rafters, hoping to avoid any nails, and pulled himself up. Sam was only five-eight, so he could stand straight in the very center without hitting his head.

It took a few moments for his eyes to adjust to the lighting difference, but soon vague shapes became boxes and cartons and bird cages and aquariums and all kinds of other odds and ends that people shove up into their attics. Sam realized he had never been in an attic before, but this is about what he expected. Although, when he'd seen attics in movies they were never this full. On the attic floor, there was just the tiniest opening between the piles to get around. Juan had said the boxes belonging to Roberto would be way in the back. The question was, in which direction?

He picked one and started heading down the little opening. After fifteen or twenty feet, he could just make out the back wall through the shadows. There were stacks of boxes on both sides. The problem was, the light from the bulb had all but faded this far back, and he couldn't read any of the writing. He waited to see if his eyes would adjust to the dimmer lighting, but it didn't work. He really needed a flashlight.

After carefully making his way back to the ladder, he called out to Juan. "You still here, Juan?" He heard the front door close, then open.

"Did you say something, Sam?" Juan yelled from the foyer.

"Yeah, glad I caught you. Would you have a flashlight handy? It's too dark to see in the back areas of the attic."

"I do. I'd get it for you but I gotta run. You can find it in the garage. Should be resting on my workbench on the right side."

"Okay, thanks." Sam was off the ladder now and headed for the garage. The front door closed again. Once inside, he spotted the workbench then heard Juan's car starting through the garage door. Then another car pulled up into the driveway.

Juan started talking. "Hey, Lieutenant. You got here quick. Sam is already in there. He was in the attic, but now he's in the garage getting a flashlight. Just go on in the front door. You'll see the hallway on the left and the attic ladder hanging from the ceiling."

"Okay, Juan. Thanks."

Sam quickly found the flashlight and headed back toward the ladder. He wondered if he should wait for the Lieutenant to join him. Probably would be the right thing.

. . .

JOE AND HANK got out of Joe's car and watched Juan's car head down the road.

"Can't believe this guy's leaving with us going through his attic," Hank said. "A few days ago, there we were confronting him at Sam's cabin. What a turnaround."

"Yeah," Joe said. "Maybe he's just the trusting type, or maybe he figures we don't seem like crooked cops. You got a flashlight?"

"Yeah, got one clipped to my belt. It's small but bright as the sun."

"Can you reach in the glove compartment and grab mine. Sounds like we're going to need them."

As they walked to the front door, Hank handed Joe the light. "Glad it's not summer," Hank said. "I had to get up in my attic last summer, thought I was going to die."

Joe opened the front door. "Sam, you in here?"

"Just down the hall on the left," Sam said. "By the attic steps."

They found him a few moments later already ascending the ladder.

"There's plenty of light right around the center of the attic, but hardly any in the back areas. That's where these boxes are supposed to be. I'll check the area to the right. Hopefully, one of us will find them."

"You go on up," Joe said. We'll be right behind you."

At the top of the stairs, Sam said, "Guess we had the same idea again, eh Lieutenant?"

"Looks like we did, Sam. Any idea what you're looking for, in those boxes I mean?" Joe never told Sam about his

conversation with Jack Turner, about Roberto possibly
writing personal research notes in the margins of the books
themselves.

"Yeah. Think I told you I let Roberto borrow some of my
camera equipment, specifically one of the first camcorders
ever made. They had just come out then, spent a small
fortune on mine. You're probably too young to remember,
but most video cameras back then were really big and bulky.
And the recorder part was a separate unit. I had a really nice
setup, professional quality. I didn't let Roberto borrow that. I
let him use my new smaller camcorder. The resolution
wasn't great compared to now. I mean, my phone now is so
much better. But it was small and super easy to use. Roberto
said he wanted it to dictate notes to himself about the documentary, so he wouldn't have to write everything down.
That's what I'm hoping to find. Not just the camera but the
videotape inside it, where Roberto is talking all about the
documentary. Sharing the kind of stuff he'd never say out
loud."

"Wow," Hank said. "That would make our job easy, if you
could find something like that."

"Yeah, it would," Joe said. "So, go ahead and start looking.
Hank and I will go in different directions. Hopefully, one of
us will find them."

For the next fifteen minutes, they roamed about the attic
searching for boxes with Roberto's name on them. Joe had
just reached the last group of boxes in his section with no
luck. "I struck out," he yelled. "How you making out Hank,
Sam? See anything yet?"

"Not me," Sam said. "Inhaled enough dust to shave a few

more years off my life. Think I'm like you, though. Nothing in my area with Roberto's name on it."

"I've got one more group of boxes to check out," Hank said, "if I can just get this old racetrack moved out of the way, so I can see clearly."

Joe shined his light over toward Hank. Saw him manhandling this big round sheet of plywood with a figure-eight racetrack nailed to it.

"Bingo," Hank yelled. "Here they are. Three boxes, good-sized ones, all with Roberto's name on them.

"Way to go, Hank," Sam yelled. "I'm closer to him, Joe. You're closer to the opening. How about I help him get the boxes over to the opening, and you head down the ladder? And we'll hand them down to you?"

"Sounds like a plan." Joe made his way to the opening, shut off his flashlight, then lowered himself to the floor. He heard a bunch of moving and scraping sounds then Sam's face appeared. "Ready whenever you are."

One by one, they handed down the boxes and Joe guided them to the floor. When they were done, Hank and Sam came down. Joe had already opened the first of the three boxes, the heaviest. He rightly guessed they'd contained the World War II books.

While Sam and Hank each opened one of the other boxes, Joe lifted out the thick book about the SS and Nuremberg trials. Opening it from the back, he started flipping through the pages. He couldn't help but smile as he saw several handwritten notes in the margins, especially on one page with several black and white photos. He showed it to Hank.

Hank smiled. "Guess Jack knows what he's talking about."

"Oh. My. Goodness," Sam said. "There they are. I was about to give up, but I lifted this burlap bag covering the bottom, and look. Here's all my stuff."

"The camcorder too?" Joe said.

Sam reached down into the box and pulled something up. "Yeah, here it is."

Joe remembered seeing camcorders like this when he was young. It looked huge compared to how small they finally became. Until they were all replaced by smartphones. "I think my dad used something like that to record our family events."

Sam pressed a button and the side of the camera opened up. "Look," he said all excited. "There's a tape in it. This has to be the last tape ever used on this machine."

"Anything written on the label?" Joe said.

"No, it's blank. But I can see half the tape's been used."

"Can you turn it on?" Joe said. "Rewind it a bit, and see if you see Roberto talking on screen."

Sam pressed a button, then pressed it again, then pressed it again.

"The battery's dead," Hank said.

"Hope that's all it is," Joe said. "That thing's been up here for over thirty years. The heat isn't bad now, but like you said Hank, attics in the summer can get hot enough to kill you."

"Yeah," Sam said. "The camera might not work. Hopefully, it's just the battery. I'll take it back to my cabin, see if the charger still works."

"I'll bring this box of World War II books back to the

office," Joe said. "See if I can start making sense of all these notes."

"I'll bring the middle box back up in the attic," Hank said. "The one that's just filled with junk. And guess I'll text Juan, let him know we borrowed some of his stuff."

30

SAM WAS ABOUT AS EXCITED AS HE COULD BE ON THE DRIVE back to the cabin. The reason was sitting beside him in the passenger seat. The box with his camcorder and gear in it. He couldn't wait to see what was on that tape. It had to be Roberto filming himself at his dining room table, right where Sam had seen the camera set up the day he'd gone there to confront Roberto. Wouldn't it be crazy if he could see Roberto laying out the details of his "top-secret documentary" right there on tape? He'd finally know who the film was about and, likely, the identity of the killer.

Another reason he was excited was the conversation he'd had in Juan's driveway with the Lieutenant and Hank just before they'd left. He'd told them all the things he remembered about the day Roberto was killed, brought back to the surface the moment he'd opened Juan's door and stepped into the foyer. The way Roberto's body literally blocked the front door, so that Sam had to push it out of the way just to get in. And that the front door was unlocked and opened a few inches. When Sam explained how this proved he couldn't have struck Roberto with a dumbbell when he opened the door—like the prosecutor had argued during the trial—both Joe and Hank agreed.

Joe had even said, "If you'd hit him hard enough to cause a fatal blow, he'd have gone flying back away from the door." Then Sam told them about the bloody drag marks on the floor extending several feet away from Roberto's body into the room. They agreed that didn't make sense if Roberto had been killed by the front door. Then Joe had asked about the crime scene photos. Did Sam ever see crime scene photos shared during the trial? Sam couldn't recall. Joe said he'd look into it, and that he'd be shocked if information like that never came up during the trial. If Roberto's body was blocking the door when Sam had arrived, someone else had to have put it there.

Sam turned left onto the dirt road that led to his cabin. It dawned on him that he might have uncovered enough evidence to get a judge to consider a new trial. That is, if the videotape of Roberto delivered the goods.

As he pulled up to the cabin, another thought hit him...*what good would it do to get a new trial if they were just going to have to turn around and arrest him for killing the man who ruined his life?*

ON THE SHORT drive back from Juan Sanchez's house to the station, Joe and Hank had mostly talked about some of the obvious holes they were seeing in Sam's case. It was kind of free-flowing, brainstorming discussion but as they pulled into Joe's parking spot, Joe decided to turn it into an assignment for Hank. "I think we're on to a few things here that could really prove substantial in getting Sam a new trial."

"I agree," Hank said. "The more we talk about it, the more pathetic it gets. I don't know who the joker was they got to defend him, but he wasn't worth a dime."

"Glad you agree, because I want you to spend some time on it. I mean, a serious effort. I'm gonna take some time with these books, especially that one. Why don't you sit down and hammer out something of a proposal, listing all these things we've been chatting on. Think of it like something we're going to pitch to Pendleton to convince him to go to bat for us with the DA."

"I can do that. Let's run down the list real quick, make sure I'm not missing anything that matters. I'd start with that thing Sam said about Sanchez's body being right up against the front door. If he had to push it out of the way to get in, and there was so much blood right there that he got it on his shoes, we should see some smearing on the floor that would prove the body slid as he opened it."

"Yeah," Joe said, "which means we gotta dig up all the crime scene photos. And hope whoever took them did a decent job. If you do see that smearing on the floor — and I really hope you do — take a duplicate shot and blow up that area. It will help drive home the point that Sam wasn't making up some kind of story. To me, if that body was against the door when Sam got there, case closed. He didn't kill the guy. If it happened the way they told it at the trial, Roberto's body should have been in the middle of the room, where it landed after Sam supposedly bashed his head with the dumbbell. Shouldn't have been a big pool of blood by the front door at all."

Hank shook his head. "How does something like this get missed? I mean, you and I can see right away what this means. Why couldn't they?"

"Sad to say, but they probably didn't want to. I've seen this kind of thing too many times dealing with these cold cases. Especially with high-profile crimes. You got all this public pressure to find the killer quick, and then someone sets up a guy like Sam to take the fall. They look at all the staged evidence, figure it all points to the guy they just nabbed, and they run with it. They hide any evidence that contradicts their new narrative, and there's nobody to call them on it. Because Sam had no money, he gets some public defender who's just not bright enough to read what's happening, or maybe too intimidated by the DA to challenge him properly. However it went down, the wrong guy gets sent to prison, so they can call it a win and move on to the next case."

Hank sighed. "It's really sad when you think about how many guys – especially back then — were wrongly imprisoned by this kind of thing. We're supposed to be the good guys."

"We are the good guys, Hank. We can't do anything about the corruption in the past. But maybe we can do something about it now. That's why we need to get this thing right for Sam." They spent the next several minutes going through the other key items then headed into the office. Joe couldn't wait to dive into this Nazi book, the one with Roberto's notes in the margins.

He just hoped he was clever enough to figure out what it all meant.

31

SAM HAD BROUGHT THE BOX IN FROM THE TRUCK AND LAID OUT everything on the dinette table. It felt strange seeing and holding all these things again. He remembered buying each and every one of them, most from Sullivan's Photo, a great little family-owned store in the downtown area. All the photography students at Culpepper's Journalism department got their gear there. Probably had to close up shop years ago, especially now with cameras built into these smartphones.

Sam had just played around a little bit with the camera app that morning after breakfast. It was absolutely ridiculous. The clarity and resolution of the pictures was stellar, better than the best camera he'd ever worked with back in the day. The video camera on the phone was also phenomenal. An entire manual had come in the box with his '85 camcorder. But this? Point the phone, touch the camera button, hit the red dot, and start recording. Move the camera around, no need to worry about lighting...it auto-adjusted itself. No need to worry about distances or focusing...did it all for you. The resolution was better than his eyesight, which was twenty-twenty.

He sighed, thinking about all of the innovations in camera technology he had missed out on between the camcorder on the table and the smartphone next to it. Just one more thing *Mr. Infamous* had stolen from him.

The first thing he did after bringing the box inside was to put the battery on the charger. He knew it would take several hours since it was totally dead. But he also knew that the camcorder he bought could be run just by plugging a cord directly into the wall. It took him several minutes to find it buried at the very bottom of the box. He plugged one end into the camera then realized it was too short to reach the nearest outlet. The next ten minutes were spent searching for an extension cord. Finding none, he added it to his list of things to buy and carried the camcorder over to the left side of the couch. After setting it on the end table, he reached down and plugged it in.

The moment of truth had come.

He pressed the power button, stared at the little green light waiting for it to come on, but it didn't. He pressed it again, then again. Nothing. He double-checked the connections. They were solid. His heart sank. This could only mean one thing. The camera had died. It had sat up in that attic for too many years.

This was terrible. How could he watch what was on that video?

He sat there for a few minutes, bewildered, perplexed. There had to be a way to see what was on that tape? He couldn't have come this far only to be stopped now. He had a thought to pray but decided against it. Back in prison, after going to some church services and listening to some decent visiting preachers, he had begun to pray and try to reconnect with the Lord. With some success. He'd even dared to believe that God had something to do with him finally getting paroled. But he'd barely prayed a single time since.

He knew why.

Seemed like the Lord didn't want to hear from him ever since he got it into his head that he had to spend however much time it took to figure out who really killed Roberto, and then make them pay by killing them himself. The idea of forgiving them seemed impossible. Even though he knew that's just the kind of thing the Lord would want him to do. He'd heard too many sermons on mercy to think otherwise. For a little while, he toyed with the idea of proving who did it then letting them face the justice of man, meaning the police and the courts. But he quickly gave that up. Look at how horribly the courts had handled his situation. He couldn't trust man's justice. They might let the killer go on some kind of technicality. That stuff happened.

He couldn't take that chance. He was just hoping that after he did kill the real killer, the Lord might have mercy again and be willing to take him back.

An idea popped into his head. He was looking at his old camcorder then at his new phone. Since camera technology had leaped so far since he'd been in prison, then surely they must have figured out a way to convert old 8 mm tapes into something he could watch on his phone. He got up, grabbed his phone, and sat back down. He went on Google, now aware that he could talk to it by pressing the little microphone icon. He said aloud, "converting 8 mm videotapes."

In seconds, a whole page of options appeared. The first few articles talked about how easily this kind of thing could be done now. He clicked on one and read the first few paragraphs. Apparently, a number of companies had been created specifically to convert people's old videotapes — in any format — into digital files that could easily be watched on any device. Big-screen TVs, laptops, tablets, and smartphones. The article went on to say a number of these companies used to be your neighborhood camera stores, which had to find a way to survive in this new digital age.

"Sullivan's Photo," he said aloud. Could it be? He pressed the Google microphone icon again and said, "Sullivan's Photo, Culpepper Georgia."

There it was! And they had a website. He clicked on it and instantly started reading. The photo in the header was just like the store he remembered, in the very same location. Below that was a picture of the owner, Dan Sullivan, the son of the original owner, Buck, who'd passed away in 2012. He remembered Dan used to be in the store on Saturdays. Back then he was maybe ten years old.

How about that? It was almost like an answer to prayer. But he hadn't prayed. Either way, he was grateful. He got up and hurried toward the table, popped the videotape out of the camera and put it in his shirt pocket. "You and me are headed to the camera store."

He grabbed his keys and headed out the door.

32

If Sam had any hopes for this trip to Sullivan's Photo being some kind of sentimental journey down memory lane, he was quickly disappointed as he pulled into the parking lot. It was in the same building, what they used to call a strip mall. Maybe they still did call them that. And it occupied the last storefront on the end where it had always been. But that's about the only thing that was the same.

Virtually every other store was something else. Except the two in the middle that were empty. And the Sullivan's Photo sign had been completely changed. As he walked onto the sidewalk and glanced through the glass store windows, again, nothing even remotely similar to what he used to see on display. But, of course, this would be the case. Pretty much everything he'd learned in college about photography and videography had gone through a digital revolution. Every teenager walking around now with their heads fixated on their phones, carried a far superior arsenal of photographic equipment than the best gear available in the Photo Lab at the University when he'd attended there.

Sam opened the door and experienced perhaps the one and only nostalgic moment he'd have today. The little bell hanging from the door hinge. It rang just as pleasantly as it had back in the day. He glanced up and saw, yes, it was the same bell. And almost every time it used to ring, old man Sullivan would look up and greet whoever was coming in. If he was in the back of the store, he'd yell, "Be right with you."

But no one said anything today. Apparently, the heir to the Sullivan dynasty didn't share his father's gregarious nature. In fact, looking around, Sam didn't see anyone in the store. Nor did he recognize any of the merchandise. Even the layout of the aisles and shelves had undergone a total makeover. He walked around hoping to find the son, but the store seemed empty. When he came back around to the counter, he noticed a bell by the cash register, a little sign that said: "Ring for Service." He pressed it once, then a few seconds later, again.

"Be right with you," a male voice yelled out from a doorway behind the counter.

Well, he'd at least inherited his father's greeting-phrase. "Okay," Sam yelled back.

Less than a minute later, Dan Sullivan came walking through the back room doorway. "Sorry about that, working on some online orders back there. These days that's more than half my business."

Sam wanted to say something meaningful in reply but wasn't sure what online orders were and how they had anything to do with photography. "No problem," he said. "I saw on your website that you can convert 8 mm videotapes into a digital format."

"That's true," Dan said. "Do a whole lot of that these days. Usually comes out pretty well. Of course, we charge extra if you want us to do any editing or make improvements to the quality of the original...you know, in the copy we give back to you."

Sam looked up at Dan. In line with everything else about the store that was different, Dan looked absolutely nothing like the kid Sam remembered. "Well, I won't need any editing or any improvements made. And I only have just the one tape." He pulled it out of his shirt pocket and set it on the counter.

Dan picked it up carefully, looked it over. "Yeah, we see a lot of these. Especially from folks in our age bracket." He looked at Sam apparently intending to mean they were in the same bracket.

This was news to him.

"You know," Dan said, "Your kids get older, you start having grandkids. They want to see these old videos we shot back when they were young, but we can't show them. Let me guess...your old camcorder doesn't work anymore."

Your kids get older, you start having grandkids. They want to see...that stung down deep...a dark reminder of what had never been. "You're right, it doesn't work. Sadly, it's been stuck in a box in an attic for over thirty years."

Dan made a face denoting serious disapproval.

"Wasn't me," Sam said. "Believe me, I'd never treat camera equipment that way. So, can you convert it to digital and how much will it cost?"

"I definitely can convert it. You said it's just the one tape?"

Sam nodded.

"Well, right now we're running a one-tape special for 29.99. That includes the content being transferred to either a flash drive, or an SD card. If you want to put it on both, it's ten dollars extra."

Sam had no idea what he just said. "Which is better, a flash drive or the...*card* you mentioned?"

"All kinds of opinions on that," Dan said. "Really, I think it just comes down to what you prefer. How do you hope to watch this? On a big screen TV, laptop, a tablet —"

"Is this the kind of thing you could watch on a smartphone?"

"Certainly. But if that's what you want, you definitely want to go with the SD card. Smartphones usually don't come with a USB port."

USB port? He was about to ask then realized Dan had just said to go with the SD card. "Okay then, guess we'll go with the card." He pulled out his smartphone. "When you give me back this card, how do I watch it on my phone? You'll probably find this hard to believe, but I got this less than a week ago. And I've never used one before that."

"Oh." Followed by a startled look. "Okay, hand me your phone. I'll show you how it works."

Dan quickly pushed a button on the side of the phone, and this tiny little drawer slid open. He lifted a little black square from it and showed it to Sam. "This is just a dummy card, like a placeholder. When I give you the SD card with all your movies on it, you just put it right in here and slide the drawer back into the phone. It'll usually recognize the memory card and ask you if you want to see what's on it."

"Wait," Sam said, "the thing you're going to give me back

— with all the converted video footage — is only as small as that little black square?"

"Oh, yeah. They're all that small. But our special includes a 1 TB card, so you have plenty of space for other things."

Sam could not comprehend what he was hearing, or what he was seeing. "You're saying that everything on this 8 mm videotape will fit on that little card? If I recall, the tape could hold up to sixty minutes of footage."

Dan laughed. "You really haven't been keeping up with this, have you? Sir, this little card can hold 250 full-length movies. I mean, that's bigger than most people's movie libraries. If you just put pictures on it, you could hold 250,000 of them."

Sam could not comprehend how this was possible. But obviously, the matter-of-fact way Dan was saying this, it had to be true. "Okay. And yeah, like you said, I haven't been keeping up with this. So, let's do it. Thirty dollars seems like a fair price." Then he had a thought. Joe and Hank would definitely want to see what was on this tape. "And I'll go ahead and pay the extra to have it copied onto...what did you call it, a flash drive? That's the one people can use to watch it on laptops?"

"Right, laptops, computers, most tablets. Will there be anything else?"

"How long will this take?"

"My usual turnaround time is seven days."

"Seven days. Man, that's gonna be too long for me. How much extra to have it done in two?"

"Two days." He made a face. "I've got a lot of orders ahead of this one. I can do it but afraid it's gonna cost you, like, an extra twenty-five dollars."

"That's okay. It's worth it to me to have it done quicker. Guess you need my name and phone number?"

"And email address, if you have it."

"Sorry, not hooked up for email at the moment."

"Not a problem, let me write this all up. Just give me your name and phone number, and I'll fill in the details of what I'll be doing and how much it'll cost."

My name. Should I give him my name? "The name's Bill, Bill Evers." Why not go with that, he figured? Then he gave Dan his cell phone number.

"Okay, Mr. Evers. If you come back Sunday at say, 5pm, I'll have this ready for you. We close early on Sundays."

Sam said thanks and headed out the door, feeling equal parts excited and dumbfounded that his mission had been a success.

DIRECTLY ACROSS THE street from Sullivan's Photo was a convenience store. And walking out of that store at the very same moment, holding eight brand-new copies of today's Culpepper Gazette was the city's recently-named Teacher of the Year, Mr. Albert Dietrich. This was the third convenience store he'd visited in the last hour. His goal had been to collect fifteen copies, some to keep, some to give away to family and friends.

You see, today was Friday. Tonight was the big banquet at the school. And in this edition of the Gazette — headlining the local section — was Tom Hazelton's article all about Dietrich. He wasn't going to get all these papers until his wife had insisted. He'd already read the article, sent to his email by Hazelton. It had come out just fine, made Dietrich seem like a much greater man who'd made a much greater contribution to the welfare of this town than Dietrich had ever imagined about himself. And as it turned out, he had no reason to worry that Hazelton would spend too much time on his German heritage. He'd only written one paragraph, and nothing was said that would stir any interest in anyone.

Just as he opened his car door, Dietrich looked across the street...and froze.

Coming out of Sullivan's Photo was a bearded man about his own age wearing a big smile. Something about him looked very familiar. He watched as the man got into an old red pickup and turned it on. He backed out of the parking space then drove down the street right past Dietrich without looking in his direction. But it gave him a clear view of the man's profile.

That's when it clicked.

He quickly got into his car, set the copies of the Gazette with the others in the backseat. Then reached for a slightly older copy of the paper written several days ago. It also was the local section but featured quite a different headline: NOTORIOUS CONVICTED KILLER FROM THE 80's BACK IN TOWN. Dietrich had brought it with him to the coffee shop that morning. He wanted to read it again, see if he could figure out any clues as to why Samuel Clemens would have come back to this town after all these years.

He turned the paper over so that he could see the bottom half. There were the pictures of Samuel Clemens, a front and profile view. Taken many years ago, perhaps from prison when Clemens was in his forties. He'd gone in at twenty-four, but maybe he'd done something inside to justify these mugshots. He didn't have a beard in the photos, but Dietrich could clearly see...the man who'd just come out of Sullivan's Photo and drove past him in that pickup was most definitely...Samuel Clemens.

Dietrich set the paper back on the seat and felt his insides tensing up. He hadn't seen this man — in person — for so very many years. Long enough till he had become nothing more than a vapor or a mist, stricken to regions of his mind almost entirely out of reach.

But now, here he was. Dietrich knew at some point in a town as small as Culpepper, he would eventually see Clemens. But why did it have to be today of all days? His appearing now threatened to mar a day and evening intended to create one of the finest memories of his life.

As Dietrich drove the opposite direction down the road, he looked to his left and wondered...why would Clemens be coming out of Sullivan's Photo? He then read a big sign in the window advertising a special: *Let Us Convert Your Old Family Videos – Just $29.99 – Ask Inside.*

This wasn't good. Not good at all.

Potentially, it was a disaster.

33

JOE CAME BACK TO HIS DESK AFTER SPENDING THE LAST HOUR briefing Captain Pendleton on the Clemens' case. It wasn't a planned session. Joe had just set the World War II book on his desk, ready to dive in, when Pendleton had called wanting to hear the latest. Fortunately, off the top of his head he was able to share quite a lot. He told him all the things they had uncovered and the implications of each one. Pendleton was shocked when Joe got to the part about their belief that the real killer was either a Nazi war criminal, or someone working closely with him.

Of course, he zeroed in on that, wanting to hear the proof they had to back it up. Joe had to do some fast talking, sharing all the various and separate pieces of the puzzle, and help him see how they were all pointing in one direction. Joe felt confident they'd have some real evidence — the kind they could take to court — very soon.

He hoped he hadn't oversold that part.

He ended talking up the proposal Hank was working on

to highlight all the specific holes they had found in the pros-ecutor's case against Sam, coupled with the pathetic defense put forth by Sam's court-appointed attorney. They weren't just aiming to find the real killer but to make a case for the original verdict to be tossed out. Pendleton thought that was probably a tall order, but he did seem satisfied with their progress.

The one contribution Pendleton had made to the discus-sion came after that. He'd asked Joe if he had talked with Clemens about where this thing was headed, if they really did figure out who the real killer was. Joe said he'd touched on it briefly but hadn't talked about it in any detail...yet. Pendleton had spent the next ten minutes lecturing Joe about the need to pin Clemens down on this. "You can't leave this to chance, Joe. I can see someone like Clemens losing it completely you guys uncover who really did this. He's not gonna be okay with just seeing him walk off in handcuffs. Think if I were him, I'd wanna kill the guy."

The Cap had a point. Joe had agreed and promised he'd make sure Sam agreed to let justice run its course, not vengeance.

As he sat in his chair now, Joe set his coffee cup on its usual place on his desk and opened up the book about the SS officers and Nuremberg. He spent a few minutes reading the introduction, just to get a feel of what the main thrust of the book was about. But he had no intention of reading every page. In fact, right after the intro he began skipping through the pages in search of Roberto's handwritten notes.

In the first third of the book, Roberto didn't leave any notes. He underlined quite a few places and wrote question marks in the margins but no words. Sometimes he'd write in one question mark, other times two or three. Joe figured these must be things he didn't understand or notes to himself to look into these things further. Most of the ones with three question marks had sentences underlined, as well. Joe noticed that all these three-question-mark items were about SS officers running the concentration camps.

He finally got to the section where Roberto had written the majority of handwritten notes. It was called, "Hitler's Final Solution To the Jewish Question." Joe read the first few pages but realized he wasn't learning anything new. The book just made the case of how Hitler and his henchmen had come to believe all the remaining Jews had to be exterminated. They were considered sub-human and toxic to the welfare and future of the Reich.

Sadly, this was well-known now. Concentration camps were built throughout various parts of Germany and other occupied countries like Poland, manned almost entirely by SS officers and guards. Their entire aim was to kill as many Jews as efficiently as possible and as quickly as possible. Joe had seen too many documentaries on this through the years.

Then he came to a chapter that talked about how puzzling it was that many of these SS officers and guards had become so vicious and ruthless in such a short time, especially when you consider ninety percent of them had never served in the military prior to the war. Many had lived entirely normal, regular civilian lives. Some were school-teachers, pharmacists, bookkeepers, and merchants. Yet here they were committing wholesale acts of sadistic violence and horrendous atrocities without any regard for the pain and suffering of their victims.

Joe turned the page and found the first of Roberto's

handwritten notes. It was beside a group picture of SS officers posing for the camera, smiling, eyes bright and lively as
though attending some recreational event. They didn't look
like they had a care in the world. Then Joe read the caption
under the photo. It said these men were the officers of the
Kaufering IV Concentration Camp, near Dachau. They
supervised the routine killing of thousands of Jews right up
until the day they all fled the camp as the Allies approached.
As of the date the book was printed, none of these men had
been captured or held accountable for their crimes. The
author explained that was because they didn't rate a spot at
the Nuremberg trials.

Under the caption, their names and ranks were listed.
Joe's eyes were instantly drawn to the second man from the
left. It wasn't because of the fierce look of confidence on his
face, or that he appeared to be the youngest of the four men
depicted. It was because Roberto had underlined his name
three times, and only his name. He had even drawn an arrow
on the photo pointing right to the man's head. Over in the
margin, Roberto had written the words: "*Could this be Al's
father?*"

That's all it said.

But that was saying a lot. For some reason, Roberto
thought this particular SS officer was someone significant.
Not especially because of what he'd done during the war, but
because he apparently looked like *Al's father*.

Who was Al? Could this man Roberto was pointing to be
the Nazi war criminal Roberto was after? The infamous
target of his documentary? He had to be. Why else would he
zero in on only him?

Joe put an envelope in this page as a marker then started

looking through the remaining pages of the book, searching for anything that might reveal more about this man. The SS officer's name was Obersturmbannfuhrer Hans Zander.

Was that Al's last name? Zander?

Unfortunately, by the time Joe got to the last page containing notes in the margins, none of them mentioned anything more about Al or this officer, Hans Zander. He flipped to the very last page, in case Roberto had written any final message. He hadn't. What Joe did find was an old black-and-white photo, by itself, of a large family gathered around what looked like a Thanksgiving dinner. Judging by the hair-styles and clothes, he guessed it was sometime in the 1950s. An arrow had been handwritten on the photo pointing directly to the man sitting at the head of the table. But no words.

Joe turned the picture over and read — in what looked like Roberto's handwriting: *Took this from Al's family album. Could this be his father? The SS officer in the book? Is this Hans Zander?* Joe grabbed the photo and quickly flipped back to the page he had marked. He held the family photo right up to the picture of the SS officers in the book. His eyes darted back-and-forth between the two men Roberto had pointed out. The resemblance was very strong. So strong he could definitely see why Roberto would be asking such questions.

Joe couldn't help being excited by this development. But still, it was so...incomplete.

The main thing was...*Who. Was. Al?*

34

A SHORT TIME LATER, HANK CAME BACK FROM WHAT HE WAS doing. He saw Joe sitting there with the open World War II book. "Dig up anything worthwhile yet?"

"As a matter of fact, I did. Let me run by you what I got, see what you think." He filled Hank in on everything he just uncovered, showed him both pictures and Roberto's notes.

Before Joe shared his conclusions, Hank said, "They are definitely the same guy. The guy at the family table is just a slightly older version of that SS officer in the book. And you know what this means—after the war, that SS officer somehow made his way from that concentration camp to the U.S. Last I heard, they don't celebrate Thanksgiving in Berlin."

"I agree," Joe said. "This guy is definitely in the U.S. when this picture was taken. I just wish I knew who Al was.",

"Yeah, too bad he didn't write his last name at least once. You see if he shows up anywhere else in the book?"

"Already looked. He's just on this page. And in that separate photo. But did you see the back of the photo, the part about him taking this out of Al's family album? Means they had to be close enough for this guy, Al, to show him his family photos. Don't know about you, but I never show mine to strangers."

"Agree. And to support the point, he calls him *Al*. Leaves off his last name. I get that this was a note to himself, but it means he knows this guy Al. Doesn't feel the need to write in a last name."

Joe nodded. "Maybe we could find out if Roberto had any friends named Al. If so, we could show him this picture."

Hank shook his head. "That'd work if this wasn't a cold case. Sadly, most of the people who would know the answer to that question are dead."

Hank was right. "Well, wouldn't hurt to ask his cousin, Juan, anyway. And maybe I'll call that retired guy from the TV station."

"You hear anything from Sam about that video? Seems like he's had enough time to get home and check it out."

"No, I'll call him, too. How you coming with the proposal about the holes in Clemens' case?"

"Almost done. Should have it to you by lunch tomorrow."

"Great. I told Pendleton about it."

"You did? You tell him I'm the one writing it up?"

"Of course. Because you are."

Hank made a face.

"C'mon, Hank. You don't need to hide behind me anymore. Pendleton respects you now."

Hank made another face.

"Okay, maybe not like me, but hey...you're paying your dues. You do this thing right, your stock'll keep climbing."

JOE SPENT the next ten minutes following up on the idea about whether Juan Sanchez or the retired TV guy, Barry Carmichael, could remember any friends Roberto might've had with the first name *Al*. Both were dead ends. Next, he found Sam's number in his phone.

Sam answered, now familiar with the idea of how these phones worked. "Hello, Lieutenant. How's your day going?"

"Pretty well. Making some progress with one of those World War II books we got from the attic. Thought I'd give you an update and see how you're making out with that tape from the camera."

"Well," Sam said, "First, thought I had hit a dead end. Couldn't get the camera to work for nothing. Then got an idea for a workaround, thanks to this crazy modern age. Brought it down to my old camera store who now is in the business of converting old videotapes into these obscenely small digital devices."

Joe laughed. "Know what you mean there. You are starting to get the hang of this. So, how long till we get to see what's on that tape?"

"Paid extra for two days. I'm hoping we'll both be able to see Roberto on screen telling us who this Nazi is, and maybe even who the killer is, if it's not him."

"That would be great," Joe said. "Think I may have uncovered the Nazi's real name from the book, and maybe the first name of that blonde guy you saw sitting out in the car."

"Really? Can you tell me more?"

Joe spent the next few minutes filling him in. Unfortunately, after he did, Sam told him that he didn't know anyone named Al and didn't know whether Roberto knew anyone named Al, either. But he agreed with Joe's thinking that this SS fellow, Hans Zander, had to be the Nazi war criminal Roberto was going after with his documentary. Of course, they both knew that wouldn't be the name the man in the Thanksgiving family pic used once he snuck into the U.S. But whatever it was, Sam suggested, it was probably the same last name as this fellow Al that Roberto had mentioned.

"When can I get a look at that picture?" Sam said. "Really, I'd like to see both when you get a chance."

Joe looked at his watch. "How about now? There was something else I wanted to talk to you about anyway. Something I'd rather do in person. I'll make you my last stop of the day."

"Am I in trouble?" Sam said.

"I don't know. Have you done anything wrong?" Joe was smiling.

"I don't think so."

"No, you're not in any trouble. I'll be there in about fifteen minutes."

JOE PULLED up to Sam's cabin, parked right next to his truck. He picked up the book and headed for the door. Sam opened it before he knocked. "Here you go," Joe said. "I stuck the family photo in the same page where Roberto had marked up the photo in the book." They walked inside and Joe closed the door.

Sam brought the book under the brightest lamp in the living room and opened right to it. Seeing both pictures together brought a look of astonishment on Sam's face, like he'd opened a chest of buried treasure. "I'm sure this is the man," he said. "This guy, Zander, has got to be the Nazi war criminal. I'm sure of it."

"And hopefully, that tape of yours will confirm it," Joe said.

With that, Sam closed the book and turned to face Joe. "So, you said there was something you needed to talk to me about...in person."

"Yeah, I did. Let's see...what's the best way to jump into this?" Joe thought about the last words Captain Pendleton had said when he'd urged Joe to have this conversation with Sam: *Think if I were him, I'd wanna kill the guy...* "Sam, we're making good progress here. And we may even be on the verge of wrapping this thing up — depending what's on that tape. And so far, I've been pretty pleased with how we're working together on this. But there's something I gotta nail down before we go any further."

"What's that?"

"I gotta know that if we do figure out who this guy is, and he's still alive and in this town, you're not going to do anything stupid."

"Like what?"

"I think you know what I mean," Joe said. "I gotta know you're going to let this guy face justice, not your wrath."

Sam looked down, sighed. He didn't reply.

"Your hesitation tells me I've got reason to be concerned."

Sam looked up. "Justice," he said. "You think that's what he's going to get, Lieutenant? What if we go through all this, he even goes to trial, but gets off on a technicality? You know stuff like that happens. Will that be justice...for me?"

"He won't get off on a technicality, Sam. That's not how I build my cases. For what it's worth, no one I ever nailed in almost twenty years has gotten off on a technicality."

"Well, that's good to know. But I ask the question again... even if he does go to jail, will that be justice for me? You gotta figure he's an old man at this point. The murder happened thirty-six years ago. All that time, he's been living a full life. Probably got to get married to a woman he loves. They probably had kids. Probably had a successful career and now he's retired, or close to it. Gonna get to spend time with those grandkids they've had. Maybe some time to perfect those hobbies he's been working on all these years. You know what I been doing all that time? The kind of...*hell* I been living in?" Sam's eyes filled up with tears. He shook his head back and forth, like flashes of his worst memories were bombarding his brain. "See, he goes in as an old man, he'll never see the horrors I faced as a young man in my twenties. Most inmates treat old fellas way different. No one looks at them like fresh meat. I'll just leave it at that. No, it's even worse than that. See, even if he does suffer some, at least he'll know he brought it on himself. He really did what he's in there for. I went through all that...all of it...all the while knowing I hadn't done a thing wrong to no one. Can you imagine that, Lieutenant? Having all that done to you, all of that taken away from you?"

Joe's heart was about to break for this man. What could he say? Compared to everything Sam had just said, *justice* really did seem too weak a word to describe what the real killer would get...if and when they caught him. He looked at Sam. He had to say something. He wished his friend Jack was there at that moment.

He was always so good with words.

35

Both men just looked at each other for what felt like a full minute.

Finally, Joe said, "I don't think I'm going to have the right words, Sam, to even make a dent in all the heartache and hardship you been through. I could put ten of my worst moments together and they still wouldn't add up to one of yours." Well, Joe thought, that was a start. He wished there was some way he could bring God into this, but he suspected a guy like Sam — if he even believed in God — was probably mad at him for letting his life turn out the way it did.

"That's okay, Lieutenant. I ain't expecting you to have any magic words for me. But I think I do get what you're aiming at. You got a job to do, to uphold the law. I know there's no way you'd ever condone a guy like me taking the law into his own hands."

Joe waited a moment, but Sam didn't say anything else, and that didn't sound anywhere near like a promise to behave. "Sam, it's actually more than that for me. Yes, I'm a lawman. And best I can, I stay within the lines. I don't always like it myself. All the years I've been doing this, I've seen plenty of times when justice — at least our version of it — falls woefully short of the kind of punishment some of the bad guys get. Not to mention all the ones that seem to get away with it, at least in this life. But the alternative? I'm telling you, Sam, you don't want to be going down that path. Sure, you take this guy out, I don't doubt it will feel very good for a while. Maybe a day or two. Maybe even a whole week. But you'll be living that week, and every other week of your life, for the rest of your life, behind bars again. Is that what you want? Look around here? Look at this place compared to the inside of a cell. Walk around outside. Spend some time on that lake, sitting in a chair, drinking in the view. Then imagine trading that in for the concrete walls of the state prison, lined with barbed wire. It can't be worth it, Sam."

Sam just looked at him a few moments. Joe could tell he was chewing it over.

Then Sam said, "What did you mean when you said *at least in this life*? You were talking about times when justice comes up way short."

Joe took a breath. Seemed like Sam was opening a door. He wanted to walk through it slowly, so it didn't get slammed shut too soon. "Well, it's kinda like this. I'm a Christian, Sam. A churchgoing man. That's what I meant when I said I'm a lawman, but there's more to it than that for me. I'm by no means perfect, and I'm certainly nobody's judge. I'm just trying to say it the way I see it, for me I mean."

Sam smiled. "I can tell when a man's beating around the bush. Just say what you mean, Lieutenant. I asked."

"See, the way I see it, and the way I think the Bible explains it, this life is totally messed up. My pastor calls it a fallen world in his sermons. Another way to say it is, everything's broken. And in this life, it's not going to get fixed. Not the way any of us likes it. Since the days of Adam and Eve it's been like this, broken I mean. Men have been doing horrible, terrible, selfish things to each other. If these are the end times — like a lot of folks who read the Bible think it is — it's only going to get worse till the Lord finally comes back."

Sam got this look on his face. "You believe that, Lieutenant? That we're living in the...end times?"

"Yeah, Sam. I think I kinda do. But even if I'm wrong, doesn't change my main point, which is...this life is not all there is. This is the fallen world, the broken world. The world where it seems like evil men get away with things, and that the people they hurt just seem to suffer for no reason. And even if we catch this guy and put him in prison for the rest of his life, you're right — after what he put you through — he's getting way less than he deserves. But see, I believe there is another life, the one we all face after this. The Bible teaches pretty plainly that every one of us will face God and give an account of ourselves to him. And if people die in that condition, where they've rejected his mercy and his offer to wipe the slate clean, they are going to face some *real* justice, I'm tellin' ya. Not the kind we have here, but God's kind of justice. Where no one gets off scot-free. Because he sees everything. And if folks don't take his offer of mercy, they will face *his* justice."

Sam smiled. "Believe it or not, I know what you're talking about. When you talk about God's offer to wipe the slate clean, or like you just said, his offer of mercy...you're talking about the gospel, aren't you?"

"Yeah, I am," Joe said. "And I'm sorry for getting into all that. I don't even know if I made any sense."

"No need to apologize, Lieutenant. You didn't do a half-bad job. Heard plenty of stuff like that in chapel. Used to go quite often. Not in the early years. Truth be told, I hated God for more than half the time I was in there. After a while, I guess about the time I gave up all hope of ever getting out, I said yes to one of the guys who kept asking me to go to one of them services. Heard enough to keep my interest, so I kept coming back. Eventually, I made my peace with the part of God I was mad at. One of the chaplains gave me this pamphlet to read, called, *The Scandal of Mercy*. Don't remember who wrote it, but I must've read that thing a dozen times. Kinda helped make sense of the nightmare I'd been living in and even got into some of the things you were talking about."

"Scandal of mercy," Joe repeated. "Don't think I've ever heard that phrase. Heard lots about God's mercy before, but usually *scandal* is a word used for something bad."

"I know. Think that's what got my attention. But it talked about God's justice and God's mercy a good bit. Think it might've been written especially for people like me, mad at God for the way their life turned out. People suffering because of what other people had done to them."

"So," Joe said, "how did this pamphlet explain the scandal part?"

"As I recall, he was talking about how mercy — by its definition — is always undeserved. I don't deserve God's mercy. You don't. The man who ruined my life certainly doesn't. None of us do. What we all deserve is justice, to get what we have coming to us. But God *is* merciful, and the only way any of us gets in, that is, can get close with him, is if he shows us mercy. Meaning, he treats us in a way we don't deserve. We deserve punishment, but instead we get shown mercy. Now to those who receive that mercy, they're happy as can be. But to the folks who were hurt by the folks he showed mercy to, it seems all wrong. Like God's doing something wrong."

"Something *scandalous*," Joe said.

"Right. Now you're getting it. The scandal of mercy. Happens every time God shows mercy to someone, because none of us deserve it."

"And I guess," Joe said, "We all want God to show *us* mercy, but when he shows it to someone we think should get justice...it's a *scandal*?"

Sam made a face. "Guess that's true, too."

Joe wanted to keep this going just a little more, because it seemed like it was doing Sam some good. "I got one more question. *Who* does God show mercy to, and *how* can he do it if they don't deserve it?"

Sam looked like he was thinking. "Think I remember the basic idea on that one, too. The reason he can show mercy is because of the cross. Yeah, that's how the pamphlet ended. God poured out the punishment we deserve on his Son, on the cross. Jesus took the hit for us, so to speak. But we have to accept what he did and put our trust in him. We do that, and all the mercy God has can then be given to us. It seems like we got off scot-free, because we didn't pay the price of justice. Jesus did. That's what they mean when they say he died for us."

"Scandal of Mercy," Joe repeated. "You still got that pamphlet? I might like to read it myself."

"Wish I did," Sam said. "Lost it somehow. Good thing I read it so many times. Actually, I had no idea I remembered so much of it till you asked about it just now."

"You know what all this means though, don't you Sam? All this stuff you been explaining to me."

"Not sure I do. Or at least what you mean."

"It goes right to what I've been saying to you about not taking justice into your own hands with this guy. You gotta put it in God's hands. Let him decide whether this guy gets mercy or justice. Maybe he goes to prison, which may be all the justice he sees till he faces God. Maybe in prison, he hears what you heard and asks God for mercy. Or, maybe he doesn't and he faces God's justice. Either way, you're in the clear. You don't have to take him out. Do you see what I'm saying?"

Sam got a look Joe couldn't quite decipher. Joe decided he shouldn't try any more convincing. "What do you think, Sam?"

Sam let out a sigh. "Definitely given me something to think about. Either way, did my soul some good remembering the things in that pamphlet. Sure wish I hadn't lost it."

Joe wondered what Sam meant by *either way.*

36

Last night ended perhaps the most emotionally exhausting day Albert Dietrich had ever spent.

Well, maybe the second hardest. The first-place award for that spot still had to go to that horrendous event back in 1985.

It was something that had to be done, even though he hated doing it with all his heart. He had tried everything he knew to avoid the terrible task, but nothing had worked. In the end, he simply had no choice. He couldn't allow his father's name, really his entire life, to be destroyed like that. That's certainly what would have happened had Dietrich not done what he did. Father would have been paraded before the entire town — and after making the national news, the entire country — as some kind of sadistic monster. The shame would have killed him and, likely, his mother too.

And it wouldn't just have ruined their lives, but his entire family's life, as well. Dietrich's future would have forever been tainted by the stench. Could last night have ever happened had he not made that drastic decision so long ago? Hundreds of students, spanning over three decades, attending a banquet in his honor. One by one they came up to the mic to proclaim the significant impact he had made on their lives. And not just to students, but numerous colleagues he had worked with over the years.

If Roberto Sanchez had been allowed to carry out his scheme, look at all of the lives that would've been negatively affected. But Sanchez gave no thought to any of this. He couldn't care less. He only cared for the chance to further his selfish ambitions and steal his chance for glory and fame.

He had to be stopped. It was the only way.

And sadly, Dietrich was having to face the very same dilemma this morning. Another man — for very different reasons — had set his sights on the ruination of Dietrich's good name, and his family's honor. Only this time, the stakes were infinitely higher. If Clemens was allowed to continue his search, he would undoubtedly uncover what Sanchez had been up to, which would undoubtedly lead him right to Dietrich's doorstep. He knew this the moment he'd seen Clemens come out of Sullivan's Photo.

There could only be one reason Clemens was visiting that store. Somehow, he had found the tape. It was the one, perhaps the only, loose end left over from that ordeal.

As Dietrich sat there in the car he had rented for the day, a plain beige four-door sedan, he remembered the horror of that moment when he'd realized his mistake. He had just struck Robert that fatal blow. He'd instantly fallen to the floor. The act itself shocked Dietrich, even though that's what he'd come there to do. There was just so much blood.

In all his years of school, he had maybe been in a handful of schoolyard fights. Only once, he had bloodied a kid's nose. But this...what he had done was horrible.

It sent his mind into a panic. Because he knew Sam Clemens was coming there shortly, expecting to pick up his camera equipment. He learned about this a few days before when he had been sitting in his car by Roberto's house and saw Clemens pull up into the driveway. He could see the anger and rage on Clemens' face all the way from the road. So, he'd decided to wait until Clemens left to confront Roberto about the documentary. He had his car windows down. They were arguing so loudly, he could hear them from the street. He couldn't tell what they were talking about, so he got out and snuck up closer to Roberto's house. He had to make sure Roberto wasn't telling Clemens anything about his father.

That's when he heard the fight had to do with Roberto deciding to work with someone else on the project instead of Clemens. Clemens was angry about that but even more so it seemed, because Roberto hadn't paid him the five hundred dollars he owed. He demanded Roberto give him back his equipment. Roberto pleaded with him to give him a few more days. Clemens said he'd be back that Saturday.

It sounded like their argument was ending, so Dietrich hurried back to his car before Clemens left. He didn't know why, but he drove off down the street and waited ten minutes at a nearby convenience store before returning to confront Roberto himself.

It hadn't gone well.

October 10th, 1985
Gibraltar Road, Culpepper, Georgia

DIETRICH LOOKED both ways down Roberto's street to make sure Sam Clemens' was nowhere in sight. He didn't know why he was so concerned about being seen, but he was. As he headed up the walkway to Roberto's house, he tried to calm himself. He had to get Roberto to give up this awful documentary idea about his father, and he knew he was better at persuading people when he was calm. He rang the doorbell.

Roberto answered a few moments later. "Oh, Al, it's you. Come in."

"Were you expecting someone else?"

"No, just not expecting you. But I'm glad you stopped by. Have you had some time to think about what I said? I could really use your help with this film project. To have someone from his own family speaking out about this would be so compelling. I know you said how much you hated Hitler and the Nazis, and all they stood for. And look, I know it's gonna be hard doing something like this, seeing that he's your —"

"I'm not going to do it, Roberto," Dietrich said.

"What?"

"I'm not going to do it. I'm not going to help you."

"But why? You and I talked for almost an hour about this. It was pretty obvious to me you hated what the Nazis did even more than me. Why are you now —"

"That was before you told me the Nazi war criminal you were going after was my father. I didn't believe you then, and I believe you less now. I have known this man all my life. I can tell you, there's no way he was the monster you were describing."

"But Al, I'm not making this up. I've got proof." He held up a plain composition notebook. "It's all in here. All my connections. All my sources. I got interviews lined up with thirteen people. I've shown them the pictures, and they have confirmed. The SS officer, Hans Zander, and your father are the same man. And when you hear the kinds of things that he did. Not just once or twice, but dozens of times to hundreds of people —"

"Where are these pictures?" Dietrich said. "Last time you said you were going to show me proof."

"Fine. But you can only look, not touch." Roberto walked over to a table, picked up hardback book and a big brown envelope, and brought them over. He opened the book to a page marked with some kind of scrap paper. Then he pulled a single photo out of the brown envelope. It was black-and-white and fairly good sized. Roberto held the book up close enough for Dietrich to see another photo on the right page. Also a black-and-white photo of a group of SS officers smiling at the camera.

"You see this guy?" Roberto pointed to one of the men. "See his name, Hans Zander? Now, look at the guy in this photo, the one sitting at the head of the table."

Dietrich immediately recognized the photo. "Wait, where did you get this? This is from our family photo album. Did you take this when you were over at the house that day?"

"I borrowed it," Roberto said. "I'm planning on giving it back. But would you look at —"

"I wondered why you wanted to see our family photos. I can't believe you did this."

"Okay, I'm sorry for deceiving you. But would you look at the picture? You said you wanted proof of what I'm saying. Look at the Nazi in the book and look at your father in this family photo. And you tell me that's not the same guy."

Dietrich was fuming inside. For just a moment, he glanced down and compared the two pictures. As soon as he did, he knew they were both of his father. But he couldn't think about that now. He looked right at Roberto. "You shouldn't have done this. There's no way I'm going to help you destroy my father. And there's no way I'm going to let you use a picture you stole from our family album." He grabbed the picture and started walking toward the front door.

"Go ahead," Roberto said. "I've got a copy."

"Where is it!"

"It's in a safe place. It would've been nice to have your help on this, but believe me, I don't need it."

37

THE PRESENT

So NOW, as Dietrich sat here on a Saturday parked outside Sullivan's Photo, he remembered *that* was the moment he'd decided Roberto had to be stopped, by any means necessary. And he had the perfect person to pin the blame. Sam Clemens would be coming back for his equipment on that fateful day, also a Saturday. And Dietrich would get there first to take Roberto out and set things up for Clemens to take the fall.

It really couldn't have gone better. It was as if Dietrich had — without a tremendous amount of planning — committed the perfect murder. It wasn't until after he'd left Roberto's house and watched from some bushes a few houses away, as Sam Clemens approached the front door, that he had remembered one very important detail.

While in the house, he had taken Roberto's notebook

with all his documentary schemes and plans, but he'd forgotten all about pulling the videotape out of the camcorder. It had been sitting right there on the dinette table. In the panic after the killing, it had totally slipped his mind. He did spend some time searching for the copy of that Thanksgiving photo which Roberto had bragged about but didn't find it. He felt sure, though, that was a bluff. It was the videotape he was really concerned about.

As things turned out, what he had feared would be the one mistake that could ruin everything, never materialized. The videotape and the camcorder had never made an appearance in the trial. The police seemed totally satisfied that they had gotten their man. Had all the evidence they needed; the motive was the money. The trial unfolded, Clemens was found guilty, and he was locked away for good.

But now this.

So, here was Dietrich wearing a ridiculous disguise, putting into motion a plan he despised. But he had no choice. He must carry it out and see it through. He needed to confirm what he'd suspected...that Clemens had visited Sullivan's Photo to have an old videotape made into a modern, digital copy. And if that was true, he would have to get that tape, destroy it, and Clemens would have to die.

Before he got out of the car, Dietrich lowered the visor to look at himself once more in the little mirror. He didn't change too much. Bought a half-decent man's wig, light brown hair to cover up his mostly silver hair. Donned an Atlanta Braves baseball cap, to hide some of his face and hair, especially the part, which didn't look all that real. And he wore a pair of sunglasses. It was pretty sunny out, and he knew a lot of people these days didn't take them off when they went inside stores. He also wore an old faded T-shirt and some faded jeans, which he'd picked up at a nearby Goodwill store this morning. Nobody had seen him in a T-shirt and jeans since his twenties.

The last thing he'd be adding to the insoluble was an exaggerated good old boy southern accent. People had always commented on his refined, Southern-gentleman accent. So, obviously that had to go once inside.

He got out and looked around. No other cars in front of the store. Good. Hoped it would stay that way. He walked in, surprised by a bell ringing above his head. Didn't see anyone inside. He walked around and still didn't see anyone, then a fellow came out from a doorway behind the register.

"Afternoon," the man said. "How can I help you?"

Dietrich figured he was about mid-forties, nice face. "Afternoon to you, too. You the proprietor of this here place?"

"Why, yes I am Dan Sullivan. My dad started the business a long time ago, but I take care of things now. What can I do for you today?"

He sauntered up to the counter, rested his elbows on it like a cowboy at a saloon. "Well, not here to buy anything from you today. Hoping though, you could help me with some information."

"I will if I can."

"Good," he said. "I was driving by your store yesterday, when I saw a man come out and get in this old red pickup. Soon as I saw him, it struck me. I recognized that fella from a long time ago. I was sure it was this guy I used to go to school with a very long time ago. Course, he looked much older, but I knew it was him. He had a beard, kind of grayish with some dark parts still left in it. But as he drove by, I could still tell it was him. Got down the end of the street and thought, I'd really like to connect with him again. So, I turned my car around and drove back this way, but he was gone. I don't know if he was coming here to pick something up, or drop something off. But I wonder if you remember someone that looked —"

"Yeah, I do remember him. Best I can recall, only had one older guy in here with a beard yesterday. He was dropping something off, taking advantage of that sale we got posted in the window." He pointed to the sign. "We take folks' old family videotapes and convert them to digital, so they can start to enjoy them again."

"Is that what he said was on his tape? Footage of his family from back in the day?"

Dan thought about it. "I don't recall if he said what was on it. He just had the one tape. Usually, folks come in with a box of them. But he just had the one."

"I see. He didn't by any chance give you his address, did he? I'd sure like to stop in and surprise him."

"I don't know," Dan said. "He might have. Let me check. Be back in a minute." He headed back through the doorway and turned left. A few moments later he reappeared holding a slip of paper. "Here it is. Bill Evers, that's his name. Don't have his address, just his phone number."

"Bill Evers," Dietrich said. "Yep, that's his name." *Who the heck was Bill Evers?* He knew it had to be fake. "Didn't leave his address, though, eh?"

"No, he didn't. But if you want to see him, he'll be coming back tomorrow at 5 PM to pick up his order. You could connect with him then."

"5 PM? That's a shame. I gotta head back home by noon.

But hey, that's okay. Thanks for trying. You have a good rest of the day." With that, he turned around and walked right out the door. He'd gotten what he needed. No reason to waste a moment more in that place.

He quickly got in the car, turned it on, and drove down the road. Now that he'd confirmed Clemens had somehow found Roberto's old videotape, the rest of his plan would have to be set in motion. He had no choice. His next task — which would still require his disguise and the rented car — would take place in Dunedin, the county seat. About a forty-minute car drive from here.

He'd have to buy a gun, illegally. Preferably, one with a silencer. Something like that, even with a disguise, he wanted to be far enough away where the chances of bumping into someone he knew were zero.

38

OFF AND ON THROUGHOUT THE DAY, SAM HAD GIVEN A LOT OF thought to what the Lieutenant had said. All that talk about mercy and Sam having to rehash all the things he'd learned in that pamphlet on the subject. They were messing with his mind a good bit. Didn't help that it was Sunday. Back in prison, he'd been a good boy, gotten into the habit of going to chapel every Sunday. But he hadn't been to a chapel or church since he'd gotten it into his head to kill the man who ruined his life. Felt like that would be the only thing could satisfy all the anger and dark feelings inside.

In fact, for a good while he thought it was a settled matter. But now, he wasn't so sure.

Was this path of mercy a legit option? Just figure out who did it, let the law handle it, and show the guy mercy? Part of him felt like that's what he was *supposed* to do. Fair to say, it was the thing God would want him to do. But somehow the very idea made him feel so empty inside. Didn't feel like it got him even halfway to balancing the scales. The guy would be getting off way too easy.

The Lieutenant was right about one thing, though. If he did kill the guy, the life he'd been enjoying lately — especially since moving in at the cabin and driving around his very fine truck — would all go away. Just like that, he'd be back inside.

Permanently. That certainly had to count for something.

He was going over all these things on the short drive from the cabin to Sullivan's Photo. It was just up ahead on the left. The owner, Dan, had said to come by today by 5 PM, and he should have it ready. Sam looked at his watch. Less than fifteen minutes from now.

He couldn't wait to see what was on that tape. It would be so strange just to see Roberto's face talking into the camera. Alive and well and totally full of himself, like he was all the time back then. He'd be going on and on, talking about this documentary as if it was going to be the biggest deal in the country once he got it made. Something everybody would be talking about.

He had no way of knowing, not only would no one see his documentary, it would never be finished. The infamous Nazi war criminal Roberto hoped to expose would wind up living out his life in peace and tranquility, probably died of old age surrounded by loving family. And just a few days after Roberto's last entry onto the video, he would himself become this war criminal's final victim.

Well, no, Sam thought, as he pulled into the parking lot of Sullivan's Photo...Sam was this Nazi's final victim.

He got out of the truck and saw Dan standing behind the

register through the store window. Sam walked inside, smiled as he heard the little bell above the door.

"You came back," Dan said.

"I came back. Were you able to get the 8mm converted over okay?"

"Got it all set for you. Checked out the SD card and the flash drive. I was able to watch the video on both with no problem. Watched the SD card on my phone and plugged the flash drive into my laptop. The picture's pretty good on both. Course, the resolution leaves a little bit to be desired. Only because of how much things have improved since then. Nothing wrong with the copies."

"So, you watched the videos?"

"Yeah," Dan said, "Not the whole thing, but I checked it at different spots to make sure it was looking okay. Looked fine every time I checked, but it was kind of an odd thing to see. Are you aware of what's on there?"

"I think I am, but it's been so long since I did anything with it."

"Yeah, it was just this guy pretty much filling up the screen, talking into the camera. Nice looking guy, had a nice voice, too. But that pretty much was it."

"Did you listen to any of it?" Sam said.

"Just a little. Once I knew the audio was working fine, I shut the volume off. On my end, you know, for privacy reasons. But the audio was nice and strong through the whole thing. The part I listened to seemed like the young man was talking about some movie he was making. Heard him refer to what he was doing as production notes. Something like that. Don't know if that's disappointing to hear.

Maybe you were expecting some old family movies, or something."

"No, I'm okay with that. I know the guy you're talking about, the one on the video. He was a friend. He's passed away, so it'll be something just to see him alive and well again."

"Okay then. I've got the bill right here. You paying with a card?"

Sam said that he was. Paid Dan what he owed, checked the bag to make sure the two items were both in there, thanked him, and was just about to head back to his truck.

"Oh, wait. Almost forgot," Dan yelled. Someone came by yesterday looking for you. Said you guys were old friends. I guess he saw you when you came in to drop this off. Not here in the store but outside, as you drove away."

"Said he was my old friend?" Sam repeated. As far as he knew, he didn't have any friends left in this town. "What did he look like?"

"Well, he was maybe a few inches taller than you. Hard to say exactly. He was wearing a baseball cap. Had light brown hair, a bit on the long side. Wore dark sunglasses, so I couldn't tell you anything about his eyes."

"He leave a name or number?"

"No. He asked if I knew your address. Course, I told him I didn't have it, but I did tell him you'd be by today, about this time, if he wanted to connect with you then."

"What did he say to that?"

"He said it wouldn't work out. He had to leave town early this morning. So, I guess you two won't be having any big reunion anytime soon."

Sam wanted to say, "*I wouldn't be so sure about that,*" but held his peace. He knew this had to be the killer. Who else would come looking for him like that, pretending to be some old friend? "Well, guess it wasn't meant to be," Sam said. "Thanks again for doing this."

When he got back into his truck, he quickly got out his phone and called the Lieutenant.

39

Joe was feeling pretty good. This was turning out to be a fairly relaxing Sunday. Went to church with the family in the morning, had a nice dinner together at Cracker Barrel after. Joe got what he got most of the time, the fried shrimp. Go figure a place like Cracker Barrel would make great fried shrimp, but they did. He liked it better than most of the seafood places he'd been to that specialize in that kind of thing.

Right after they got home, Kate took Kristin out shopping for a new purse. Seemed to him, that should take twenty minutes. Kate said he was dreaming. They wouldn't be back for three or four hours. Joe Junior was hanging out with his best friend, playing Xbox. So Joe had the rest of the afternoon and the house to himself. He had just woken up from a soccer nap. He liked soccer ever since his kids got into it, but for some reason if he watched on TV by himself, he'd fall asleep within fifteen minutes. The only thing that made him sleep faster was golf.

He grabbed the remote, thinking he might watch a World War II movie he had saved on a streaming channel. Then his phone started ringing. With Kate and both kids out of the house, better get up and look at it. It was Sam. "Hey Sam, what's up? Everything okay?"

"You hear me okay? Got this thing on speaker. Trying to drive with both hands on the wheel, like they want you to."

"I can hear you fine. What's going on?"

"Wouldn't normally call you on Sunday. But something just happened that made me think I should."

"Don't worry about it," Joe said. "What happened?"

"Well, I was just leaving the photo place. You know, where I dropped off the tape, so he could convert it to digital. Got a flash drive for you and Hank, by the way. I can get it to you tomorrow somehow. Anyway, as I'm leaving, Dan says — that's the owner — some old friend of mine had come in yesterday asking about me."

This didn't sound good. "You don't have any old friends left in town, do you?"

"No, I don't. You see the problem."

"Yeah, I do. What did this old friend say to this guy, Dan? How did he know to come there to find you?"

"He said he'd seen me leaving the store on Friday, the day I dropped it off. Must've been some kinda chance thing, I guess. Like he was outside at one of the stores nearby and saw me."

"You shave off your mustache and beard?" Joe said.

"No. Still hairy as ever. I don't know how he recognized me. But I'm thinking, it's got to be the killer."

"Yeah, this isn't good, Sam. I'm thinking you could be right."

"So, what do we do? What should I do?"

Joe wasn't sure. If Sam wasn't an ex-con, he'd tell him maybe now's a good time to get to a gun store. "You see anyone trailing you lately? Anyone suspicious hanging around the cabin?"

"No. Course, not like I been looking, either."

"Well, maybe you better start. Just in case. Guess the main thing is, go home and watch that video, see if it IDs who this guy Al is, or at least his father, so we can get a last name. We get that, it changes everything."

"I agree. On my way to the cabin right now."

"Did this photo shop owner say what the guy looked like?"

"He did, but sounded to me like he was trying to hide his looks. Baseball cap, long light-brown hair, wearing sunglasses...in the store. Thinking the hair's probably a wig."

"You're probably right," Joe said. "If it is the killer, he's gotta be at least your age."

"Yeah," said Sam, "and if the killer's that young blond fella I saw outside of Roberto's house, by now that blond hair probably turned totally grey, if not white."

Joe smiled. Sam really had a good head for this stuff. "Okay, you just get home and watch that tape. Call me the moment you know anything we can use. You want me or Hank to head out there and keep an eye on things? I can maybe get one of the patrol guys to swing by."

"I don't think so. I'll keep looking out the window. I see anything doesn't look like a deer, I'll call you right away. You guys aren't that far away. Last time you got out here pretty quick."

"If you're sure," Joe said.

"I'm okay to use a bat if anyone actually tries to get inside, right? Bought one at Walmart."

"Yeah. Anyone tries to get in, you're okay to whack 'em with a bat." They hung up and Joe immediately called Hank to tell him what was going on.

FOLLOWING five cars behind Sam Clemens was Al Dietrich.

Yesterday, the camera store owner had said Clemens would be back today at five and, sure enough, he was. Dietrich had been parked at the convenience store across the street, watched him go in and come out.

Of course, following him now through Sunday traffic was a breeze. Culpepper's traffic wasn't that bad on weekdays. Didn't have anything you could call a rush hour. On Sundays, traffic was half as much. What made following Clemens even easier was that old red pickup truck he drove. Stood out like a sore thumb.

Clearly, he wasn't trying to blend in. Dietrich figured it had to be the only antique red pickup he'd seen in town. What was Clemens thinking? If he were Clemens, he'd be driving a boring beige sedan, like the one he rented.

Then Dietrich remembered something. That's right. Back in '85 when Clemens had visited Roberto's house, he'd been driving an old red pickup. Probably not the same year but something similar. That was why it had been so easy for police to find him after Dietrich had killed Roberto. He'd watched nearby as Clemens fled the house. Then he quickly rushed to the closest phone booth to report "sounds of some guy screaming his head off inside this house." He'd given the police Roberto's address.

"Oh, yeah," he'd then said, "he was driving this old red pickup."

So, that was it. Clemens, now out on probation, had decided to reward himself with an old pickup, similar to the one he drove back in college.

Whatever the reason, Dietrich didn't care.

Sure made his task now a simple one. There was no way he'd lose Clemens as he made his way home, wherever that was. He decided not to try and take him out today, didn't even have his new gun and silencer in the car with him, just in case he got stopped for some reason. But he had decided to wear his disguise. Again, a precaution.

No, today was about sizing up the situation and forming the perfect plan. But he knew he'd have to execute that plan very soon. He couldn't wait more than a day or two.

The anxiety surrounding this whole affair was becoming unbearable.

40

SAM MADE IT BACK TO THE CABIN WITHOUT ANY PROBLEMS. HE was half-tempted to plug that SD card into his phone and start watching Roberto's video on the drive here from Sullivan's Photo, but knew he'd probably miss a curve and smack into a tree. He got out of the truck and was just about to unlock the door to the cabin when he thought he better pause. Make sure no one had followed him. A few cars had gotten his attention on the way here, but they were so far back he felt sure they were no cause for trouble.

After a minute or so without seeing or hearing anything, he went inside. As he closed the door, a strange thought floated up. He imagined how nice it would be to be greeted by a friendly dog. Had one back in college, some kind of terrier mix he'd brought home from the pound. Another casualty to chalk up to his arrest and imprisonment, another thing the killer had stolen from him. The dog's name was Rex, and he gave the best greetings whenever Sam came home. Even if he'd just been gone an hour.

Of course, before he'd even seriously consider getting a Rex Number Two, he had to settle the idea of whether to show this killer mercy or justice. Wouldn't do to bring a dog here, start getting attached, only to lose it again if he had to go back to prison. And if he did decide to show mercy, he'd have to make the second Rex a bigger dog. He was kinda enjoying life out here in the woods. Might make more sense to get a woodsy kind of dog, like a hound or a lab mix. The kind that would stay by you if you went out hunting or fishing.

He set the bag from the photo store and his phone on the dinette table. Felt the need to visit the bathroom, and as he walked toward it he passed the baseball bat he'd bought at Walmart. When he saw it, he thought about what he'd said to the Lieutenant on the phone, about whether he could use it if the killer ever tried to get inside the cabin. Of course, that was only said for the Lieutenant's benefit.

If that guy ever did try to get inside, he'd plug him with his Colt 1911. A quick double-tap, one to the head, one to the heart. He might go to jail for a little while, as a convicted felon in possession of a firearm, but then again, they might go easy on him since it would be a clear case of self-defense. As he opened the bathroom door, he had another thought. Maybe he wouldn't go to jail at all, if they could prove the guy breaking in was the original killer.

Would that be a sweet thing? To kill the guy who'd ruined his life and clear his name at the same time?

Now, which dirt road was it?

Dietrich had been driving around these lakeside country

roads for the last fifteen minutes looking for Samuel Clemens. He couldn't remember the last time he'd been out this way. Had to be over ten years. Then it came to him. He and his wife had been asked to visit his oldest son's family. They had rented one of the cabins for a few weeks that summer and were celebrating their grandson's second birthday. Yeah, that was it.

A much more pleasant reason to be out here.

He was surprised when Clemens' red pickup had turned left at Hilden Road, started coming out this way. Never figured Clemens to be a man of means, especially after spending thirty-six years in prison. Dietrich had expected to follow him to one of the poorer sections of town, maybe to some kind of group home for inmates. Made following him pretty tricky. There weren't that many cars out on these country roads during the week, much less on Sunday. That forced him to stay way back from Clemens' truck.

The fact that it was bright red helped. Could see it from a good distance away. He was able to tell when he turned and did his best to keep up without getting too close. But somehow, after three or four turns he lost him. So, he'd been driving down different dirt roads hoping to spot his red truck in front of one of these cabins. So far, he'd spotted six different cabins on the lake. Four of them looked empty, the other two had regular cars parked out front.

Of course, a significant upside to this dilemma was... eventually he would find where Clemens was staying, and when the time came to take him out, he wouldn't have to worry about doing it at night.

Especially if he used his silencer, there was no chance anyone would hear him out here.

.   .   .

WHEN SAM CAME out of the bathroom, he decided to do a walk around, peeking out the curtains from each room to make sure everything was okay. He didn't see anyone and hoped it stayed that way, but while on the john he couldn't stop thinking about the fact that just yesterday the guy he'd come back to find had managed to find him. Of course, he had some help with that stupid newspaper article. Even though Sam had a beard and longer hair now, he really hadn't changed much from the pictures included in the article.

Besides that, the real killer knew Sam's identity. So far, Sam still didn't know his. Hopefully, that was about to change.

He made sure all the doors and windows were locked, got his Colt pistol, and brought it to the table where he was about to sit. Might not be a bad idea to keep it close to him in the cabin, in case the guy busted through the door at some point. Wouldn't be that hard to do, considering the condition of the door. That happened, and it wouldn't help Sam if his gun was on the other side of the room.

He turned on the light and sat down. Finally figured out how to open the little slide door on his phone and inserted the SD card. Just like Dan had said, his phone seemed to recognize the intruder. A little window opened up on the screen asking if he wanted to see what was on it. He clicked YES.

This was it. The big moment.

41

A few moments later, Sam was looking at a video of... something. A little bit grainy, but it appeared to be an off-white-colored wall. On the right, he could see half of a painting or poster of some Italian-looking countryside. He hadn't spent enough time in Roberto's house to know if this was —

Suddenly, it didn't matter. Roberto came into the picture.

Oh my gosh. Look at him. He's so young. Looks like a boy almost.

Sam had forgotten how long Roberto's hairstyle was back then. It looked silly. But then, maybe Sam's looked just as bad.

Roberto sat and started talking. He adjusted the camera slightly to make sure he was centered properly, then said:

"Okay, *this video is really just for me. Decided to kill two birds with one stone. Give me some face time practicing in front of a camera, but also save my hand a ton of writing, so I'm going to share a bunch of my production notes and other thoughts I'm having about this documentary on this tape. I find it a lot easier to brainstorm if I don't have to write everything down. If anyone else sees this — and I certainly hope they don't — don't laugh when you see me start to change in a few moments. From this point on, I'll be using my professional on-camera voice and facial expressions. Again, just to get in some practice. Even if I'm just talking shop. Don't plan to use anything on this tape in the actual documentary. Well, I mean the footage on this tape, not some of the content. This is a borrowed camcorder I'm using. The resolution quality isn't good enough for the documentary itself. Okay, here goes..."*

SAM WATCHED for the next thirty minutes. After getting over the initial shock of seeing Roberto alive and so vibrant again, he was mostly bored by what he saw. It was just Roberto going on and on about the details of the documentary. He must've made a half-dozen different entries. With each one, he was dressed differently and would give a short intro. Then he proceeded to talk about some new idea or some better way to approach a scene idea. A few times, he mentioned where he might like to integrate some of Sam's B-role footage into the interviews he planned, which was interesting. He also said some fairly complimentary things about the footage Sam had shot, which was nice to hear.

At one point, he did speak about a list of questions he would like to ask the SS officer, Hans Zander, if he ever got the chance to speak with him one-on-one. Then Roberto spelled out the questions. There were eight of them. Good questions, but none of them gave any clue as to the false identity of Hans Zander. His new American identity.

Finally, Sam could tell the video was almost at its end, Roberto came into the picture once more. It kind of freaked Sam out. Roberto was wearing the same clothes he wore on the last day of his life.

WELL, this may be my last entry on this tape, at least for a little while. I may have mentioned I'm using a borrowed camcorder. Unfortunately, the guy I'm no longer working with is coming back today to reclaim it. If I can get him to give me a little more time with it, or find someone else to let me borrow theirs, I'll make some more entries on this video. But alas, this may be it. Thought what I'd do is make an entry I should've made a few days ago after my meeting about Al's father.

SAM'S EARS perked right up. He sat forward in his chair staring at the screen.

I HAD HOPED to convince Al to cooperate with me in the making of this video. In an earlier conversation with him, I got him to admit even though he was of German descent, he was raised to despise Hitler, the Nazis, and all they stood for. I thought I could build on that when I showed Al the photos of his father. The one from the book showing SS Officer Hans Zander, and the family photo of Al's father at a Thanksgiving dinner back in the 1950s. It was clear from his reaction that he believed his father was in both pictures. I could tell — without a doubt — he realized his beloved father was actually a Nazi war criminal guilty of some heinous war crimes. But instead of agreeing to work with me, Al lost it. He told me he'd never help me destroy his father's life, grabbed the photo, and left. Fortunately, I had a copy made. Which I will use to prove my case in this documentary. Sadly it seems, without Al's help.

THEN IT ENDED.

"But what is Al's last name?!" Sam yelled at the screen. He double-checked to make sure it was over. Yes, that was it, the last entry. He couldn't believe it. He'd listened to the whole tape, but Roberto had never once mentioned Al's last name.

42

Sam couldn't believe they'd gone to all this trouble to find the tape, get it converted, and it turned out to be a bust. He'd actually rewound it to the beginning and watched it one more time, just to make sure he hadn't missed Roberto mentioning Al's or his father's last name. But nothing. He felt almost sick inside. There was nothing left to do but call the Lieutenant and deliver the bad news.

After a few rings, the Lieutenant picked up. "Hey, Sam. So, what is it?"

"What is what?" Sam said.

"You know, Al's last name. You trying to keep me in suspense?"

Sam sighed.

"That doesn't sound good."

"He never said it. I listened to it twice. He never said it."

"You're kidding," Joe said. "Of course, you're not. That's almost hard to believe. How long was the tape?"

"All total about forty-five minutes. But he made a bunch

of different entries, sounded like over a couple weeks. That's how long he'd borrowed my camera."

"Man, that's disappointing."

"Tell me about it. I kept waiting, thinking any minute now he's gonna say it, but he never did. Said Al's name a half-dozen times, but that was it. He did say at the beginning he was only making this tape for himself, so I'm thinking since he knew Al's last name, he never felt the need to say it. I don't know."

"No," Joe said. "That makes sense. But still, what a bummer."

"Haven't heard that word in a long time. They still say that...bummer?"

"Don't think so. Probably just me. Well, I'd still like to see it when you get a chance. And save your copy, too. It might come in handy as evidence if we can get you a new trial. Anything else on there you think is useful?"

Sam thought a moment. "Yeah, I guess. He talks pretty plainly about Al's father being a war criminal, and that his real name is Hans Zander. He also talks about a conversation he had with Al that didn't go so well. Apparently, he had gotten Al to admit even though he was of German descent, he was raised to hate Hitler and everything the Nazis stood for. Roberto thought that would mean Al would cooperate with him on the documentary, but Al blew up at him, said he'd never help them ruin his father. Roberto said he'd shown Al the photos, and it was obvious Al believed he was seeing his father in both pictures."

"Well," Joe said. "That sounds like something we could use. I'll tell you what, let me see if I can get hold of Hank, run all this by him. Maybe we can come up with something else to try."

"All right, Lieutenant. Appreciate all your help on this. I'm just—"

A pause. "You're just what, Sam?"

"Thought I heard something outside. Sounded like a car coming down the road then turning around in the dirt. I'm gonna go check." He heard Joe yell, "Sam, wait," on the phone as he set it down, grabbed his gun, and headed outside.

ALBERT DIETRICH TURNED DOWN YET another winding dirt road off the main road in search of the red pickup truck. He'd lost count how many of these he'd driven down so far. This one was a little longer and had a few more curves than the rest.

Suddenly, he came around one more curve and there it was. An old, red pickup truck parked in front of a cabin. But Dietrich was way too close. He didn't mean to, but he slammed on the brakes then whipped the car around in the open space and headed back the way he came. So far, he didn't see anyone outside or any movement in the front window curtains.

He hauled off down the road as quickly as he could, looking through the rearview mirror the entire time. He still hadn't seen anyone as he rounded another curve that put the cabin out of sight.

His heart was pounding. He almost blew the whole thing. Stopping at the main road, he looked around for some sign that would identify the smaller road he'd just been on.

But there was none. He did see a large rock on the far corner right at the tree line. That would have to serve as the marker. What he had wanted to do was to get out, walk through the woods back to the cabin, find a nice hiding spot, and spend some time checking the place out.

But that was too risky now. At least, he had solved the mystery of Samuel Clemens' location. That really was the priority.

He'd just have to come back tomorrow and make this thing happen.

WHEN SAM GOT OUTSIDE, he could still see a thin wall of dust gliding toward the trees. Somebody had been here. He ran toward where he'd seen the dust and could clearly see grooves in the dirt showing where a car had stopped suddenly, then made a sweeping turn to head back the other way. Looking down the road as far as he could, he didn't see anything but the trees. He thought about running toward the main road but realized whoever it was had been moving fast and was likely gone by now.

Whoever it was. Who was he kidding? Had to be the killer. And that meant the guy knew where he lived. Instinctively, he reached for the gun in his waistband but didn't pull it out. But it seemed a certainty now that he would be using it very soon.

He walked back to the cabin, walked inside, and grabbed the phone.

"Sam, is everything okay?" Joe said.

"It is now. Don't know for how long. Definitely was someone here in a car." Sam explained what he had seen.

"Doesn't sound good, I agree. Maybe it wasn't the killer. Could've been just someone looking for another cabin and realized they had the wrong one when they saw your truck. You know there's no street sign out there identifying the road."

"Could be, Lieutenant. But I don't think a tourist would've driven like that when they realized they had the wrong place. This guy tore out here, like someone who didn't want to be seen."

"I hear you, Sam. I'm going to send a patrol car out there, have them look around, just in case the guy's still in the area. Maybe you shouldn't stay in the cabin tonight. You got money for a hotel?"

"I do, but I'm not going anywhere. Let him come to me. He does, I got my trusty bat and I know how to swing it."

Joe laughed. "All right, but if you hear anything else, anything, you call me. I don't pick up right away, you dial 911."

"All right, Lieutenant."

"And Sam, next time we're talking and something happens, don't set the phone down. You know, you could have brought it with you as you ran outside?"

"Yeah, I'll try to remember that."

"I called Hank," Joe said. "Got his voicemail. We'll see what he says when he calls back. Don't worry, we'll think of some way to figure out who Al is."

After they hung up, Sam was thinking maybe they didn't need to figure out anything. Seemed like Al had already decided how this thing was going to end. Sam knew he'd come back. And when he did, he wouldn't be dealing with no baseball bat from Walmart.

43

JOE STILL HAD THE HOUSE TO HIMSELF AND WAS TRYING TO GET into this WW2 movie, but he kept thinking about his phone call with Sam. His gut told him this incident out at the cabin with the car leaving in a hurry was something bad. Couple that with a stranger going to the camera store trying to find out where he lived...it had to mean the killer was starting to make his move. Joe figured the guy came back to the store today, parked off to the side, and waited for Sam to come back and pick up his tape. He'd told the owner when he was pretending to be Sam's friend that he'd seen Sam as he'd left the store on Friday, which meant he knew Sam was driving that old red pickup. He must've followed Sam out to the cabin, lost him at some point, and started searching the area till he found Sam's truck.

Sam didn't seem too concerned for his safety, but that didn't mean he was okay. If this guy killed Roberto back in '85 to keep his father's secret intact, he'd have even more reason to keep his father's secret and his own identity a secret now. The guy was old enough to have grown kids and grandkids. The last thing he'd want is to spend his remaining years utterly humiliated, his reputation ruined, languishing all alone in a prison cell.

No. This guy had tons of motive to want to stop what Sam was doing, even more than he had in '85 when he killed Roberto. Joe paused the movie, picked up his phone, and called Hank.

"Hey Joe, what's up? Not like you to call me on a Sunday."

"Sorry about that. Did you hear my voicemail?" Long pause. Of course, he didn't. "Okay, when you hear why I called, I think you'll understand." Joe briefed him on all the details that just happened.

When he finished, Hank said, "I'm right with you, Joe. Whoever this Al guy is, he's obviously up to no good. You want me to drive out there and check on Sam?"

"No, I already called in to get a patrol car to swing by. The question is, is this serious enough to warrant twenty-four-hour protection?"

"Might be a hard thing to sell to Pendleton. You know how edgy he gets these days spending overtime money. We'd have to really prove our case. I mean, at the hunch level, I think we're already there. But if you step back and look at what we're talking about, nothing real has happened yet."

"Yeah," Joe said. "Guess you're right. I'll bring Cap' up to date on all this first thing in the morning. Maybe when he hears the new stuff, he might agree it justifies the protection idea. Say listen, that tape didn't give us the last name of this Al guy—"

"Yeah, can't believe it," Hank said.

"We just can't catch a break," Joe said. "Anyway, I know

you're pretty good at thinking outside the box. Got any ideas how we can turn up this guy's last name? I'm drawing blanks here."

Hank didn't say anything for a few moments. "This might be something," he said. "Didn't Sam say he saw a blonde-haired guy about his age sitting in a car by Roberto's house? I think it was the day he confronted Roberto the first time."

"Yeah," Joe said. "He did. It never made a showing at the trial. Even his own attorney thought it probably wasn't related."

"But Sam's thinking now maybe it was, right?"

"Yeah, I'd say he is."

"Well, let's assume it was. There's a chance *he* could be our killer. Or at least the guy who set Sam up. I remember a case I worked on last year had me checking through old yearbooks at the University library. Turns out, they have a copy of every year stored there. The lady at the desk said they go back to the first year they started making them. If this blonde guy was involved, maybe he went to Culpepper during the same years Sam and Roberto went."

Joe realized where Hank was heading. "That's a great idea, Hank."

"How about I get Sam to meet me there tomorrow morning while you're briefing Pendleton, see if he can start looking through these yearbooks. Maybe we'll get lucky, and he'll see the blonde guy who was out by the street. Wouldn't it be crazy if he did, and the guy's name was Al?"

"Do it, Hank. Really, run with this." He gave Hank Sam's phone number, and they hung up.

44
———

THE FOLLOWING MORNING, SAM STOOD OUTSIDE HIS CABIN waiting for Hank to arrive. He'd called early yesterday evening, saying Joe had asked him to run an idea by Sam. As soon as he heard it, Sam agreed it was definitely worth a try. Sam had suggested meeting Hank at the library, but Hank said he'd feel better bringing Sam there himself, considering what happened over the weekend. Besides that, the guy who'd been coming after Sam — assuming he was the killer — knew what Sam's red pickup looked like. Hank thought it would make more sense to leave it parked at the cabin.

Sam looked at his watch. It was 9 AM. Right on time, he heard a car driving down the dirt road toward the cabin. He was relieved to see Hank's face through the windshield. He pulled up to where Sam was standing. Sam heard the door unlock. He opened it and got in.

"Morning, Sam," Hank said. "Ready for our little field trip?"

"Yes, sir. Sure am. Hope it proves to be fruitful. That was certainly a good idea you had, doing this I mean."

"Thanks, hope it turns up something, too." Hank looked at Sam's face. "Man, I just realized...you shaved off your mustache and beard."

"Yes, I did."

"You look...well, younger for one thing."

"Really? I thought so, too. More gray in my beard than on my head. With the beard gone, I was thinking I didn't look so old. The Lieutenant had asked me to keep it on after that article came out, so people wouldn't recognize me. Figured it didn't matter much anymore. No one else in town seemed to care and the guy who's after me recognized me somehow with the beard anyway."

"I'm sure Joe will be fine with the change." Hank turned the car around and headed back toward the main road. They drove a few minutes in silence, then Hank said, "How do you like that cabin? Guess it must be about the exact opposite of where you been hanging your hat the last thirty-plus years."

"I like it...a lot. Can't wait to get this nasty business behind us, so I could maybe start taking better advantage of the place."

"You mean like fishing?" Hank said. "Lake Samson's got some great fishing spots."

"Yeah, like that."

"You're just renting, right?"

"Yeah," Sam said. "Just booked it for a couple of months. Figured by then I'd be adjusted enough to life on the outside to make a more permanent step. The realtor gal told me the place was available to buy, if I was interested."

"You thinking now you might be open to that kind of

thing?"

Sam thought a moment. Hank had touched on more than small talk here. The real reason Sam had booked the cabin for two months was, he figured by then he'd have learned the identity of the real killer, killed the man, then get sent back to prison for life. "I think I might be wide open to that, Hank."

Hank's phone began to ring. It displayed on his computer screen, showing it was Joe. Hank touched the hands-free button. "Hey, Joe. You already through meeting with Captain Pendleton?"

"YEAH, Hank. Just finished five minutes ago. We met at 8:30."

"How did it go? I got Sam here with me in the car, just to let you know."

"Thanks for the heads up," Joe said. "Hey, Sam. Guess you guys are heading to the library?"

"Yes, sir, Lieutenant. Hank and I are just shooting the breeze, getting to know each other a little better."

"Good. Hope you guys find this guy. So, Hank, the meeting went well. Cap's on board with everything we discussed. In fact, he agrees with our concern that this mystery fellow could very well be the bad guy. So, he approved the idea of Sam receiving some protection, at least for a few days till we see if this guy's going to keep active. After we get off the phone, I'll be sending someone out there to the cabin. But I had an idea, so I'm glad Sam's with you. I'd like to get his thoughts on this."

"Go ahead, Lieutenant," Sam said. "What's your idea?"

"Well, before I explain it, if you're uncomfortable with it, even a little. Just say so."

"Got it."

"The idea is not having him parked right there next to Sam's truck, but somewhere out of plain sight. You know that area off to the left of the trees, when you come down that road and first see the cabin? If we parked his car there, someone coming down that road to the cabin wouldn't see him until they drove past him. Which means, he would definitely see who it was before they had a chance to turn around, like that guy did yesterday."

"So, we're hoping for a chance to catch the guy," Hank said, "instead of just scare him off?"

"That's what I was thinking. We'd use Sam's truck as bait to get him to drive far enough down that road to where he'd have to go past our guy. But hey, Sam if this makes you feel —"

"No, Lieutenant. I like this idea," Sam said. "I'm for whatever it takes to get this guy."

"Great. Then that's what we'll do. I'll get that happening right away. You guys have fun at the library." Joe hung up.

ABOUT TWENTY MINUTES later on the west side of Culpepper, in an area considered to be rather upscale, Albert Dietrich backed out of his driveway. Most people would assume this neighborhood to be beyond the reach of a high school teacher, even one with so many years under his belt like him. But as with most math teachers, he was good at numbers, and he'd applied this skill to build a significant portfolio in the stock market.

Yet another reason why he couldn't let Samuel Clemens

continue on this path to uncover what really happened all those years ago. He had way too much to lose.

No. Today, was the day.

He was driving his regular car to a paid parking lot in town where he'd parked his rental car, after figuring out where the security cameras were. A few moments ago, he'd kissed his wife goodbye. Where was he going? Oh, he had to run some errands at a few places like Lowes and Home Depot, maybe a few others, so he could get started on some of those projects he wanted to tackle once his retirement became official.

It hadn't started yet. He'd taken today off as a personal leave day. Had a ton of those stored up. Once he switched cars, he'd don his disguise and head out to that cabin on Lake Sampson where Samuel Clemens resided.

Hopefully, when he got there, he'd find everything as it should be and be able to put a quick end to this dreadful task. That included not only killing Clemens but staging the scene to look like a robbery. Of course, the only thing he absolutely needed to steal was that digital video copy Sam had made at Sullivan's Photo. That, and the original. Everything else he'd take would find a home in some downtown dumpster.

If things went according to plan, Sam would appear to have died at the hands of a thief who had no regard for human life. Judging by the scene, they'd surmise he was probably a drug addict rummaging for things he could quickly convert to cash.

No one would even know that the videotape had ever existed. Life could go back to normal, the way it was always meant to be.

45

HANK AND SAM ARRIVED AT THE CULPEPPER UNIVERSITY library parking lot. Took a few extra minutes to figure out where it was in the sprawling complex. A security guard finally helped them solve the riddle. The parking lot was half full. They found a spot right by the front door.

"A whole lot more buildings at this place than I remember," Sam said.

"That's right," said Hank, "you went to school here."

"Guessing that was a few years before you were born." As they got out of the car, Sam looked around. "I'd heard the School of Journalism got shut down some years ago. We drove past the buildings where I spent most of my junior and senior year. Looks like they use them for the Computer Science department now."

Hank opened the front door to the library. "Ever spend any time in here?"

"Not if I could help it."

They walked up to the main desk. Hank greeted the

middle-aged woman standing behind it, showed her his badge. He looked at her name tag. "Hi Doris, my name is Sergeant Hank Jenkins. I called about an hour ago, don't know if I spoke with you about us coming here."

"Don't think it was me. I just got in thirty minutes ago. How can I help you, Sergeant?"

"Well, whoever I spoke with confirmed that you keep all the college yearbooks stored somewhere. Would you know where they're kept?"

"Yearbooks? I believe we do keep them here, but I'm not sure where. Give me just a moment, and I'll check." She walked toward a room, also behind the desk, about twenty feet away. She opened the door, peeked inside, and spoke to someone. "Okay, fine," she said. "I know where that is." She came back. "We don't keep them out here on the main floor. They're down in our basement area. It's not really a basement. It still looks like part of the library, but it's mostly for storing things people don't ask for that often."

"So," Hank said, "guess it's fair to say y'all have never converted them to digital?"

She laughed. "Not hardly. That would be a very low priority I'm sure. I've worked here for about eight years, and you are the first people who've ever asked to see them. At least when I was working" She came out from behind the desk and started walking toward the far corner of the library.

Hank and Sam followed.

"Is this some research you're doing for a case?" she asked.

"You could say that," Hank replied. "If we do find what we're looking for in one of them, will we be able to check it out? I mean, neither one of us go to the school."

She reached the door with a sign labeled *Stairwell*. "I'm

sure we'll be able to make an exception if it's official police business." She opened the door and the three of them went down the stairs one floor. The door opened to what looked like a much less impressive library, but a library just the same. No windows, just fluorescent lights, and row after row after row of books.

"Right this way," Doris said. "It's about halfway down the aisle." Eventually, she turned left and they continued down several racks.

Sam could see up ahead the shelves filled with yearbooks.

"What years are you looking for?"

"Probably 1981 through 1984," Hank said. "That sound right to you, Sam?"

"That'd be my guess."

"That should be easy enough to find," she said. "Since they're stored by year." They got to the correct rack and stopped. A few moments later, she pulled out the four yearbooks and handed them to Hank.

"Are there some table and chairs down here where we could work? If not, we could go upstairs."

"There are," Doris said. "When we go back out to the center aisle, I'll go right, back toward the stairway. You go left about the same distance, and it will open up to a sitting area on the left. When you're done, just bring up any of the yearbooks you want to borrow and put the others right back here."

"Great," Hank said, "thanks."

With that, she left. Hank and Sam followed her directions and easily found an area to work. Hank handed the ones labeled 1983 and '84 to Sam. "Why don't you work your way through these? I'll take the other two"

"Sure, but how will you know if you spot him? You've never seen him."

"Good question. How about I limit my search to blonde-headed guys with the first name Albert, or Allen, or Alvin. I see any of them, I'll stop and show it to you."

"That'll work." Sam said. "We find him in one of these, what then?"

"Guess that'll be up to Joe. But we find a guy that looks a lot like the guy you saw in the car that day, and his first name's Al? Yeah, Joe's gonna want to hear that."

46

AL DIETRICH MADE HIS WAY THROUGH TOWN DRIVING HIS rented car and wearing his silly disguise. Might be an unnecessary precaution, but he still felt it prudent to do so. From teaching in a small town at the same high school for decades, he always ran into former students. They always recognized him. He got their names right less than half the time.

When he got out into the country roads, he thought about taking off his disguise but decided against it. He only needed to wear it another thirty minutes or so. That should be enough time to get there, take care of Clemens, stage the scene, and drive back to town. He could put up with the charade until then.

He saw the road up ahead with the big rock at the corner then turned left when he reached it. Fortunately, he hadn't seen another car the last five minutes. He drove slowly down this last road aiming to keep his ambush a surprise. Just before he got to the last curve, he reached over and opened the glove box. He pulled out his gun, a full clip already in place, silencer attached, and set it on the seat beside him.

He slowed a little more as he came into the clearing, saw the cabin and Clemens' red truck parked in front. As he got closer to the truck, he stopped, thinking maybe he should back up and park further back, in case Clemens looked out the window. That would ruin his element of surprise.

Suddenly, he was startled by flashing blue lights and the piercing sound of a police siren. His heart started pounding.

He turned and looked over his left shoulder. A Culpepper SUV squad car was parked in the far corner, totally out of sight as he'd driven up. "Oh, God. Oh, God. Oh, God." What should he do? An officer was getting out of his car. The cop's hand was on his gun. Quickly, Dietrich grabbed the gun and shoved it under the seat. Then he yanked off his disguise: the hat, the wig, and the sunglasses. Crammed them under the seat with the gun. The cop would ask for his ID. It had his picture on it.

He looked back at the cop. He had pulled his gun out and was pointing it toward Dietrich. Still walking slowly toward him.

"Roll down your window, sir," the cop yelled. "Let me see those hands."

Dietrich did exactly what he was told. "I don't under-stand, Officer. What have I done wrong?"

"Keep those hands right where I can see them," the cop said.

Dietrich had put them flat on the dashboard in front of the wheel. "I'm not moving. Can you tell me what the problem is?"

"What are you doing back here? I know you don't live in

that cabin, so why are you here?" The cop was only a few steps away now.

Dietrich looked up at him. He looked vaguely familiar. "You're right, I don't live here. And as soon as I saw the red truck there, I realized I came down the wrong road. I'm supposed to meet a friend to fish at the lake. He drives a blue Ford Taurus. There's no road sign back there, so I took a chance this road might be his—"

"Mr. D? Is that you? My gosh, it is you."

Dietrich looked at the cop's face. He was all smiles now and putting his gun back in its holster. Most of his former students called him Mr. D when they bumped into him around town. Al looked at the cop's nameplate. It said Dobbs. Then he remembered, *Johnny Dobbs.*

"I'm sorry to scare you like that, Mr. D. You can put your hands down now. Let me go shut off my lights. I'll be right back."

Dietrich started breathing normally again. It seemed his life wasn't about to be destroyed. He quickly opened the car door, got out, and shut it. Dobbs was walking back toward him. "Johnny Dobbs. Good to see you, young man. I didn't know you had become an officer."

Dobbs walked up, extended his hand. "Yeah, quite a few years now. Guess we haven't run into each other before. You must be a pretty good driver."

Dietrich didn't understand.

"You know, haven't had to give you a ticket."

"Oh, yeah. That is true. Don't think I've gotten a ticket since I was your age. So you married now? Got any kids?"

"Yes, and yes. One wife, two kids. And nobody calls me

Johnny anymore. Dropped that years ago when I joined the Academy. But you can call me anything you want."

"So, what's...going on here? You about scared the life out of me?"

"Oh, just on an assignment. The fellow that lives in that cabin there's been having a little problem with a stalker, or something like that. I was asked to park over there and be on the lookout for any cars that came down this dirt road. I guess there was a concern he might be armed and dangerous. That's why I came out of the car the way I did. Sorry, if I scared you. Feel free to head back out whenever you're ready. Hope you find your fishing buddy."

"Thanks, Johnny. I mean, John. Great to see you again."

"You too, Mr. D." He headed back to his SUV.

Dietrich got back in his rental car and turned it around. He waved as he drove by John's car headed back toward the main road.

He stopped when he got there, looked through the rearview mirror. *That was way too close.* So, Clemens must've gotten suspicious somehow and called the cops. Then he remembered, the camera store. The owner there must've said something to Clemens about, "an old friend that stopped by" the day before. It hadn't dawned on him that something like that could lead to this. He had to be more careful.

But what should he do now? He had to rethink this thing. At least, it was clear Clemens still had no idea who he was. And neither did the police. Had that going for him. Maybe he could stick to the same plan with a slight modification. A police force the size of Culpepper couldn't afford twenty-four-hour protection for a guy like Clemens. Especially since no one had actually tried to harm him.

He looked around. The woods surrounding the cabin were pretty thick, plenty dense enough for him to hide in.

That's what he'd do. Put his disguise back on. Head to that convenience store he'd passed on the way here, pick up some food and drinks, find a place nearby to hide the car, then make his way back to Clemens' cabin through the woods. He would just sit there watching the place till John Dobbs left for the day.

Then...make his move.

Of course, this thing Dobbs said about Clemens having a stalker might mess up his robbery-gone-bad idea. They'd be more inclined to blame it on the stalker. But that wasn't all bad. As long as they didn't know who he was, it could work.

The plan could still work.

47

BACK IN THE LIBRARY, IT WAS SLOW GOING FOR BOTH OF THEM. It was mostly turning page after page after page, stopping occasionally to mock the 80s hairstyles, especially on the girls. Even Sam laughed a few times. He'd forgotten how badly they all had dressed, too. "Not a great decade for hair or fashion," he'd said. Several times, when he was looking through his yearbooks, Sam had stopped to show Hank pictures he had taken. There was his name in the credits at the bottom.

After finishing the yearbook for 1981, Hank closed it up and picked up the next year. "Found quite a few blonde-headed guys in '81, just none of them named Al. Found several guys named Al or Albert, but none of them were blonde."

Sam was still turning the last few pages for 1983. "Pretty much finding the same thing in this one. It was pretty strange seeing my senior photo and Roberto's. There we are just smiling at the camera, thinking we got our whole lives ahead of us. Graduating from a great school with all kinds of job prospects up ahead. Neither one knowing, two years from this point he'd be dead, and I'd be going to prison for the rest of my life."

"Well," Hank said, "you still got some life left, Sam."

"Yeah. But you know what I mean."

"Yeah, I do. It really sucks. Sure hope we get this guy, so at least he gets a taste of what he put you through for the time he has left."

Sam looked down at his book. "Well, just two more left. Guess he didn't graduate the year we did. Hopefully, he's in that 1982 book or he graduated the year after, and he'll be in this one." He picked up the other yearbook.

The conversation ended and gave way to the sound of turning pages. After about five minutes, Hank froze on one picture. He reread it again to make sure. "Hey, Sam. Got a live one here. Look at this guy. Albert Sorensen. Hair's mostly blonde." He held the yearbook up close for Sam to see.

Sam looked at him keenly then shook his head no. "The guy in the car had more of a round face. That guy's face's long, and he's got a pointy chin."

"Okay," Hank said. "Narrows things down even more. Blonde hair, named Al, round face."

More turning pages. Maybe ten more minutes.

Suddenly, Sam gasped. "I don't believe it. There he is. This is the guy I saw in the car. I'm sure of it." He held it up for Hank to see.

Hank looked. It must've been the guy's senior year, because there were only four pics to a page. "Albert Dietrich," Hank read aloud. "He's definitely got a roundish face. You sure that's the guy?"

"I'm sure. This is even the angle I saw him through the windshield. It's definitely him."

"Did you know him at all?"

"Don't think I ever met him before," Sam said. "Look what it says, he's studying for a bachelor's in Mathematics. Definitely didn't hang around with anyone in that crowd. But I'm telling you, Hank. This is definitely the guy I saw. And look at that last name, *Dietrich*. That's a German name, isn't it?"

"Sounds German to me," Hank said. "Well, I'll be. We have found our Al." He looked at his picture again. "Sure doesn't look like the kind of guy who could smash someone's head in with a dumbbell."

"You think I did?"

"No, not at all. I'm just saying, this guy looks like just a regular old guy. A typical college kid from the 80s, bad hair and all." He closed up his yearbook and took out his phone."

"Gonna call Joe?" Sam said.

"Yeah, but first I'm going to take his picture, so I can send it to him. Could you hold it up a minute?" After taking several pics of the yearbook photo, he texted one to Joe, then called him.

As it rang, Sam said, "Albert Zander."

"What's that Sam?"

"This guy's real name. His Nazi name."

Joe answered. "Hey, Hank. Tell me some good news."

Hank put his phone on speaker. "We found our guy. Well, Sam did. Looks like he graduated with the class of '84."

"What's his name?"

"Albert Dietrich," Hank said.

"Albert Dietrich," Joe repeated. "How certain is Sam that this is our guy?"

"Hundred percent, Lieutenant," Sam said. "We're on speaker. This is definitely the guy I saw in the car that day at Roberto's."

"And Joe," Hank said, "what are the odds that the guy Sam saw that day in the car would also be named Al?"

"I hear you, Hank. I think this has to be the guy. Albert Dietrich," Joe repeated. "I don't know why, but for some reason this name sounds very familiar to me. Anyway, great work guys. Hank, you drop Sam off back at his cabin, then—"

"Is anyone out there yet?" Hank said.

"Yeah," Joe said, "I got confirmation we've got a car out there now. Sam should be okay. You head back here after dropping him off. I want you with me when we update Pendleton on all this. And bring that yearbook with you, if they'll let you. I'll look up this Al Dietrich's info, get a current pic off his driver's license, see if he still lives in town."

48

JOE OPENED UP HIS LAPTOP AND NAVIGATED TO THE DATABASE that let him search driver's license info. His program defaulted to search first for people who lived in Culpepper, his jurisdiction. With one click, he could extend the search to the entire county. Before he typed in Dietrich's name, he paused to thank God for what he was about to do. He thought back to that conversation with Kate just a few days ago where everything had seemed so hopeless, like they'd never find this guy. Then she'd suggested he call Jack Turner, his professor buddy, who'd helped him on so many challenging cases over the last few years.

And Jack had come through.

His idea had led to another, then to another and then, pretty soon, here they were. They had discovered the guy's first name, and now they had his last. Joe felt certain when he typed this in, he'd find Albert Dietrich did indeed live somewhere in this town. He probably had lived here ever since the murder in '85. He was likely the mysterious guy who'd recently been asking about Sam at the camera store, pretending to be an old friend. And he was likely the same guy Sam heard driving up to his place then scrambling out of there in a hurry.

"But now, we got you Al Dietrich," Joe said aloud as he typed in his name. In seconds, there was a high-res jpeg of his driver's license filling Joe's screen. He *did* live in town. Joe wrote down the address. "You've done well for yourself, sir?" His street was in a pretty nice part of town. Joe noted his birthdate and quickly figured out his age. He was one year younger than Sam. He scrolled down a little to find his car registration data. Dietrich drove a blue, four-door Audi sedan.

Nice car.

Joe scrolled back up and looked at his picture. His face looked familiar, just like his name had. But why? Joe doubted he'd ever met the man. Usually remembered things like that. He opened a new tab and typed in his name on Google, along with their city.

Bingo. There it was. The reason Albert Dietrich looked familiar.

"Oh. My. Gosh." He leaned back in his chair and released a sigh. This could be trouble. Suddenly, Joe wasn't all that excited about briefing Captain Pendleton on this exciting new development. Pendleton hated this kind of thing. Joe clicked on the link to a very recent article from the Culpepper Gazette, written by none other than the illustrious reporter, Tom Hazelton. The article announced that Albert Dietrich had just been named Teacher-of-the-Year at Culpepper High for an unprecedented fifth time. He had seen the article in the paper the day it came out, including

Dietrich's picture, but Joe hadn't read more than the first few paragraphs.

He read the rest now. Paragraph after paragraph singing the praises of this man. Quote after quote talking about how wonderful he was, how he was the best teacher most of the people being interviewed ever had, other teachers saying how nice he was to work with, how he was "just super" with the kids.

"Great," Joe said. "Just great." Joe sat up in his chair, stared at his picture again. "You have just one flaw, Mr. Dietrich. You killed Roberto Sanchez in cold blood thirty-six years ago, bashed his head in with a dumbbell, to cover up the fact your Grandpa was a vicious Nazi war criminal. Other than that..."

Well, that's what mattered. The only thing that mattered.

He had to call Kate. She'd get a kick out of this. He needed to call Hank, too but figured he'd probably be back in the office by the time he finished telling Kate.

This was just crazy.

AT LEAST THE weather was nice.

Al Dietrich sat in the woods about twenty-five yards in from the tree line on the left side of the cabin. It was a little closer to John Dobbs' patrol car than he'd liked, but the trees and undergrowth were so thick between Al and the squad car, he knew he couldn't be seen. He had a better view of the cabin front door in this spot and Clemens' red pickup. He was further away from both but still plenty of trees and shrubs kept his presence hidden.

He'd found a downed tree to sit on and had some decent

snacks and refreshments to make his wait time more bearable. He wasn't sure what Dobbs was doing to pass the time, but he hadn't heard a sound from his direction since he'd arrived. Maybe he had some headphones on. Probably fiddling with his smartphone, like so many young people did today. Of course, Al had gotten one several years ago, and he did enjoy a few of its features. But he never understood how anyone could become obsessed with these things. Seemed to him, they were losing so much of what real life had to offer in the exchange.

He heard a noise.

Sounded like a car coming down the dirt road. He couldn't see it through the trees yet, but a few moments later it came into view. It drove past Dobbs' patrol car then pulled in beside Clemens' red pickup truck. He waited for Dobbs' lights to start flashing and his siren to sound off. But nothing happened. Two men got out of the car, the driver who looked to be in his late twenties, and the passenger who seemed much older. Closer to Al's age. To his surprise, the younger man looked in Dobbs' direction and waved.

Then the younger man said, "How you making out, Dobbs?"

Dobbs walked over to the man, no gun pulled. "Just fine, Sergeant." He said some other things Al couldn't decipher.

The two men talked a few moments more, as the older man walked from the car to the front door of the cabin. "Thanks for the lift, Sergeant," the man said. "Enjoyed our time together. Glad things worked out."

Al recognized the voice. He looked again at the older man.

"Me, too, Sam," the younger man said.

The older man was Clemens. He must've shaved off his beard. And here Dietrich had thought Clemens had been sitting in his cabin all this time. He must've gone out somewhere with this young sergeant. He wondered if the sergeant was going to relieve Dobbs from guard duty. He didn't have to wonder long. The sergeant said something else to Dobbs, got in his car, and drove away. At the same time, Clemens went into his cabin and closed the door. Dobbs walked back in the direction of the squad car.

Well then, an interesting turn of events. But at least Dietrich knew for certain that Clemens was in the cabin. The only thing he needed now was for Dobbs to leave.

He hoped he would soon.

49

"Joe," Kate said, "what a crazy turn of events. So, let me get this straight. The guy whose last name you all have been trying to uncover the last several days turns out to be the most popular high school teacher in town?"

"Looks like it, Kate," Joe said.

"And that means," Kate continued, "that he's probably the guy who really killed Sanchez in 1985, and then framed Sam."

"Yep. I'm sure it's the same guy. And don't forget...he bashed in poor Roberto's head with a dumbbell. From the crime scene pictures, it was a bloody mess. Kate, this guy's married almost thirty years. Got kids and grandkids."

"All things poor Sam never got to experience," she said. "And this wonderful family man did all this to cover up the fact that his sicko father was a Nazi war criminal. Wow, this is gonna make some news when word gets out."

Joe sighed. "I know."

"When you gonna arrest him?"

"Soon as Hank gets in, and we brief Pendleton."

"Would love to see the look on Pendleton's face when he gets what you're saying," Kate said.

"I'll have Hank take a picture."

"That I'd like to see."

The office door opened. Hank walked in. "Well, Hon, Hank's here. Gotta go. Love you." He hung up.

Hank sat at his desk. "Dropped off Sam at the cabin. Everything seemed fine out there. Find out any more about this guy, Al Dietrich?"

"Yeah, Hank. Way more than I wanted," Joe said.

"What do you mean?"

Joe spent the next ten minutes filling him in on who Albert Dietrich was. Toward the end of the briefing, after Joe mentioned that Dietrich was a math teacher, Hank stopped him.

"You said he taught math?"

"Yeah, why?" Joe said.

"Mr. D," Hank said. "D, Dietrich. Oh, crap. I got to call Dobbs out at the cabin."

"Why? What's going on?"

"After dropping off Sam, I went over and talked with John Dobbs. He's guarding the place. Asked him had anybody come by since we'd been gone. He said no one except his old math teacher from high school. Called the guy Mr. D, said he had just pulled into the dirt road for Sam's cabin by mistake. He was trying to find some guy to meet up with to go fishing."

"That's gotta be him, Hank. Shoot, he's still making a move for Sam."

Hank was already dialing Dobb's cell phone.

. . .

"COME ON, Dobbs, pick up the phone." He put his phone on speaker.

"This is Dobbs. Hey, Sergeant, what's up?"

"Dobbs, listen. This is extremely important. That one car that you said came by the cabin this morning —"

"Yeah, just the one, Mr. D. But I already told you, he was—"

"What's the D stand for, Dobbs?"

"I...I don't remember. We always just called him Mr. D. Why, what's the—"

"Could it have been Dietrich?"

"Yeah, now that you mention it. That sounds familiar. Why? What's going on?"

"Send him the driver's license picture," Joe said to Hank. "I just sent it to your phone."

Hank opened the file showing the pic Joe had sent. "Dobbs, I'm forwarding a photo to you right now. Tell me if this is the guy, your Mr. D?" Hank sent it.

A brief pause, then Dobbs said, "Yeah, that's Mr. D. And there's his last name, Dietrich. That's him. Why?"

"Dobbs," Joe yelled into the phone, "we believe this is the guy who's been after Sam Clemens, the guy you're guarding at the cabin. He was probably there to kill him. But you surprised—"

"Kill him," Dobbs repeated. "Who, Mr. D? There's no way. He's no killer. He's like the nicest—"

"Dobbs, stop talking and listen," Hank said.

"Dobbs," Joe said, "we don't have time to tell you every reason why we know this is true. We're not making this up.

He's the guy. And we're 99% certain he's the same guy who killed a man thirty-six years ago but got away with it, by framing Sam Clemens. The man you were sent there to guard."

"I'm sorry, Lieutenant." He sighed. "I believe you. You and Hank. I had no way of knowing—"

"Don't worry about it now," Hank said. "What kind of car was he driving?"

"Some kind of beige sedan," Dobbs said. "It was a four-door, don't remember the make."

Hank looked at Joe. "Didn't you say he was driving a blue Audi?"

Joe nodded. "Must have rented the beige car." He leaned closer to Hank's phone. "Listen, Dobbs. You see your Mr. D or that car anywhere near that cabin, you make him stop, pull your gun on him, and call for backup. Don't listen to a word he says. Treat him as armed and extremely dangerous. He makes any move toward you after that, you shoot him. Believe me, at this point, he's got nothing to lose."

"Okay, Lieutenant. I'll do it. And listen, I'm really sorry. I know you told me to stop anyone who came by and get their info, but I never figured Mr. D to be anyone—"

"I know, Dobbs," Joe said. "Just keep your eye out and be ready in case he shows up again."

DOBBS HUNG up the phone and got out of his SUV. He was so shocked at what just happened, what he'd just heard. How could Mr. D be a killer? He was like the best teacher Dobbs ever had. And the nicest guy. But he didn't doubt Hank or Lieutenant Boyd.

Especially the Lieutenant. He never got this stuff wrong.
Ever.

He paced back and forth, remembering the earlier scene
when Mr. D had stopped by. Imagine...he was really there to
kill Sam Clemens. It was so hard to grasp. Although he did
act super-surprised to find Dobbs guarding the place.

Dobbs paced back and forth some more. The more he
did, the more he regretted his mistake. He hated the thought
of Hank and the Lieutenant thinking he was such a screwup.

A way to fix this popped into his head.

He knew what Mr. D. looked like and the car he was
driving. Maybe he was still in the area. Maybe he'd parked
just off the main road somewhere between here and town,
waiting for Dobbs' shift to end. When he saw Dobbs drive
by, he'd come back and kill Clemens then.

Dobbs had to do something to make this right. If he
could catch Mr. D still in that car, or at least hold him in
place till help arrived, they'd forget all about how badly he'd
botched this up. He'd be gone no more than ten to fifteen
minutes, tops. And there was only one road that led from
town to this cabin, so there was no way he'd miss Mr. D if he
did try to come back.

Dobbs got in his SUV, turned it on, and drove slowly
down the dirt road toward the main road. He'd have to drive
slowly the whole while, keeping his eyes peeled for that
beige sedan hiding somewhere in the woods.

50

Joe had been feeling uneasy about something for the last several minutes. He knew what it was. Dobbs was a decent guy, but he wasn't the sharpest knife in the drawer. In the years he'd known Dobbs, he'd made more than his share of poor choices. Joe didn't feel totally okay with him being the only protection Sam had out there, especially knowing Dietrich had come by the cabin a short while ago.

He stood up, grabbed his phone. "Say, Hank. Think I'm going to head out to Sam's cabin. Make sure everything's okay."

"Okay, Joe. Want me to join you?"

"No, I should be okay. Dobbs is still there for a few more hours, right?"

"At least till two," Hank said. "Someone else takes his place then."

"Then I'll be fine. Just keep your phone nearby in case something breaks."

· · ·

DIETRICH COULDN'T BELIEVE IT. Officer Dobbs had just gotten inside his patrol car and drove off down the dirt road. He looked at his watch, just a few minutes before eleven. Couldn't be a shift change. He must've gotten a call to go after something else. Dietrich stood, stretched. He pulled out his gun, checked everything over again to be sure. Made sure the silencer was nice and snug.

It was now or never.

He crouched and began to walk toward the cabin. Just inside the tree line, he stopped. He had planned to kill Clemens inside the cabin. That way, if anyone came back, they wouldn't see a body lying on the ground. It would at least buy him time to get far away. But then he imagined things not going well after he confronted Clemens at the door. Clemens had been an inmate all these years. He was probably a lot tougher and stronger than Dietrich was. What if he wrestled with him and Clemens was able to get the gun away? What if Dietrich was only able to wound him?

He stood in place and thought about it until an idea began to form. Looking around the ground, he picked up a handful of decent-sized stones. Clemens' front door was in plain sight about twenty-five yards away. His red truck was parked off to the right. Al decided to toss rocks at the front door every few seconds or so. When Clemens came out to investigate, he'd be an easy target to hit. Once he was down, Dietrich could close the distance, finish him off, and drag him back inside.

This was a better plan.

SAM WASN'T sure what was going on, but he just heard a car

outside leaving. He peeked out the window and saw the police SUV driving down the dirt road toward the main road. No car had taken its place, so it wasn't a shift change. And he wasn't driving all that fast. He decided to play it safe and fetched his 1911 Colt 45. After making sure he had a round in the chamber, he stuck it in his waistband behind his back.

He had been pouring himself a glass of iced tea and started heading back to finish when he heard a knock at the door. Something that sounded like a knock anyway. Again, he peeked out the window closest to the door but didn't see anyone standing there. Could've been a pinecone hitting the roof right there near the door. He'd been startled more than a few times when that happened. He turned and headed back toward the —

There it was again. Only this time, it definitely hit the door, whatever it was. Again, he peeked out the window. No one there. Now, he pulled his gun out, cocked it, and lowered it to his side. Slowly, he opened the door halfway. "Okay," he yelled, "whoever's out there. I don't know what kind of game you're playing, but —"

Another rock came flying out of the woods, hit the cabin just to the right of the door. Shocked by the noise, he jumped, lost his footing, and grabbed for the doorknob. This caused the front door to swing open all the way. Instinctively, he ducked expecting another rock to come his way, but that's not the sound he heard. It almost sounded like an arrow being shot his way. Then a loud smack above the door, right where his head had been a moment ago. Glancing up, he saw wood splinters flying outward from a small hole.

Then another arrow sound. Another smack into the door

just above him. Someone was shooting at him...with a silencer! Quickly, he hurried back into the cabin, upended a nearby table, and took cover behind it. He had to get the door closed somehow. "Al Dietrich," he shouted. "That you? I figure it's gotta be."

No reply. Just another silenced gunshot hitting the door-frame. This time, Sam got a sense of its general direction. He aimed at a tree closest to the spot and fired a few shots.

Man, was that loud.

HE HAS A GUN. *And he knows my name.*

Dietrich did not expect either of these things. The bullet hit a tree about five yards to his left. He ducked down, got behind a tree a few feet in the other direction. Now, what?

The front door slammed shut. Clemens must've gotten to it while Dietrich was moving positions. Maybe he should run, try again some other time. No, he couldn't. Clemens knew his name now. He had to finish this. He remembered from scoping out the cabin earlier, there was a back door. While Clemens was preoccupied with the front, he decided to slip around to the back.

51

JOE HAD JUST TURNED ONTO THE MAIN COUNTRY ROAD THAT led away from town when his phone started ringing. He looked at the screen on his dashboard. It was Sam. He quickly pressed Answer. "Sam, is everything—"

"He's here, Lieutenant. And he's shooting at me!"

"Who's there? Dietrich?" Joe floored it, turned on his lights and siren.

"Yeah, gotta be him. Don't know anyone else's got a reason to kill me."

"I'm five minutes away," Joe said. "Was already headed out there when you called. Where's my officer, the one who supposed to be keeping —"

"He left. Don't know why. Just got in his car and drove off."

Dobbs. Geez.

"Just after that, heard a bang, like a rock hitting the house. Thought it was a squirrel till I heard it again a few seconds later. This time, right on the front door. Opened it to check and ducked just as a bullet smacked into the door, right where my head was."

"Where's he at now?"

"Don't know. He fired at me again, barely missed again. So, I fired off some shots in his general direction. That shut him up for a few—"

"Wait," Joe said, "you got a gun? Sam, you know better than—"

"I know I ain't supposed to have one. But I'd be dead now if I didn't."

"Okay, we'll deal with that later. Just keep your head down till I get there."

"Uh-oh," Sam said. "He must be moving around to the back. Just heard my cans jangle. Stretched some twine across a bunch of trees at ankle level back there."

"Well, stay in the cabin, Sam. And stay down. I'm almost there. If you gotta shoot that gun, try just to scare him off. You understand?"

"I'll do my best, Lieutenant."

Joe quickly called Hank, told him what was happening, said to call in for backup then to head out here as soon as he could.

SAM HURRIED to one of the back windows, peeked out through the edge of the curtain. "There you are," he muttered. Saw a man running crouched, a few yards further back into the trees. Sam broke the window with his gun and fired, aiming just behind the guy. "Thought you'd sneak up on me, eh Dietrich?" he yelled.

Dietrich dropped out of sight. Must be crawling now,

Sam thought. It was so hard not to just go right out there and take him out. There was a chance he could lose the gunfight, but he hated sitting there like a duck in a barrel. He walked over to another back-facing window, closer to where it looked like Dietrich was heading. He opened it slightly, so he could yell something else. The windowpanes to his right shattered, and the curtain flew up as the bullet tore through it. Sam fell back onto the floor, more in shock than anything else.

As he got up, he felt some pain in his right arm, rubbed it, and saw blood on his hand. Was he shot? He lowered his sleeve over his shoulder. No, a piece of glass must've cut him. He pressed his shirt against the wound and got back up into a crouch stance to the left of the window. That last shot was just inches from his heart. This was getting ridiculous. The cavalry would be here any minute, but he could be dead by then. Still in a crouch, he made his way to the front door, opened it just enough to squeeze out.

He thought if he made his way around to the corner facing Dietrich, he could wait him out, pop him if he moved. He wouldn't aim for the head or heart. Just hit him in other places enough to stop him.

DIETRICH WAITED, staring at the window he'd just shot through. He'd heard the sound of Clemens falling to the floor, but he knew it wasn't a clean hit. A moment later, he'd heard the window opening, took the shot without seeing him clearly through the curtains. Way too much glass breaking to be a kill shot. And with Clemens armed, it was still too risky to barge in there and hope for the best.

Just then through the torn curtain, Dietrich saw the front door open slightly and close. Clemens was going on offense. He had left the cabin. Crawling, he got to a place where he could see the front corner through the trees. He could just glimpse Clemens body peeking out from the edge. He was just standing there, with his pistol aimed toward the woods.

This was his chance. He slowly turned around then crawled more quickly in the opposite direction toward the other end of the cabin. When he was sure he was out of Clemens' line of sight, he stood and trotted through the woods toward the far corner. When he got there, he started walking against the cabin wall in Clemens' direction.

52

JOE MUST'VE BEEN GOING ABOUT NINETY WHEN HE PASSED Dobbs' SUV going in the opposite direction. For just a flash, he caught the look on Dobbs' face as he flew by. Sadly, he'd seen that look on Dobbs' face way too often. As Joe glanced in his rearview mirror, he saw Dobbs hit the brakes, whip his car around, turn on his sirens and light, and start moving in Joe's direction.

Joe knew the turnoff for Sam's cabin was just a few blocks ahead on the left. He got an idea, slowed his car down, turned off his lights and siren. Sam was in the cabin with a gun, so he wasn't helpless. And Dietrich knew this, since Sam had shot at him several times. So, he wasn't likely to storm the cabin. If Joe dashed in there like gangbusters, Dietrich would likely take off into the woods before any decent backup arrived. Then the whole thing would dissolve into a massive manhunt that could take days to resolve.

By the time Joe had reached the dirt road toward the cabin, Dobbs had closed the distance. Thankfully, he'd taken

Joe's cues already and turned off his siren and lights. Joe heard a crack of static, then Dobbs' voice.

"What's going on, Lieutenant?"

"Shots fired at the cabin, Dobbs. Already been talking with Sam. He's fine for now. But he's exchanged shots with a shooter outside, likely Dietrich. I want to go in there quiet, guns drawn, till we get closer. You stay at least twenty yards behind me, watch my six."

"You got it, sir."

Joe had slowed his car way down, then stopped just before the last curve. He pulled over, got out, drew his gun, and walked toward the cabin. He glanced back and saw Dobbs doing the same. Just as he cleared the last clump of trees and could see the cabin, he was about to call out to Dietrich, expecting him to still be in the woods. Joe was shocked to see him out in the open, his gun drawn, walking along the back cabin wall.

Clearly, he hadn't seen them yet.

DIETRICH TIPTOED along the wall toward the front corner. Just a few more steps. When he reached it, he glanced around and looked toward the other corner, the one closest to the water. There was Clemens, still in position, his back facing Dietrich. His gun pointed toward the woods in the wrong direction.

Should Dietrich take the shot now? Clemens' head was partly obscured, but he could clearly fire several shots into his back near his heart. He couldn't miss from this distance. He stepped out from the corner, got in the stance he used at the gun range, and aimed.

Should he say something first?

Just then, "ALBERT DIETRICH, FREEZE! THIS IS THE CULPEPPER PD. DROP YOUR GUN NOW. DO IT NOW!

Dietrich was stunned by the voice screaming behind him. Without thinking, he turned to face the sound with his gun still drawn and pointed.

Two shots rang out.

He felt like he'd just been hit with a baseball bat in the side and left leg. He fell to the ground in more pain than he'd ever known. What was happening?

He was staring up at the sky. A beautiful blue sky.

A moment later, a face blocked his beautiful view. A man was standing over him, looking down at him. A clicking sound. Dietrich's eyes focused on the barrel of the pistol pointing at his head.

He heard someone yell off in the distance, "Sam, don't do it! Put the gun down, Sam."

SAM HEARD WHAT JOE SAID. But he kept his gun pointed right at Dietrich's face.

This was the man who had destroyed his life. Who'd taken away everything that was supposed to be his life. He'd stolen it and lived it for himself. For all these years. He got to fall in love, got married, had kids, had a career — a successful one. Made plenty of money. Drove nice cars. Went on vacations. Even had grandkids. Tears filled Sam's eyes. "You took all of that away from me."

"Sam. C'mon, buddy. Drop the gun. Please." It was Joe. No longer yelling. Closer.

Sam stayed focused on Dietrich. "Look at you there on

the ground. Only it was supposed to be me, laying there, you had your way. Weren't for the Lieutenant, it would be me." He sighed. Tears fell from his cheeks, landed on his gun. He looked past them to Dietrich's face. "You don't deserve mercy." He felt such a strong urge to squeeze the trigger.

"Sam," Joe said, just a few feet away. "You're right. He doesn't deserve mercy. No one does. Remember the pamphlet? None of us do. Let me make sure he at least gets justice. Let's do that instead, Sam. Give me the gun."

THE SOUNDS of multiple sirens could be heard in the distance, headed their way. Joe turned to Dobbs, still about twenty yards back. "Call for a Medevac, tell them we got gunshot wounds."

"Already took care of it, sir."

Sam looked up at Joe, wiped his tears on his sleeve, handed him the Colt .45. "All right, Lieutenant. Mercy it is." Sam stepped away from Dietrich, still conscious but looking totally confused.

Joe kicked Dietrich's gun out of reach, put Sam's gun in the waistband behind his back, and looked at Dobbs. "Don't say anything about this gun to anyone. Not till we talk."

"Sure thing, Lieutenant. Want me to bag the other guy's gun?"

"Yeah, but take a picture first. Send Hank up as soon as he gets here. Brief the other guys as they arrive, start working the scene."

Joe handcuffed Dietrich from the front because of his wounds, read him his rights, then walked over to Sam, who'd already stepped further away from Dietrich. Tears were still in his eyes. "I wanted to so bad," he said.

"I know, Sam. But you didn't. That's what matters." He put his hand on his shoulder, then noticed the blood coming through his shirt. "You get hit?"

"No, just by some glass when he shot out a window. Missed me by inches, though. And weren't for you, he'd have killed me for sure. I didn't even hear him coming up behind me.

"Probably right about that."

"Thanks, Joe."

Joe smiled. "You didn't call me Lieutenant."

Tears welled up in Sam's eyes again. "A man saves your life like that, guess we gotta be something like friends now, right?"

"We are friends, Sam. Proud you did the right thing back there. Would've really hated to have to shoot you, us being friends and all."

"Would you? Would you have shot me?"

Joe nodded. "If you made a move for that trigger, yeah, I would. Took an oath to serve and protect...even scumbags like Dietrich." No one said anything for a moment.

"I saw where you hit him," Sam said. "The side and the leg. That on purpose?"

"I could've killed him easy," Joe said. "But then he wouldn't get his chance."

"His chance?"

"To taste everything he put you through all these years. No way he wiggles out of it now. Slamdunk for premeditated first-degree attempted murder. His age, he'll never get out again. And who knows, maybe after he's in there a while someone'll hand him that pamphlet they gave you."

"The Scandal of Mercy?" Sam said.

Joe nodded. "Sure did you some good."

An unmarked car slammed its breaks on as it arrived, sirens and lights going. Joe saw Hank get out, Dobbs talking to him. Hank looked over to Joe, nodded, headed his way.

"Sit tight, Sam. If you want, you can head back into the cabin, wait there."

"You're okay with that?"

"Yeah, go ahead. Let me talk to Hank."

Moments later, the Medevac pulled up, followed by several squad cars. Dobbs directed the paramedics to Dietrich, still lying in the same spot.

When Hank got close, Joe spent the next few minutes giving him the rundown. Pretty much play-by-play. When he finished, he said, "Could you take charge of things from here? Think I could use a minute, catch my breath. Maybe down by the lake."

"Sure, Joe. Take as much time as you like. Want me to call Pendleton on this?"

"No, I better do that. But first I want to call Kate. Don't want her hearing anything about this till she hears from me first."

53

AFTER TAKING A FEW MINUTES DRINKING IN THE SIGHTS AND sounds down by the water, a few more minutes thanking the Lord for how the situation back there worked out, Joe pulled out his phone and called Kate.

"This is a nice surprise," she said. "Don't usually get a call from you this time a day. Tell me it's because you're tired of my cooking and wanted to take me out to your favorite place to eat tonight?"

Joe laughed. "Okay, which place is that?"

"Okay, one of your favorite places then."

"Well, I'm not tired of your cooking, so no luck there. But I think after you hear what I'm about to say, going out some-place nice might be just the thing." He didn't know why, but he got choked up. Maybe it was just hearing her voice.

"Joe, what's wrong? You okay?"

He breathed in deeply. "Physically, yeah. I'm definitely okay."

"That doesn't sound too reassuring."

"Kate, I just had to shoot a guy. Not fifteen minutes ago."

"Oh, Joe. I'm so sorry." Then she chuckled. Muttered, "sorry" again.

"What's that?" he said.

"What's what?"

"I heard you giggle after you told me you were sorry I had to shoot a guy. That's what."

"It's nothing. I really am sorry you had to shoot a guy."

"I believe you. You sounded sorry. But then you did giggle, which, you know, isn't usually what someone does after offering you their sympathy."

"You're not going to let this go, are you? Okay, yes I giggled. But it was a totally inappropriate giggle, so I kept it to myself. I should think that would be considered progress."

"Probably is some progress. But what made you giggle?"

"Well, after you said you just shot a guy, my first thought wasn't the sympathetic thing I said."

"What was it?"

"I thought, *Again*? But see, I caught myself."

"Again," Joe repeated. "That was your first thought? Does it feel to you like I do this a lot? You know, shoot people?"

Kate laughed. Then Joe couldn't help it. He laughed, too.

"Well, Joe," she said, "I suppose that's sort of a relative thing, don't you think? When we first moved down here to Culpepper, I thought your shooting-people days were over. Now, I'm more adjusted to the idea that they're not. That they happen...less times."

"A lot less times," Joe said.

"Okay, a lot less times. That's why I didn't say it. And you wouldn't even have known I thought it if you just could have let my giggle go by. We'd be way past that now, and I could've told you a dozen other things — all sympathetic things — that would've made you feel a lot better."

Joe took a moment, took in the scene in front of him, and this wonderful crazy woman talking to him on the phone just now. "You know what, Hon? I do feel a lot better. I don't care if you giggled. And I do see your progress. And I love you more than life itself. Pretty sure, the guy I shot will be okay. Only, because he's a very bad guy, he'll be locked up the rest of his life."

"After he gets over being shot," Kate said.

"Yeah, that. And the best part is, I think I saved Sam's life in the process. Maybe even a little more than that."

"Well, how about that?" she said. "I'm so proud of you, Joe. I mean that, sincerely. No giggles to follow. But you know what this means? You're going to be a hero again in this town. It'll be all over the news in a day or two."

"I'm not so sure," he said. "Maybe not this time."

"Why not?"

"You know who I shot...just the best school teacher this town has ever seen."

"Yeah," she said, "Pendleton's probably gonna have something to say about that part."

EPILOGUE

8 WEEKS LATER
Culpepper City Hall

CAPTAIN PENDLETON WAS TALKING. ON AND ON AND ON.

They were at that part of the event when he should have wrapped things up and turned everyone loose to the refreshment tables, but Pendleton could never miss a moment to share everything on his mind with the troops.

Joe figured most of them, like him, had stopped listening. But all the relevant things that had taken place today did get him thinking about the events of the last several weeks.

The days following the shootout at Sam's cabin had been crazy, to be sure. Culminating in this...Joe, Kate, Hank, and pretty much the entire Culpepper PD had been gathered for the last hour in a big room down at city hall for an inter-department award ceremony.

Even Sam was there. Beside him were Juan and Alonzo Sanchez.

Considering the major fiasco that had erupted in town right after the news broke about the "Five-Time-Teacher-of-the-Year" being arrested for murder and attempted murder, Captain Pendleton thought they should keep this ceremony on the down-low.

That suited Joe just fine.

Joe and Hank had already received their citations for "breaking wide open a significant Cold Case from 1985," as Captain Pendleton put it. "As well as righting a major injustice done to a man wrongly imprisoned for a murder he did not commit thirty-six years ago." Of course, everyone in the room clapped. Then Joe was brought up again and given, basically, a hero award for saving Sam's life at the cabin. Kate, Hank, and Sam stood for that round of applause, which obligated everyone else to do the same.

Tom Hazelton of the Gazette was the only member of the press who'd been notified and invited to the ceremony. His stock had gone way up over the last two months, covering every story surrounding the case since the cabin shootout.

Joe glanced over at Tom, standing off to the side along a wall, his face beaming. A man reborn. Yesterday, he told Joe he'd just signed a deal with a major publisher for a "pretty hefty advance" to write a true-crime book about the case. They wanted the whole story, from beginning to end, including the Nazi war criminal components. Tom promised them he'd deliver a bestseller, especially after securing the cooperation of Juan and Alonzo Sanchez. For a decent fee, they'd agreed to let him use all of Roberto's materials for the book, and be interviewed as often as needed. He'd made Sam a similar offer. Sam was still mulling it over.

Tom said he'd already started interviewing several key

players in town, mostly the people he'd talked to when he'd written that glowing article about Dietrich, after they announced his Teacher-of-the-Year award. Of course, Tom had said, the contrasting perspectives of these people now compared to then "was simply stunning." In short, the town was devastated by the news. "*Mr. D was actually a ruthless, heartless killer,*" they said. "*And his father was a Nazi criminal? Who knew?*"

It was the only thing the locals talked about for weeks.

A few days ago, Dietrich had been quietly released from the local hospital and transferred to the medical facility at a state prison. Joe wasn't surprised that he quickly agreed to plead guilty to all charges, once they'd presented him and his attorney with all the evidence they had gathered. It substantially proved he was the one who had actually murdered Roberto Sanchez thirty-six years ago, then framed Sam Clemens to take the fall.

And as for the more recent attempted murder charge of Sam, it was a total open-and-shut affair. Both Joe and Officer Dobbs saw what happened at the cabin with their own two eyes. Dietrich had decided pleading guilty to everything was his only hope of protecting his family from all the horrible things that would come out during a prolonged trial.

Of course, it was a false hope, Joe thought, with Hazelton's crime book on the horizon. Tom wouldn't miss a thing.

The matter about Sam being in possession of a loaded firearm went away nice and quiet. When Joe had gone back to talk with Dobbs about it the day after the shootout, Dobbs told him he never saw Sam with a gun. Only Joe and Dietrich. Made Joe smile when he heard it. How about that Dobbs? Bounced back pretty good on that one.

To Joe, the best piece of news happened for Sam. After the dust settled, and at Joe's suggestion, Sam had contacted a well-known organization that specialized in getting fair settlements from the government for people who'd been wrongly imprisoned for many years. After reviewing Sam's case, the team instantly agreed to represent him and had already had several meetings with Georgia state officials.

Because of how soon Dietrich accepted the blame for everything, Sam was quickly exonerated by a state judge of all charges. Even though Georgia had no law yet guaranteeing Sam a settlement, they had begun to move in that direction. In recent years, they had awarded numerous wrongly-accused victims substantial payouts. Sam's new legal team told him he would likely be receiving no less than a million dollars in a settlement, and it could go as high as two.

Since hearing this, Sam wore an almost permanent smile on his face.

But he told Joe, his happiness wasn't rooted in the money. Not mostly. Mostly he was glad he hadn't pulled the trigger on Dietrich that day at the cabin, and he couldn't stop thanking Joe for talking him out of it. Really, for all Joe had done for him. The money was nice, but knowing the whole world knew now that he wasn't a killer...that was priceless. People all over town looked at him differently now, he said. Some even smiled and said hi.

He had decided to buy that cabin at the lake and make Culpepper his home for good.

When they had arrived at the ceremony today, Sam told Joe he'd like to take him up on his offer and visit the church he and Kate belonged to this Sunday. Joe hadn't had a chance to tell Kate yet.

Joe looked up at the podium. It looked like Captain Pendleton was finally winding up his little speech. Joe leaned over and whispered to Kate, "Remind me to tell you something Sam said when we get in the car. It's something good."

She whispered back, "Remind me to tell you something in the car, too."

"Is it good?"

She nodded. Then said, "I can't wait. Joe Junior's gonna have a baby brother."

"What?" He forgot to whisper. Everyone looked. Joe nodded his apologies. When their eyes all focused back on Pendleton, he whispered, "I thought we weren't going to know for another month."

"We weren't. But when they did the ultrasound yesterday, well, the little guy made himself known...if you know what I mean."

Joe squeezed her hand, pretended to listen to Pendleton's final few words. *I'm gonna have another boy*. It made him so happy. *Wonder what we should call him*?

Kate leaned over again and whispered. "I was thinking... maybe we should name him Sam."

Sam, Joe thought. *Samuel Boyd*.

"What do you think?" she said.

He looked over at his friend Sam, leaned toward her, and said, "I like it. Sounds like the name of a real somebody."

WANT TO READ MORE?

If you haven't read any of Dan's other suspense novels, you'll be happy to learn *The Scandal of Mercy* is actually Book 3 of the Joe Boyd Suspense series. The first book is, *If These Walls Could Talk*, and the second is called, An Inconvenient Death. We're sure you'd enjoy both of them, even if you read them out of order. Here are the Links:

- If These Walls Could Talk - https://amzn.to/2XDJfOi
- An Inconvenient Death - https://amzn.to/2PfRZaJ

If you have read the first two, maybe you weren't aware the Joe Boyd series is actually a "**Sequel Series**" to Dan's best-selling 4-Book *Jack Turner Suspense Series*. The events and mysteries unfolding in those 4 books take place a few years prior to this book and include many of the same characters and places.

All of Dan's novels (over 20) are similar in genre and style to *The Scandal of Mercy*. Except half of them (including his 4 Christmas novels) feature more heart-impacting, spiritual themes, and some have a stronger romantic thread.

As of now, Dan's novels combined have received over 15,000 Amazon reviews (maintaining a 4.7 Star average). They've won multiple national awards and received rave reviews from publications like USA Today, Publisher's Weekly, Library Journal and RT Book Reviews magazine.

Here are some quick links to a few of *Dan's other novels*:

The Jack Turner Suspense Series (*over 2,600 Amazon Reviews, 4.7 Star Avg*)

- When Night Comes - http://amzn.to/1xNat4G
- Remembering Dresden - http://amzn.to/1RO7WvN
- Unintended Consequences - http://amzn.to/2pvSvmG
- Perilous Treasure - https://amzn.to/2HOgpl7

The Forever Home Series (*Dog Rescue Series - over 3,900 Amazon Reviews, 4.8 Star avg*)

- Rescuing Finley – http://amzn.to/1Hn0vrg
- Finding Riley - http://amzn.to/2c7xdWY
- Saving Parker - http://amzn.to/2g9vKkA

You can check out all of Dan's other novels by going to his Author Book Page on Amazon. Here's the link:

http://amzn.to/2cG5I9o

WANT TO HELP THE AUTHOR?

If you enjoyed reading *The Scandal of Mercy*, the best thing you can do to help Dan is very simple—*tell others about it* (Leave a Brief Review). Word-of-mouth advertising is the most powerful marketing tool there is. Better than expensive TV commercials or full-page magazine ads.

Leaving a good review is the best way to insure Dan will be able to keep writing novels full time. He'd greatly appreciate it if you'd consider leaving a rating for the book and writing a brief review. Doesn't have to be long (even a sentence or two will help).

Here's the Amazon link for the book. Scroll down a little to the area that says "**Customer Reviews**," right beside the graphic that shows the number of stars is a box and says: "**Write a Customer Review**."

https://www.amazon.com/dp/B09H4XH1F5

SIGN UP TO RECEIVE DAN'S NEWSLETTER

If you'd like to get an email alert whenever Dan has a new book coming out or when a special deal is being offered on any of Dan's existing books, click on his website link below and sign up for his newsletter (it's right below the Welcome paragraph). Also, **every first-time visitor to his site can choose to receive one of Dan's bestselling novels for FREE** (see the Tab for the Free Book in the Menu).

From his homepage, you can also contact Dan or follow him on Facebook or Goodreads.

www.danwalshbooks.com

ACKNOWLEDGMENTS

There is really one person I absolutely must thank for helping to get *The Scandal of Mercy* into print. That's my wife, Cindi. Her editorial advice and input on this book was indispensable.

But I also need to thank my great proofreading team. They help catch any of the typos or other little distracting errors in the book before it goes to print: Patricia Keough-Wilson, Debbie Mahle, Jann Martin, Terri Smith, and Rachel Savage.

Dan Walsh

ABOUT THE AUTHOR

Dan was born in Philadelphia in 1957. His family moved down to Daytona Beach, Florida in 1965, when his father began to work with GE on the Apollo space program. That's where Dan grew up.

He married Cindi, the love of his life in 1976. They have 2 grown children and 5 grandchildren. Dan served as a pastor for 25 years then began writing fiction full-time in 2010. His bestselling novels have won numerous awards, including 3 ACFW Carol Awards (he was a finalist 6 times) and 4 Selah Awards. Four of Dan's novels were finalists for RT Reviews' Inspirational Book of the Year. One of his novels, *The Reunion*, is being made into a major full-length feature film.

CPSIA information can be obtained
at www.ICGtesting.com
Printed in the USA
LVHW011726221221
706958LV00011B/1341